D0463444

# feuds

# feuds

AVERY HASTINGS

st. martin's griffin
new york

y

HASTINGS

RODGERS MEMORIAL LIBRARY

NOV 13 2014

$ 18.99

This is a work of fiction. All of the characters, organizations, and events portrayed
in this novel are either products of the author's imagination or are used fictitiously.

FEUDS. Copyright © 2014 by Avery Hastings. All rights reserved.
Printed in the United States of America. For information, address St. Martin's
Press, 175 Fifth Avenue, New York, N.Y. 10010.

www.stmartins.com

Designed by Anna Gorovoy

The Library of Congress Cataloging-in-Publication Data is available upon request.

ISBN 978-1-250-05771-6 (hardcover)
ISBN 978-1-4668-4532-9 (e-book)

St. Martin's Griffin books may be purchased for educational, business,
or promotional use. For information on bulk purchases, please contact Macmillan
Corporate and Premium Sales Department at 1-800-221-7945, extension 5442,
or write specialmarkets@macmillan.com.

First Edition: September 2014

10  9  8  7  6  5  4  3  2  1

# feuds

# I

## DAVIS

It was the grand pas classique. She felt it: not as a well-practiced variation but as an emotion, rich and complex, swirling through her. She was lifted; she flew, unfettered. Everywhere she turned, a thousand duplicates turned, too, her image reflected in hundreds of mirrors, spinning endlessly.

The entrechat, the grand jeté. There was one final pirouette, a simple dénouement. She lifted, her body weight focused on the tips of her toes, her energy channeled into a single column. And then . . .

Her knee gave, and her whole body became a marionette, failing.

*Suddenly there were faces, everywhere, surrounding her, jeering at her as she fell.*

*Imp faces.*

*She could tell from their skin and pockmarks and jagged scars. The Imps were laughing. Howling.*

*No.*

Her eyes shot open to a gentle beam of filtered, green-hued sunlight seeping through her shade. Normally, the sunshade eased her into wakefulness, but Davis bolted upright in bed, panting. The shade only used the green filter when it registered Davis's neural transmission—and anxiety levels—as abnormal.

The clock in her headboard read 5:00 a.m., which meant she was twenty minutes late.

Davis pulled herself out of bed, reaching for yesterday's workout gear, wrinkly and wadded up in the corner by her bureau. There was no time to root around in her drawers for something clean, and she just had to pray none of the other girls would notice.

She caught a glimpse of her mother dancing across her wall. Her mom's larger-than-life image magnified the brilliance of her perfection as she performed her own flawless *grand pas classique* to a sold-out crowd. Davis swiped a corner of the screen and her mother faded as the screen saver came on: a random slide show of images of Davis and her friends.

Davis tugged rose-hued leg warmers over her black tights and swept her hair into a messy bun. She gave herself a cursory glance in her mirror, allowing it to register her vitals, swiping quickly through the displayed results: hydration levels were in the normal range. Neural transmission, heart rate, and blood pressure were still a little funky but making a steady progression back to optimum. Davis flicked off the mirror feed and slipped out the door, pausing only to kiss her mom's Olympiad medal on her way.

Davis headed for the kitchen, pausing briefly in front of Sofia's room. A beam of light stretched from underneath her little sister's door, causing Davis's figure to cast eerie shadows on the walls. Sofia was always leaving the light on after reading late. Davis pushed the door open soundlessly and padded into Sofia's yellow-and-orange-spackled fortress, which was digitally painted across every inch of the floor-to-ceiling, touch-screen walls. Fia's latest work in progress was displayed: a vibrant self-portrait.

Fia's dark curls—inherited from Terri, but even more striking than Terri's when contrasted against Fia's lighter skin—were illuminated by the headboard lamp. A paperback lay open on her chest. Davis reached for it and Fia stirred, but her breathing pattern continued uninterrupted. Davis glanced at the cover and couldn't help smiling. *A Brief History of Nearly Everything*. It was a classic their dad had loved . . as a teenager. Fia had stolen it from the glass cabinet where the collectibles were kept. As a print book and a first edition, it was extremely rare and very valuable—or at least it had been valuable before Fia had gotten her hands on it. She was only eleven and had already read it countless times. Fia always insisted that dog-earing a page gave it character. It was the reason she even bothered reading her dad's ancient paper editions despite their funky smells and brittle textures, like leaves on the verge of disintegrating.

Davis leaned over her sister, brushing her cheek with a light kiss so as not to wake her. Then she flipped off the lamp with a quick swipe of her finger and padded softly from the room, securing the door behind her.

She stopped in the kitchen to grab some fruit and a protein shake.

"Sweetie, what are you doing?" Her stepmother appeared in the doorway, her thin figure complemented by her silk robe, and her skin radiant—not a trace of puffy eyes or dark circles, even though Davis was sure she'd just woken up. Terri's coarse black hair tumbled over her shoulder in long, thick waves; her dark lashes were always bold and upswept, even then, so long they hit the base of her brow line. Her cheeks wore a healthy flush against the natural chocolate hue of her skin. But her most notable features were her big, sympathetic eyes. She was beautiful, but it was her kindness that set her apart, illuminating her entire expression.

"Class," Davis answered. It came out a little stiffer than she'd intended.

"Class? But—" Terri interrupted herself, staring at Davis with concern. "It's Kensington Day, sweetie. There is no ballet."

*Crap.* Davis had forgotten.

"I know," she said anyway. "More time to practice." The second she said it, she was glad it was true. While she knew she could always get in a small workout at her building's gym, she preferred the sanctity of the dance studio—it always improved her mood. And since it was a holiday, she'd probably have the space all to herself.

Barr Kensington was a national hero, and the man responsible for a better, more perfect human. Kensington had pioneered all the in-utero optimization: Mozart and Brahms piped directly into the womb, math lessons, linguistics practice. He had engineered superior humans. He had *made* the Priors—made Davis, and everyone like her.

Thanks to Kensington, every portion of Davis's brain was more developed than it would have been otherwise. Diseases like AIDS and malaria that wiped out entire populations hundreds of years ago would never affect her today, even if she were somehow exposed. But Kensington had been more than a scientist. He had also been one of the most renowned politicians of his generation; her dad had a copper bust of him in his study. It had been nearly seventy-five years since Kensington's death in 2062, but his political agendas were stronger than ever among conservatives like her father. Davis's father had told her horror stories of what the city had been like back when the Imps were fully integrated. Crime— rapes, shootings, theft—was through the roof until Kensington started pushing segregation.

If it weren't for Kensington, the city of Columbus might never have survived and endured all the instability that caused dozens of major cities—Chicago, Los Angeles, portions of New York that still existed after the floods—to crumble, leaving most of the country uninhabitable. Every aspect of her life—the city she called home—was safer and better.

And soon, as long as her father defeated Parson Abel for city prime minister, steps toward total segregation and an even more ideal Columbus would be implemented. Columbus was truly becoming the perfect place to live.

"Why don't I wrap you up a vitamuffin for the road then," Terri offered, breaking Davis's reverie. She moved farther into the kitchen and patted Davis on the shoulder as she passed. Davis leaned into Terri's touch instinctively before she remembered herself.

"No. Really." Davis turned from Terri, rummaging in the fruit bowl on the table. "Thanks, though." Terri's offer warmed her— she was always so sweet and thoughtful. Still, something in Davis resisted.

"Well, how about an enhancer? I was just about to make one for myself—"

"I'm fine," Davis said, grabbing a banana from the basket by the fridge. "I promise." She gave Terri a perfunctory kiss on her cheek, trying to ignore the disappointment in her stepmom's dark eyes. Davis hesitated when she reached the door to the apartment, turning back at the last second. She could just leave. Or . . .

"Terri?" she called back.

"Yes, sweetie?" Terri's voice was soft, hopeful.

"Maybe you could make me one of your revitalizers when I get back from dance? I'll probably need a pick-me-up. If you aren't too busy, I mean."

"I'd love to."

Davis could tell she meant it.

The elevator descended quickly from their fifty-second-floor apartment. Davis opted to walk the few short blocks to the monorail; her dad had specifically forbidden her to use the car after she and Vera had drunkenly reprogrammed the nav system. She passed through the turnstile marked PRIOR at the uptown monorail, pausing briefly for her P-card to register, then stopped at a kiosk and entered her destination via DirecTalk. The monorail was brightly lit and full of security like it always was. Several officers nodded hello to her, and Davis returned their greeting. Were there more police than usual? It seemed that security had been tightening, maybe because of the election. She felt a flash of worry. *Irrational,* she assured herself. *Everything will be okay.* She heard laughter behind her and looked over her shoulder from where she stood on the monorail platform, waiting for the train to arrive.

Several officers were clustered around a girl wearing the wide armband of an Imp. They were patting her down, three of them at once running their hands over her body in an elaborate search effort. She watched as the girl wriggled away from the men's grasp; then another guard grabbed her arms, pinning them behind her back, his laughter ringing through the air as his colleagues prodded her with their guns and touched her body in places Davis was sure weren't necessary for a normal pat-down. Davis saw them run the standard test for antibodies: a series of halogen lights swept across the girl's slender frame.

Maybe there was a reason for it—the girl must have been sick or hiding something. Still, the girl's humiliation and fear were palpable. No one should have to feel that way. Davis had never known what it was like to be patted down like that—it looked awful, and her chest constricted instinctively as she watched.

A Prior monorail car labeled with Davis's destination and already carrying several passengers pulled up and she stepped inside, turning just as the officers let the Imp girl go. The Imp caught Davis's eye through the train window as she hurried to her own Imp car. She looked furious—maybe close to tears. Davis looked away, feeling embarrassed without knowing why. Part of her almost wanted to call out, to say, *I've suffered, too; I've lived my whole life without my mom*, but the girl would have thought she was crazy; and anyway, sadness and suffering don't alleviate more sadness and suffering. Davis sighed, focusing on the sparkling beauty of the buildings rising up outside her car window. The sky was a startling blue in contrast—so pure its beauty almost took her breath away. If only everything could be so beautiful. If only there were no suffering, no humiliation, no death—for anyone, Imp or Prior.

Thoughts of Imp and Prior relations turned her mind to the election. What would happen if her father lost the race to Parson Abel? But that wouldn't happen; her father had already gained a solid margin. Soon he'd be in office, and he'd keep her—and the rest of the city—safe, peaceful, and segregated. Worry-free, with cleaner boundaries established, everyone happier. The Imps and Priors didn't belong together—anyone could see that. Segregation would be better for everyone involved. Despite the carefully delineated borders, Davis couldn't help feeling like the Imps were moving closer all the time, like she had to wedge herself into a tinier and tinier space of the universe to feel safe. The sanitization checkpoints—arched gateways that administered automatic spray-downs to anyone who walked through them—kept her anxiety in check, but barely.

After all, the Imps had killed her mother.

At the thought, Davis felt hatred bubbling deep in the pit of her stomach, just below her heart. It was all their fault.

As the monorail ascended, the blurred landscape outside the high-speed train changed from grays, blues, and yellows to browns and reds. The train was soaring through Columbus, weaving through the canyons formed by the towering buildings, and beyond the river coiling like a snake to Davis's left were the dirt-covered shanties of the Slants. Davis was glad they were too blurry to see.

It was rare that Davis got the studio all to herself, and when she opened the door to the familiar room with her P-card, a tiny thrill climbed its way up her spine. She didn't bother signing in; there was no one at reception. And although she half expected to hear the familiar pitch of the Leon Minkus that her studio partner Emilie always practiced to, the room was quiet.

Davis slipped on her worn-in pointe shoes and walked onto the floor, taking pains not to make any noise. The fear of waking someone—some spirit, maybe—flitted through her mind unbidden, but she knew she was being silly. She wrapped her arms around herself, staring at her reflection on four walls. Green eyes stared back from a heart-shaped face framed by tousled chestnut waves. The dance room was a large space the length of a city block and nearly as wide, and the whole thing was covered with floor-to-ceiling mirrors. There were even mirrors *on* the floor, a detail all new students found disconcerting—so had Davis when she was small, always tripping over her own image—but Madame Bell had always insisted that a girl became a dancer when she could see herself at every angle and remain immersed in the music. The Apex rink, the famous landmark where the Olympiads took place, was mirrored on all sides, even the ceiling. She would see herself in the eyes of thousands of people, and in the reflection of their eyes, and in the reflection of that reflection . . .

She stripped off her overcoat and tossed it in the corner, wishing every day could be a holiday. It was so much different being there alone—so much freer. She ran across the expanse of the room, doing a series of jetés that made her feel as though she were flying. She hadn't bothered to stretch, but she didn't care. This was what she loved about ballet: it was this feeling of floating, like she was suspended in time. Anything seemed possible, then—it even seemed possible that if she turned to look, she'd see her mother watching her from the sidelines, or dancing just one step behind her.

And for whole minutes at a time, Davis felt free.

# ⚔ 2 ⚔

## COLE

Sweat dripped down Cole's forehead and stung his eyes. It moved along his spine, then his face and neck and hands, as if he were one great machine meant for producing water and blood and rage. He *was* a machine, at least in the ring. *An animal. Fighting to entertain the vultures.* The thought didn't stop him from wanting to connect. *Body on body. Fist on face.* It was all he was good at; it was the only thing he'd ever known how to do without trying.

Kenny wasn't down yet, but Cole could tell he was fading fast. It was their last round in the cage. Cole leaned against the metal supports, feeling the cold, slick bars against his back.

The bell rang, signaling the start of the final round. So far they were tied, which was no surprise to anyone. Kenny and Cole had been neck and neck in the FEUDS since they were boys. Before that, before the FEUDS had meant anything to them, they were friends. It was hard to remember now the days they spent playing down by the abandoned railway tracks. But Cole couldn't let those thoughts distract him—he couldn't pity Kenny, because Kenny wouldn't do the same for him.

They each had their families to think of, and sponsors to attract.

Priors and Geneserians alike had started placing bets on the qualifying round months ago. Whatever happened in the ring these days could determine who would have enough money to finish school. Or better yet, move away.

Kenny moved forward, raising his fists to his chin. He was a rat-brawler. He'd always been unpredictable in the ring. Violent. No brain and all muscle. Cole had heard some people whisper that Kenny *liked* the FEUDS, that he craved the violence. Cole was glad he wasn't as transparent as Kenny—they'd never know that Cole was the one to be afraid of.

Kenny took a swing and Cole feinted left. Cole was light on his feet—that's what everyone always said, and just the right size for a fighter. They circled each other like dogs, teeth bared, moving with the rhythm of the frenzied shouts of the Gens above them.

Cole forced himself to take long, slow breaths. *Focus*, he thought. Kenny was big but he was too slow. He didn't use his head. And he depended on his fists too much. He didn't know how to grapple or use his weight, didn't understand that fighting wasn't the same as brawling. You had to be as good at dodging hits as doling them out. You had to be smart.

*Cole* had to be smart.

The Priors—some overweight businessman lab rats; a couple of blinged-out women, probably call girls; a minor celebrity Cole recognized from TV—hung back in the observation decks, enclosed in air-conditioned glass rooms into which the audio was piped. The Priors' shit-eating grins made Cole want to spit. They were there to make money off him.

His eyes flitted across the room, settling finally on Michelle. Her beautiful crystal eyes were wide. She had one hand pressed to the base of her throat, the other wrapped around her waist as though she was hugging herself. She was worried.

Kenny swung clumsily at Cole. Cole blocked easily and delivered a thrust to Kenny's jaw that knocked him back a few steps. But Kenny regained his footing within seconds.

Kenny leaped at Cole, and the weight of him threw them both to the ground. Kenny lifted his fist. But Cole reached up and deflected him, grabbing hold of his wrist. Cole shifted his weight and pivoted his hips forward, freeing his legs from beneath Kenny's bulk. In another second, he had Kenny completely immobilized in a triangle hold—eyes bulging, fat face red, shocked, and gasping.

The fight was over.

Then Cole felt Kenny's teeth sink into his thigh. Pain ripped through him. He saw the blood in Kenny's teeth. An overwhelming wave of nausea washed over Cole's body from stomach to throat to mouth. Instinctively, he broke the hold, rolled away. Kenny was fighting dirty now—and the Priors loved it.

He staggered to his feet, his vision swimming red, his head spinning. He inhaled for the count of three, exhaled for the count of three. No panicking. Let Kenny panic.

Kenny came at him again. Cole dodged him, ducked, kept moving, dancing on his feet. He waited for the right opening. Let Kenny tire himself out.

Then he saw it: his chance. Cole struck with his foot, hitting

Kenny squarely in the chest. Like he'd expected, Kenny was unprepared for a kick. He stumbled backward, bumping up against
the cage. The screaming of the crowd grew to a single note, like an
alarm.

Cole pounced. He pummeled Kenny's head hard, bringing him
to the ground, his knuckles crushing against skull, intense pain
radiating from the contact point to his wrist. Cole released all the
rage and sorrow he usually ignored, barely even feeling the crushing
pain in his knuckles. *Wham.* He hated fighting for money. *Smash.*
At night, when he dreamed about it, he was afraid. *Crack.* Parson
wouldn't own him right now if he'd withdrawn from the fights
when he should have. *Thud.* He hit Kenny again and again. Six
times, then seven. He couldn't distinguish Kenny's eyes from his
mouth from his nose. It was all slick with blood. Cole's heart
pounded, and his own blood pulsed in his ears. *End it,* a voice said.
*If he's out, you win.*

Kenny managed to raise two fingers. The signal of defeat.

The final buzzer rang and cheers erupted from the crowd.

Cole's world began to shift back into focus. He glanced back
into the crowd for Michelle's wide-open face, but she was gone.

A medic had already slipped into the cage to tend to Kenny's
skull. Kenny was half dead, and the realization made Cole lurch
backward, grabbing his stomach. His muscles clenched as he
bent over his knees, vomiting at the edge of the cage. The audience
gasped. *Let them,* Cole thought. *Let them soak up the drama.* Killing wasn't forbidden in the FEUDS, but it was against Cole's rule
book. How would he be able to look his mom in the face after
killing a guy? It was all blood money, but there were limits.

The noise around him increased to a roar, and Cole was glad
for a brief second that he was protected by the cage. Supposedly in
one of the FEUDS long ago, a winner was trampled to death by

revelers before he could even receive his prize. Hands grabbed the cage bars, eager to touch him. Gens hoisted other Gen girls into the air, some wearing only little beaded bikinis and waving signs with his name on them.

Through the haze, Cole could see the motion of the Priors cheering beyond the risers. They'd be gone soon, back to their luxury homes in Columbus, back to wash off the dirt that clung to them.

"Great fight, Cole." Cole stiffened as Parson Abel's palm connected with his shoulder. "Let me walk you out." Parson Abel, the CPM, was the only one with a key to the cage—despite the fact that the FEUDS were technically illegal. Then again, when had politicians ever *not* been corrupt? In addition to running Columbus, Abel's duties apparently included being the person designated to lock fighters in and—if both were still alive in the end—let them back out.

"Whatever you want." Cole avoided Parson's attempts at eye contact. Parson reeked like the cigars he liked to smoke. His white hair glistened with oil and shone silver like the blade of a knife. Cole wondered where his security contingent was; usually they followed Parson like puppies. Vicious pit bull puppies, teeth bared.

"Nice fight, nice fight." Parson Abel kept his trademark smile frozen to his face, chin dimpling as his cheeks stretched wide. He propelled Cole out of the cage and through the crowd. "Now all you have to do is beat out Brutus James next weekend, and you're clear for finals."

"Right. Win against the guy who beat 'Tommy the Toro' within inches of his life. That's it," Cole mumbled.

"What was that?"

Cole shook his head.

Just before he and Parson Abel reached the old tunnels, Cole felt a light tug on his wrist. Michelle stood behind him, her coal-black hair falling all the way to her naked waist. She was wearing a tiny red cutoff top. Her skin was dark and shimmery, making her look like a metallic statue. Her nails glittered against the skin of his forearm.

"You looked good out there," she told him, throwing her arms around his neck and pressing her torso into his.

"Thanks," he replied, making an effort to extract himself from her embrace. But it only made her push against him more.

He and Michelle had been friends for years, and although they had never actually hooked up, he knew that Michelle cared—that she probably even wanted to be more than just friends. But he wasn't exactly in a place to get close to somebody. He couldn't afford to lose focus over a girl. The last thing he wanted to do was hurt her.

"I wanted to talk to you—" Michelle started.

"The time, Cole, the time," broke in Parson Abel.

"I'll catch you later," he told Michelle, peeling her fingers from his wrist. He signaled to Parson Abel that he was ready to go.

"Don't know how you say no to that," Parson Abel said with a low whistle, smirking at Cole. "I hear they're wild in bed." Cole ignored the question in his statement, because Parson didn't mean Michelle in particular—he meant Gen girls. No, *Imp* girls—the derogatory term used only by Priors.

Abel led him into one of the dozens of offices that dotted the bottom of the site—shanties for the workmen who'd been running the demolition, now empty, abandoned—and closed the door. The "office" was lined with filth and rot, and it was dark. A rat skittered across the floor when Abel switched on a lamp, one of the dozen or so that had been installed to help the players and spectators navigate the underground.

The FEUDS—which technically stood for Fights Established

Under Demolition Sites—were held in various arenas that had been hastily constructed in the basements of the crumbling buildings that used to comprise the city, before reconstruction and modernization efforts made Columbus one of the wealthiest and most powerful cities in the New Americas. As a result, the fights were dirty. Everyone got dirty and fought dirty; you couldn't help it. It was a voyeuristic sort of thing: you left with a sheen of dust and a gritty sense of satisfaction.

"How much?" Cole asked when Parson closed the door. He wanted to take the money and get out of there. He needed to study, and pay the electric bill . . . and there was probably no food in the house.

"You beat Kenny to a bloody pulp out there," Parson remarked, ignoring Cole's question. "It's dangerous to lose control, Cole. Remember that."

Cole met his eyes, careful to keep his face impassive. Abel was always unpredictable. "I didn't lose control," he lied. Then he couldn't help it; his eyes flicked again to the envelope.

"It's yours," Parson said, extending it toward Cole.

Cole reached for it a second faster than he should have.

"Wait," Parson cautioned, lifting the money just outside of his grasp. "I forgot to take my cut. You know, Cole," he said, counting out his 50 percent of the cash. "If I hadn't spotted you, if I hadn't *sponsored* you, you'd be going nowhere fast."

Cole looked away. Even though it killed him to admit it, Parson was right. It was Parson who pushed Cole for the games in the first place, who paid his entry fees, who kept his meager salary coming. Parson Abel resumed distributing the stack of dollar bills and handed back the envelope. Cole sifted through his winnings against the dim light of the makeshift office. It would last two weeks, maybe three if he was careful.

"Thank you," Cole said stiffly as he stood up.

"Wait!" There was an unmistakable command in Parson's tone. "Stop right there." Cole sat back down, sighing. The simple motion of bending his knees hurt. "I have a business proposal," Parson said, leaning forward. "Actually, consider it more of a prerequisite. For the final rounds."

"What is it?" Cole asked.

Parson pulled a small photograph from his wallet and extended it toward Cole, his fingers touching only the edges of it, as if it were something precious he didn't want to spoil. Cole grabbed it carelessly, gripping it between his filthy thumb and forefinger on purpose. Parson Abel offered him a tight smile. Cole had won that round.

"I need you to get close to her," Parson Abel said. "I'll pay you for it. Ten thousand dollars. That's what you need to get into the finals, as you know. I'm not quite sure how you could come up with that sum of money without my assistance."

Cole bent over the photo.

"Here." Parson Abel reached out and brightened the lamp, illuminating the photo. Cole squinted at the face in the picture and felt his heart stop. At first he thought it was Michelle, but then he saw that the features were too regular and perfect, the coloring a shade or two lighter. The image lacked all of Michelle's defiance and rough edges.

She was flawless. Soft brown hair floated to her shoulders, and bright—almost surreal—green eyes shone out at him. Cole ran his fingers over the photograph for a second time, and he could feel the hair beneath his fingers and the softness of her skin. Was that a mole on her chin? Cole touched it lightly. No. Just a speck of dirt.

She was perfect.

A zing of curiosity rushed through his whole body.

"Lifelike, isn't it?" Parson Abel commented, seeing Cole's wonderment.

Cole had never seen anyone so breathtaking. That morning when he'd woken up, he'd been convinced that Michelle was the most beautiful girl in the world. Now he knew he was wrong.

But the girl in the picture wasn't one of his kind.

"A Prior," he whispered, more to himself than to Parson. "You want me to get close to a Prior."

"Yes," Parson said simply. "A Prior."

"Why me?" Cole looked up.

"Let's just say I've heard you have a way with the ladies." Parson Abel jerked his head, indicating the hall down which Michelle had retreated. "It's no secret that you're a good-looking guy, Cole. Don't you hear the way people react to you in the fights? No? Of course not." Parson Abel smiled thinly. "People are *hot* for you out there. Men, women, everyone. That's why I need *you* for this. It can't be anyone else."

Cole frowned. None of it made sense. "How—?" he started to ask.

"Leave the details to me," Parson assured him. "And meanwhile, try to keep that pretty face of yours from getting hammered in the cage. Are we on?"

Kissing a Prior was illegal. Even getting close to one could get Cole arrested. "Do I have a choice?" he said.

Parson smiled without humor. "Smart boy," he told Cole, slapping him on the back.

# 𝟥

## DAVIS

"Welcome, Miss Davis." The automated voice boomed out after Davis swiped her P-card at the front door of Emilie's building. She crossed the lobby and stepped into the elevator, her six-inch heels ticking on the floor.

"Reflection, please," she commanded the system.

She stretched her legs as she waited for her image to register. Her calves were sore from the extra two hours of practice she'd put in that morning.

The elevator's hexagonal design allowed Davis to check herself out from every angle as it shot to the 102nd floor, where Emilie's party was being held on the building's communal observation deck. Her legs were her best feature, muscled and defined from a lifetime of ballet, but now she tugged on the hem of her dress, worried that it showed too much. The glitter on her shoes drew attention to her slim ankles—but should she have worn heels that were a little lower? Fia had helped her select a navy dress that clung to her frame, and her chestnut hair spread over her shoulders in uniform waves. She thought her hair and makeup looked subtle enough; she just hoped she didn't look like she was trying too hard.

Davis smiled to herself as she remembered the gravity with which Fia had selected her outfit. Her sister's eagerness to please was sweet—she so badly wanted to be grown-up. She'd asked Davis at least six times to take her along, even saying she'd bring a book so she wouldn't bother anyone. Davis had kissed her cheek and promised her, as always, *Won't be long until it's your turn.* She wished she could tell Fia to slow it down a little, enjoy being a kid. There'd been a brief second when, exiting the house, she'd caught a glimpse of Fia leaning up against Terri's shoulder on the sofa, Terri's arm draped around her as they laughed at something on TV—and in that second, Davis wanted to swap places with Fia.

Davis caught her reflection in the mirror—her eyes looked big and sad, and she righted it quickly, taking a breath and squaring her shoulders. She smiled at herself in the mirror, hoping the emotions would follow. She was just a few minutes shy of seeing her best friend in the world and having a night of fun. She needed this—a light, easy night with her friends.

She turned sideways to catch a glimpse of her back. Fia had chosen well, she thought. She narrowed a critical eye, twisting to see better for signs of areas that needed improvement. Davis had always loved the lean sexiness of backs. They reminded her of old pictures of racehorses she had studied in history. The beautiful creatures had gone extinct fifty years before she was born, afflicted by a mysterious virus that some claimed to be a direct result of the last bad Tornado Decade. She always wished she'd been alive to see one, to sit on one's back and fly through the city, *away, far away from here.*

She straightened her shoulders. The shoulder blades floated, she knew, attached to the back by muscles and nothing else. This was what made the back so flexible but also so vulnerable. It was up to the ballerina to develop the connections that lay underneath. Discipline and strength were what kept everything from being too soft, from falling apart. She opened her purse and took out a small pill case full of her optimizers, shaking them into her hand. Davis swallowed the first pill, a little blue cylinder that was supposed to develop her spatial perception. Then she swallowed the purple one, the one that allowed her to take in more oxygen with every breath. Last was the pink pill, meant to help with brain cell regeneration. She might actually need a little extra regeneration-oomph that night, depending on how much she decided to drink. Just in case, she also took a yellow pill to help her more efficiently metabolize whatever Emilie had persuaded her parents to buy them.

The counter ticked down from forty-two floors in a hologram above her. Emilie's building was more than a hundred stories tall, but Davis wouldn't trade it for her family's more modest, sixty-story building if someone paid her. Davis's bedroom window overlooked the river, but from Emilie's you could see beyond that to the Slants.

The elevator opened to a blast of cool air from the observation decks. Davis took a quick look around. As usual, Emilie had gone overboard with her party's theme: Black Magic.

An Imp waitress wearing a dark corset, feathered skirt, glittery black heels, and a white beaked mask carried a tray of steaming shots, the dark alcohol within the glasses smoky.

A huge hologram of a pentacle lined one end of the roof, and the balcony was draped with sparkling red lights. Davis stepped around a cluster of velvet wing chairs: they were a nice touch, as were the gilded mirrors and brocade draperies that gave the roof deck the intimate feel it otherwise lacked. Trails of smoke seeped from every surface, obscuring Davis's view but giving the rooftop an eerie effect, as though it was distinct from the building itself. Besides the absinthe, the servers were toting around trays of foie gras and champagne and wearing top hats and black bow ties. Emilie's parents spared no expense for her legendary bashes. Emilie was notorious for using that money for a fully stocked bar, even though most of the guests were still a few months shy of the drinking age—eighteen in Columbus.

Davis brought her necklace to her lips, eager to find Vera. The mouthpiece of her phone was hidden in a gold necklace she wore at all times. It bore her initials—D.M.—but it also masked her DirecTalk. All the girls she knew wore jewelry to hide their DirecTalks, but a lot of them switched it up from time to time. Most girls had a dozen gaudy diamond bracelets by the time they turned sixteen.

But Davis preferred the simple gold chain she'd always had, a copy of one she saw long ago in a picture of her mother. The chain itself was a little flimsy—and Davis knew it was impractical. She ought to have reinforced it with a stronger, hardier one, but every time she thought about it, something held her back. She'd always loved the delicate quality of her mother's original chain, and the way this one mimicked it.

"*Connect Vera,*" she said into the device, clutching it in her palm. There was a minute of ringing, and Vera picked up. Davis held the necklace close to her ear, her voice connecting with Vera's somewhere in the sound waves between their accessories.

"*Hey girl, you here?*" Davis heard. Vera's DirecTalk never failed to put Davis on edge. DirecTalks were supposed to sound like their owners, but something always rang a little off about them. There was a quality to a human voice that the machines could never capture, in Davis's opinion.

"Yup. I'm standing by the bar on . . . the east side, I think? Where you at?"

"West corner by the white leather lounges."

"We're about to play spins, hurry up!"

"Be there in a minute! I'm going to grab a drink first. You want?"

"No way. I've taken like five shots already."

Davis could tell Vera was tipsy, but she didn't mind. She was so excited to see her friend that she found herself smiling broadly with anticipation. Vera was unpredictable and never boring. Some people were like that—they made every situation better, more vibrant. Davis loved traveling in Vera's orbit. They had so many ridiculous memories together. Like the time Vera had flashed the bartender at one of Davis's dad's political functions for a free bottle of Grey Goose, and they'd downed a third of it in the stairwell behind the stage before pouring the rest out since it was disgusting to drink straight. Or the time she'd snuck Davis out at three in the morning to sing at the top of their lungs to "Fire Walk" on the roof of her building in honor of the new year, even though Davis was grounded. Or the time she'd picked up a kitten on the street on the way home from Oscar's and insisted on taking it back to her place, where she'd promptly forgotten all about it and passed out and woken up the next morning to find that it had shredded half of her wardrobe.

A bunch of top hats soared over the rest of the crowd, tipping her off to the closest bar, which was right on her path toward Vera's side of the party. Davis pushed her way toward the velvet-and-brocade-draped station, sidestepping a crowd of about a dozen partiers who were clustered in the middle of the dance floor.

It wasn't hard to spot Emilie in the center of the crowd. She swayed on top of a mirrored, rotating table just next to the bar, matching the pulsing rhythm of the music. Her eyes were closed, and her drink sloshed a little over its brim as she danced, her silver boa trailing behind her. She moved with the kind of confidence and fluid precision that even copious amounts of alcohol couldn't strip from her. Her tiny body and boyish, muscular frame were perfect for ballet. Those were partly inherited and partly, of course, her parents' engineering.

Davis turned away and motioned to the bartender, trying to get his attention.

"I'm *fine*," someone shouted, bumping into her from behind. Davis whirled around to see a younger girl—Caitlyn, she thought—struggling to stand up straight. Her thin body looked overly gaunt in her tight white dress. Caitlyn's red hair was sweaty and clung to her face. The girl didn't look good; Davis felt her eyes widen in concern. Where were Caitlyn's friends? Why weren't they looking out for her? Davis reached for her arm, drawing her closer toward the bar where she'd be out of the way of the crowd.

"You look like you could use some water," she said, pouring her a glass from the pitcher at the edge of the bar. Caitlyn's eyes were unfocused; Davis helped her bring the glass to her lips and smiled reassuringly when the girl met her eyes. "Feel better?" she asked. Caitlyn nodded a little, pushing her champagne glass away from her, in the direction of the bar top. Davis grabbed it before it could spill, and pulled up a bar stool with her free hand. "Sit," she told her.

"I'm fine," Caitlyn said, but she settled herself onto the stool, leaning toward the counter as she sipped her water. Some of the color had begun to return to her cheeks.

"You sure?" Davis asked. "Where are your friends? Want me to wait with you?"

Caitlyn smiled, and her eyes looked a little more focused. "No, that's okay," she told Davis. "Thanks though. For the water. I think ... I just didn't eat enough today. I'll stick to water now. I'm fine, really." Davis nodded and smiled, then headed off in the direction of her own friends. For a second she wondered if she should have stayed at the bar with Caitlyn, but Caitlyn had dozens of friends at the party, and anyway she was just a little drunk, no big deal.

She headed toward Vera's spot, taking a large gulp of the champagne from Caitlyn's glass. The bubbles instantly went to her head.

"Come here often?" said a deep, unfamiliar voice.

Davis turned around, taking in the handsome guy standing behind her. He was cuter than the other guys she knew, who were also very cute. He was perfect like all the rest, but something was *different* about him. Davis had never seen him before, and Davis knew a lot of the kids in Columbus. Other guys were carved out of stone, similar to the sculptures of Adonis and David that she and Vera had giggled over in ancient history years ago. This guy was a living, breathing Apollo: warm and vibrant.

"Use lame pickup lines often?" she fired back, trying to regain her cool.

To her surprise, the guy laughed. "Only with beautiful girls," he returned. But his lips were turned up slightly in one corner.

Davis flushed. Her palms were sweaty all of a sudden, and the hair on the back of her neck was tingling in the weird way it did when she was excited.

"Do I know you?" she said, hoping her voice sounded controlled. Despite her nerves, the way he was looking at her gave her a strange sense of glowing from the inside out.

"You do now," he returned, placing his hand softly on the exposed part of her back, sending a finger of heat down her spine. "I'm Cole."

She pulled away. "And I'm looking for my friends," she told him. She almost didn't like how tingly this guy was making her feel.

"Let me get you another drink, then," he said, taking her nearly empty glass from her hand. She noticed her fingers trembling slightly. Was she really *that* nervous?

"I'll be over there," she called to him, indicating the corner where Vera and a bunch of her other friends were seated, shoving into the crowd without bothering to check whether he'd heard her. She knew guys like that couldn't be trusted anyway. They could have anyone—and usually, they did.

"Hey!" Vera jumped up when she noticed Davis, giving her air kisses on both cheeks. "Come sit," Vera commanded, pulling her over Oscar's lap to the other side of the white divan. Vera let out a piercing squeal at the sound of her favorite song.

"What can I say?" Oscar smiled, nodding toward Vera. "She's a real treasure."

"What's that phrase?" Vera tried to joke. "When love touches—"

"'At the touch of love, everyone becomes a poet,'" Oscar broke in. "Everyone except you, I guess. Use your compendium, and then you won't have to worry about screwing up basic clichés when you drink."

Vera just tossed her blonde hair over her shoulder and laughed, and so Davis laughed along with her. She wondered whether Oscar's little jabs ever bothered Vera. They didn't seem to, but they bothered *her*; she didn't like to see anyone putting Vera down.

Davis had never said as much to Vera, because she knew Vera was happy, but Oscar reminded her of father's smarmy campaign planner, Frank, in a weird way. Maybe it was how he clenched his jaw when he was annoyed, or the way he interrupted Vera, or even the way he was always dispensing advice as though he knew best, no matter what the topic.

But even when Oscar did things Davis would never put up with herself, Vera stuck by him. They had grown up on separate floors of the same building, and were the children of two of the wealthiest, most powerful families in Columbus. They were the perfect match: Vera was unparalleled on the cello, and Oscar had scored higher on his intellectual aptitude test that year than anyone had in Columbus in three decades.

Maybe Vera loved him, maybe she didn't. She'd never said as much—and Oscar certainly never had—but Davis figured they had to love each other. But whenever Davis asked Vera what it was like—being in love like that, being sure you'd found the one—Vera laughed her off. "It's not like those lame old movies you hoard," she would say. "*Dangerous Love* or whatever," which was actually *L'Amour en Temps de Péril,* an epic love story about a couple separated when the first wildfires tore through Europe—not that Vera could ever remember the name of it despite the million times Davis reminded her. "We fit. That's all."

Davis never even bothered asking about the sex. She knew Vera would make fun of her for making it into such a big deal—and for *still* being a virgin. All their other friends swapped and exchanged on a regular basis. Anytime Vera did offer up any details, it was a half-joking reference to the awesome abs-and-thighs workout she was getting all the time.

Davis had made out with plenty of guys—that was just how it was; it was what *everyone* did—but she'd never actually slept with anyone. There was something stopping her from going all the way, and she wished she knew what it was. She just couldn't help the feeling that if she lost her virginity, she would lose something else, too.

"What took you so long?" Vera said, pouting.

"Ver, it was my dad's broadcast tonight," Davis said, rolling her eyes. "He went up against Parson Abel in a debate about segregation. This was his *last* big speech before elections."

"Oh no!" Vera clapped a hand over her mouth, her eyes widening. "I forgot. I'm so sorry!" Vera had been forgetting a lot of things lately. Davis told herself it was just a natural result of the Olympiads and the Classics, the arts competition that was looming. The stress of extra practices had been taking a toll on all of them. Still, Vera had always been a thoughtful friend. She knew it wasn't personal, but tonight's slip hurt a little.

"Everyone knows your dad's going to win. Don't stress, okay?" Vera said, clutching Davis's hand in hers. She offered Davis a reassuring smile. "The whole thing is pretty much a joke. It's not like anyone else in the campaign has a chance."

"Um, except the *current* CPM," Oscar interjected. "Stop being naïve. Parson Abel's got a lot of support. I know a few people who wouldn't mind him staying in office for another term." A shiver of panic worked its way through Davis's chest. If her dad lost . . . his career would be ruined. She didn't want to think about what it would mean for them, or for the future of Columbus.

"Whatever." Vera dismissed Oscar's comment with a wave of her hand. "Davis, you have nothing to worry about. And I'll be at the next campaign event with bells and whistles. Literally." She smiled at Davis and patted her on the shoulder. Davis laughed. She would totally not be surprised if this were true. She felt better— way better. Vera might have forgotten, but nothing in her doubted that Vera *cared*. "Here," Vera said, unwrapping the braided leather cord she always wore over one wrist. "Take my lucky cuff. It loves you. As I do. It will bring you luck, too." Davis laughed; now Vera was just being silly, but she took the cuff and gave her friend a kiss on the cheek, allowing her to fasten the cord around her own wrist.

A new game of spins was just starting. Max reached forward to spin the bottle. If her turn landed on Max, she might have to bolt. Max had been obsessed with her since kindergarten, and he had a tongue like a Saint Bernard. Thankfully, it landed on Lana Douglass.

Then Davis felt a slight pressure on her arm, and the mystery guy was back, sliding in next to her with a new glass of champagne. She felt her heart speed up—she was weirdly excited he'd returned. She took the glass—another drink wouldn't hurt. With the new metabolizers, she could have up to four without feeling it the next day.

She brought her champagne flute to her lips, trying not to notice the feeling of his skin against hers, but it was impossible to ignore. He sat next to her on the divan, and his thigh was pressed against hers. As he leaned forward, his tanned, muscular forearms brushed against her waist.

"I'd love to join in. If that's okay with you, of course," he said, addressing Davis in a low voice.

"Whatever you want," she said, once again trying to play it cool. "No need to run it by me." Her heart hammered in her chest and her palms felt cold; she was shocked and relieved that her voice didn't betray the intensity of her reaction to him.

He nodded, smiling as though she'd said something funny.

"Who *is* that?" Vera whispered.

"No one," Davis said, hoping that the new guy wouldn't guess that they were talking about him.

The new guy reached across them for the bottle, his arm brushing against Davis's, sending a line of fire trailing up her shoulder.

"What's up, man? It's my turn." This from Harrison, a guy from her history class.

"It's cool," the new guy said. "I only plan on going once."

Davis could tell his presence was affecting everyone. Even Vera seemed to have forgotten herself. She leaned into Oscar but kept her eyes trained on Mystery Guy.

The bottle spun. He spun it fast and hard, so hard that it wobbled from its place on the crystal tabletop and skittered across the table. As it came to a halt, he grabbed its neck and pointed it—directly at her. Davis's cheeks heated up.

"Looks like it found who it wanted," he said so softly that only she could hear. He grabbed her hands and tugged her to her feet.

"What are you doing?" She was trying to laugh it off as she said it, but something about the confident way he moved was making her nervous. His hands were still clasping hers, and he was yanking her away from the lounge chairs and the group toward the dim corridor that led back inside the building.

"It's no fun if people can't see," she protested. That was the whole *point* of spins—being watched. Putting on a show.

He glanced at her questioningly. "It's *more* fun," he said. But he took a few steps back toward the crowd anyway, leading her like a dancer might. When they were close enough, he hooked his arms behind her waist and pulled her toward him. For half a second, Davis felt the stares of all her friends on them. But then she noticed his heart beating against her chest. And his hands lightly grazing her bare back. And then his lips pressed against hers softly, his tongue finding its way into her mouth . . .

A chorus of laughter brought Davis back to reality. She pulled away and opened her eyes to find herself facing the lens of a video camera. She stumbled backward a little, extending one hand palm facing out to cover the lens. She'd never been a fan of being caught on video; her friends loved it, but she always managed to look awkward on film.

The guy held on to her waist, almost as if he'd guessed in advance that he'd have to steady her. Then sensation began to filter back, and Davis could feel her feet again. Davis blinked a few times, wanting more. She glanced Vera's way and was surprised to see her friend looking concerned. But in the space of a second, Vera smiled her familiar, dazzling grin.

"I think I need another drink," Davis said, moving away from the group before anyone could stop her. Only at the bar could she catch her breath.

"Can I tell you something?" He was next to her then. She was afraid to look at him in case she lost her composure altogether. She didn't know how he managed to shake her up the way he did. It wasn't all bad, feeling disarmed.

"What?" She tried to sound confident, careless.

Instead of answering, he took her hands in his for the second time that night and tugged her back toward the hallway, which was empty because no one wanted to leave a party this good, this wild. And then he was cradling her head in his palms and tipping her face up toward his, and Davis found herself wrapping her arms around his waist and touching his back under his shirt with her fingers. It was as if her body already knew how to do all of it without needing any commands from her brain. The only other time she'd ever felt that way was while she was dancing.

This time the kiss was slower, more passionate, and more intense. Her whole body reacted at once: her heartbeat flooded her veins until it felt like it was hammering against every part of her. Her head was empty. She couldn't think. It was like her body had choreographed a dance with his, something they were experts at even though neither of them knew what would come next.

She felt his hands in her hair, then touching the skin on her back, just above her waistband. He crushed her silk dress in his palms as he pulled her hips toward his. But his mouth stayed on hers the whole time, anchoring her to that spot until she no longer cared who he was or why he was there but just wanted the moment to keep going on forever. No one had ever done that to her. No one had ever made her feel so out of control.

Out of control. She was out of control.

"Stop," she said, placing her hands on his chest to push him away. They were both breathing hard; Davis had the weirdest sensation she was dreaming.

"Why?" he asked softly, stepping back ever so slightly. "Aren't you having fun, Davis?"

She stepped out of reach, shaking her head, unable to answer. "I have to go."

She needed Vera. Vera would make her feel better, would laugh off this boy's weird intensity and make her feel normal again.

It was only after she'd pushed back into the crowd, back toward the party, into the geometry of moving and swaying bodies, that she thought to wonder how he knew her name.

# 4

## COLE

Heat coursed through his body. Music pounded in his ears.

The kiss wasn't what Cole had thought it would be. It was way, way better. He'd heard more times than he could remember that Prior girls were cold. But that kiss had left him reeling, his head thick and foggy like he'd had too much to drink, and he could feel a sharp wetness on his lips where the nerves were still reacting. It was so good, he'd forgotten why he'd gone in for it in the first place. He'd forgotten to take a photo, as Parson had instructed him to do, to prove he'd been successful. The kiss had caught him off guard, and he'd completely blown it.

Parson was going to be furious.

It was his one shot. There wouldn't be another kiss like that.

Cole took off in the direction Davis had gone, following an intricate maze of red-lit paths and makeshift bars around the roof. There were people everywhere. Cole pushed past a girl in a slinky blue dress who was swaying to the indie-pop the DJ was shuffling. She grazed his bicep with her fingers as he went by, but when he met her eyes, her gaze was directed somewhere else. The place was so crowded that Cole had to fight back an instinct to shoulder people off. There was a sort of organized chaos about the whole thing: the movements of the crowds seemed choreographed in a graceful imitation of revelry. He took a right turn toward the entrance he remembered accessing when he first came in, ignoring a tray of hors d'oeuvres a woman in a puffy feathered skirt and an elaborate mask was passing around. She smiled at him.

No. Not *at* him, he realized—at the mirror just behind him. He turned and caught a glimpse of his face, where a slight hint of red, likely invisible to everyone else, emerged from beneath the makeup he'd layered on to hide his scratch from the fights. He unbuttoned the top button of the shirt Parson had given him, the nicest piece of clothing he owned. The tightness around his neck reminded him of a noose. He wasn't used to feeling nervous, but the combined rush of the kiss plus the claustrophobia of the party and the fear of getting caught had started to mess with him. He could feel a line of sweat trickling down his forehead.

*Leave,* said the voice in his head. *Just go home. You're already in over your head.*

He spotted a redheaded girl slumped over her knees as if taking a nap. The way her thin body was folded over itself, she looked like some kind of party prop. He hesitated. She was obviously sick.

Cole approached the girl slowly. If she was drunk—or if she

had a boyfriend—she might lash out and make a scene, and the last thing he needed was to draw attention to himself. But she didn't stir as he drew closer, and when he put a hand on her shoulder—a chill working its way farther up his spine every second—he knew something was wrong. He gave her a nudge, and the girl's head flopped back, her strawberry curls draping low against the chair as her neck succumbed to the weight of her skull. Her eyes were almost closed and her skin was the color of ash—almost as pale as her tight white dress. A tiny stream of blood dribbled from the corner of her mouth.

A dart of concern shot through his chest. Lab rats didn't get sick. Not like this.

"Hey," Cole said, kneeling down to speak to the girl. "Hey. Can you hear me?" He shook her gently, fighting a wave of panic. But instead of reviving her, his movements just caused the girl's head to loll to the other side of the lounge chair where she sat, her arms draped by her sides.

"Shit," he mumbled. He leaned closer and her eyelids fluttered. The sounds of labored breathing somehow reached his ears over the din of the music. She needed a doctor; anyone could see that.

Cole straightened up, glancing around the packed roof deck. The beautiful masses swayed to electronica now. A brunette near him flashed him a smile and flipped her glossy hair over one shoulder, moving her hips seductively. Soon her attention shifted past him— but not to the girl in the chair. To a mirror mounted on the wall behind him. Cole turned toward the mirror. Not for the first time that night, he realized there were a lot of mirrors at the party, and each one reflected dozens of sets of eyes trained on their own images.

Cole's stomach turned on itself. He felt a wave of revulsion, a thick blot of anger directed at every Prior, the "superior" kind of human.

Animals.

He'd have to help her on his own. *Where were her friends?*

"What's wrong with her?"

Cole had just begun hoisting the girl's body over his shoulders. The voice, sharp and afraid all at once, belonged to Davis. Cole shook his head, grunting as he changed position, holding the redhead like he might a baby. Her body was surprisingly heavy.

"I thought . . ." Davis said, her voice dying to a whisper. "I thought she was just drunk. Is she—?" Her sentence cut off, her chin beginning to tremble. Cole looked at her in surprise.

"Let's get her downstairs." His voice was harsher than he'd intended.

Davis nodded. It didn't escape Cole that she was the only one at the whole party who'd even noticed something was wrong, or cared enough to do something about it. Cole managed, with difficulty, to carry the redhead into the elevator. Davis punched furiously at the lobby button. Her eyes looked naked and frightened.

"We should call an ambulance," Cole said, breathing hard.

"We can't," Davis told him. "The Imps are on strike, remember? There aren't any drivers, there haven't been for days."

Cole turned away, trying not to flinch when he heard the word *Imps*. Of course. He'd forgotten about the strikes. For the first time, he realized how dependent on the Imps the residents of Columbus really were.

Once outside, Cole laid the girl's body gently on the pavement within the building's inner courtyard, leaning her against the cold slabs of limestone just in front of the grassy strip that decorated the base of Emilie's building. Davis knelt next to her. Thankfully, they were out of sight of anyone who might pass by—still shielded by the building's opaque entry gate, which divided the courtyard from the streets and served as the building's sole security system. It was nearly two o'clock in the morning, dark, and mostly quiet.

"What's her name?" His words came out sharply.

"Caitlyn. I think . . . Caitlyn. Should I get someone?"

"We don't have time. Caitlyn," he said. "Can you hear us?" He cupped her face in a gentle motion, squeezing, shaking her face. Her eyes fluttered open.

"Don't hurt her," Davis said.

"She needs to stay conscious. Caitlyn," he said again. "Caitlyn, where do you live? Can you hear me?"

The girl's lips parted, and the tiniest bit of blood bubbled between them. *God.* What was wrong with this girl? What had she done to herself? Priors didn't just get sick. Drugs, maybe? Some kind of OD? He had no idea what kind of shit Priors took.

She mumbled something, and her body began to shake. Then her eyes shot open, and she trained them on Davis. They were wide and vacant, as if she was having trouble focusing.

"Davis?" the girl slurred. "Can you . . . can you check . . ."

"What, honey?" Davis asked. Cole could see she was struggling to stay calm—her hands trembled. "What do you need?"

"Do I look okay?" the girl asked, her head lolling to the side. Her eyelids fluttered again, dangerously close to shutting altogether. "Is . . . is my mascara smudged?" The last part came out thick, like she had cotton stuffed in her mouth.

"No," Davis lied. "You look just beautiful." Caitlyn rested her head against Davis's shoulder, and blood and saliva trickled down Caitlyn's neck, onto the straps of her white dress. Some of it was getting on Davis's skin as well. Cole felt heavy, useless, the same way he did when he sustained a powerful hit in the ring. He recognized it as a sign of shock.

"I don't like it here," Caitlyn said. Her voice was so soft that Cole had to strain to hear it. "Take me home. Please."

"*Dammit,*" Cole said. He stood and turned in a circle, raking his hand through his hair. He shouldn't have gotten caught up in this. He couldn't take her to a hospital; it was too risky for him. He had the fake ID from Abel: a real, scannable ID that Abel had doctored with Cole's picture—but what were the odds he'd get away with it?

"What should we do?" Davis said, her voice rising. "Help me. I don't know what to do."

"Just let me think," Cole said.

"Please," Caitlyn murmured again. "Please take me home. I'm fine."

"Okay," Cole said. He sucked in a deep breath. That's what he would do. He'd take her home. He didn't have a choice. He'd let her parents deal with her overdose or whatever she was going through. "Where do you live?" he asked her.

"Sherman," she barely managed to get out. "Two . . . Sherman." *Sherman.* Cole didn't know how the hell he'd find it, but he would.

"I want to help," Davis told him. "Please."

"You can help by telling me where Sherman is, then by letting me handle this alone," Cole said. "It's better for you," he explained, his voice softer this time.

"You don't have navigation on your DirecTalk?" Davis looked confused.

"It's busted," Cole told her. *Of course* they'd have some sort of navigation device. Why hadn't Parson given Cole a cheat sheet when he'd delivered his P-card and DirecTalk?

The creases on Davis's forehead deepened, but she nodded.

"Three blocks west," she told him. "The row of vintage bunga-lows. You can't miss it." Cole didn't know what a "vintage bungalow" was, but he wasn't about to tell her that.

"Thanks." He hefted Caitlyn up from the curb, holding her in his arms for the second time that night. "You should head back inside," he said to Davis.

She hesitated. "Are you sure?"

"Yes. You shouldn't be out here alone. I've got it covered."

"Okay," she said, looking uncertain. "Thank you. Really. I . . . I hope everything will be okay."

He nodded but didn't reply. He wasn't sure he knew how to. He bent to readjust Caitlyn's arms around his neck, and by the time he straightened, Davis had vanished. They walked less than half a block before Caitlyn began to gurgle deep in her throat. Then she vomited a thick and vile liquid all over Cole's loaner button-down and onto the street beneath them. Cole turned her chin and swiped out her throat with his fingers. But it was too late.

Caitlyn was out cold.

Cole thanked God that the streets were empty, the lights in neighboring apartment buildings long extinguished. He had no idea what would happen if someone were to see and stop him. But he wouldn't be left with this girl's death on his conscience. He walked three blocks west, like Davis had told him to. He didn't see any street sign for Sherman, let alone any sort of old-fashioned house—mansion, he was guessing—like she'd described.

He heard footsteps behind him and his pulse began to quicken. He ducked his head and shuffled as quickly as he could into an empty doorway. A minute later, a guy walked by him without pausing. Cole couldn't tell whether it was a member of security enforcement, but the fact that he *could have been* hit him like a black wave, rendering his legs near-paralyzed. He could be imprisoned, even executed, if he got caught masquerading as a Prior, holding an inebriated Prior girl in his arms.

If he was caught, he didn't stand a chance.

And even worse: he was lost.

New plan. Cole would take her back to the Slants, get her help there.

He hurried toward the riverbank with renewed conviction, sticking to the shadows but not bothering much with caution. He was close, so close. Adrenaline coursed through him with every step, and then he was at the embankment, sliding down the slope covered with mud and old leaves, where everything was shadows but the glittering water.

Cole whistled twice hard and once soft for the motie. A minute went by: silence, punctuated only by the gentle lapping of water against the edge of the bank. Crossing into Columbus from the Slants earlier this evening by motie had been scary, but only because he'd never done it before. This was different. Every second it didn't show up put Cole a second closer to getting caught . . . which meant prison or worse. Cole whistled again, louder this time, terrified that the sound might draw attention from shore. His heart was practically exploding out of his throat.

Finally, the motie pulled up. Cole was still too panicked even to be relieved. The old man running the motorboat was skinny and shirtless, the outline of the bones of his rib cage showing like faint stripes along his flesh. He grinned wide at Cole once he started the engine, and Cole saw pure black where teeth should have been.

Cole stepped aboard, positioning Caitlyn next to him. His heart pounded; this wasn't what he'd signed up for, not even close. And now he was calling it a night without getting a photo, holding the wrong girl in his arms. The plan had been completely derailed, and Parson was going to be pissed. But what could he do? He settled Caitlyn in place, keeping her frame steady in his arms. The old man leered at the girl but didn't ask questions—he'd probably seen worse. Cole kept Caitlyn upright—and out of the motie's reach—against the waves that rocked the vessel. He just wanted to get home.

Worsley would help. Worsley knew everything. They'd grown up together, two doors apart; Worsley had been Cole's brother's best friend all their lives, even though he was a few years older. He was like a second older brother to Cole, maybe because he'd fought in the FEUDS himself once. Cole still had a hard time believing it, even though it was Worsley who'd gifted Cole with an ancient hard drive, salvaged from a junkyard, and equally ancient instructional videos that Cole had watched so many times he had them memorized, learning not just boxing techniques but old martial arts like jujitsu, judo, wrestling, and tae kwan do.

Worsley just didn't look the part of a fighter. He was strong but sinewy, much leaner than Cole. He was over six feet tall, with dark hair that was always flopping into his eyes. Worsley had long, bony fingers and he wore glasses, too: a prescription he'd written himself. He was the closest thing they had to a real doctor in the Slants. And he was the only one Cole knew in the Slants who had a college education. Worsley had attended university in New Pacific— the northwestern region of the New Americas—at a prestigious institution in Helena. It had been funded by his FEUDS winnings, plus a rare and coveted Columbus Academic Exchange Scholarship less than a decade ago.

Worsley could fix this.

They were less than a few feet from shore when water began to accumulate at the bottom of the wooden vessel. It lapped against Cole's shoes, the only pair of decent ones he owned. The motie saw Cole looking down at them and laughed.

"What's so funny?" Cole asked, annoyed. Tension crept through him, making him feel like he was being strangled. But the motie just kept on laughing to himself and ignoring Cole, and water kept on building up at the base of the boat.

Cole looked around him; they were maybe halfway across now, but he couldn't make out the beginnings of either side of the shore, and the water around them was pitch black and menacing.

"Turn around," Cole said to the motie. But the old man ignored him and they kept moving forward, the waves lapping at the side of the boat. Cole had no choice but to shut up and pray.

When they finally got to the Columbus border, Cole scrambled out of the boat, his already drenched shoes slapping against the muddy surface of the shore. He hefted Caitlyn onto his shoulder, reaching back only to place a single dollar in the man's hand. It was all he had.

There were roughly fifteen separate small communities in the Slants. They were really just groups of leased trailers and other "temporary" housing structures clustered around public bathrooms, schools, bars, and rec centers that were owned and operated by North Quadrant. A child peered out from behind the flimsy screen door of a trailer, and Cole held a finger of his free hand to his lips. The child nodded. Kids here grew up fast.

By the time Cole reached his own narrow three-room mobile home, he could barely feel his arms, and the girl hadn't made a sound in half an hour. He kicked open the screen door to confront five startled faces: his brother Hamilton's friends. The room smelled like stale beer and sweat. Tom Worsley was there, thank God. He jolted up so fast at the sight of Caitlyn that his glasses jumped on his nose, and he knocked over his stool. Hamilton was on his feet, too, rushing toward Cole.

"She needs water," Cole told him. "Maybe medicine, I don't know. I don't know what's wrong with her."

"Worsley," Hamilton said over his shoulder. "Do you have your bag with you? Looks like the girl's strung out on something, maybe OD'd." Worsley nodded, pushing his hair out of his eyes with one palm as he darted past Cole, presumably to grab his medical kit from his house two doors down.

Cole struggled to kneel, placing Caitlyn's body on the pallet they used as a sofa. He looked up to find Hamilton's eyes narrowing, his face set in an expression of disbelief. Cole braced himself. Even with blood trickling from her mouth, it was easy to see what Caitlyn was.

"You brought home a Prior," Hamilton growled, his voice low. The other three guys shifted, and someone let out a cry of disbelief.

"I didn't know what else to do," Cole told him. "She needed help. I couldn't go to the hospital—"

Hamilton lunged at him before Cole could finish his sentence. He grabbed Cole by the shirt collar, and Cole allowed his brother to yank him into the bedroom. He could have resisted—Hamilton was taller, but he was skinny, and Cole could have creamed him in a fight any day. But Cole's entire body felt numb. He couldn't find it in himself to fight.

Hamilton slammed the door behind them, kicking it shut with his heel.

"How could you be so stupid?" Hamilton hissed, keeping his voice low. The veins on his forehead were pulsing, and he looked more furious at his little brother than he'd ever been. All at once, he seemed to take in what Cole was wearing: his nice shirt, his clean, pressed jeans. "What the hell is going on, Cole? What were you thinking?"

"I was thinking I'd help her!" Cole snapped. "You saw her—I couldn't just leave her!"

"Where did you even find her?" Hamilton released him. "Never mind. I don't need to know. We'll talk about this later. Dammit, Cole . . ." He trailed off, still pacing the room, both hands massaging his temples.

"Hamilton," came a voice from the main room. "Hamilton, you better get in here quick, man." Cole and Hamilton pushed back into the room just as Worsley came through the front door with a large canvas bag in tow.

One of the guys from the table, a kid Cole had never seen before, was staring at Caitlyn, his face ashen. One of the other guys had left—*Not to get the police,* Cole prayed. Even though the police force in the Slants had been put in place by the Priors specifically for the Gens' protection, they were notoriously vicious. The third guy had been pressing a damp cloth to Caitlyn's forehead. But now he'd backed off. Because Caitlyn was bleeding from her ears and nose, too, now—not just her mouth. Her ears and nose were gushing blood, and her face was frozen into an expression of misery.

Worsley inserted his body between the brothers. "Let me take a look."

"Can you help?" Cole could hear that he was pleading. "Please?" Worsley didn't answer. Instead, he opened his bag and bent over Caitlyn, shielding her from Cole's view.

Cole couldn't help being relieved. He'd seen a lot of blood in his life, but never anything as horrifying as this.

"You said you were going to the mines," Hamilton said to Cole while Worsley worked. "And I thought that was bad. But this is pure idiocy! How could you be so careless? If someone had seen you—" He broke off, breathless. "You'd have been arrested, maybe worse." Cole glanced down at Caitlyn's inert body, still covered in her tight white dress—now horribly stained—and expensive shoes. He *was* an idiot. Anyone could tell she was a Prior. But he'd had no choice other than to bring her home. "Make no mistake," Hamilton continued, "if this happens again—if you *ever* go back to the other side—I'll call the police myself. I'll get you thrown in jail faster than you can throw a punch. I will *not* watch you put our family at risk."

"Hamilton," Worsley interrupted. "Be quiet and sit down. You're not helping." Worsley's voice sounded strained, as though he were speaking from a distance. He adjusted his glasses with one hand.

"I didn't know what to do," Cole said to no one in particular, hating himself for how weak he sounded, how afraid. "I thought she was about to die. I didn't mean for any of this to happen." Cole sat down heavily on a kitchen chair, unable to process everything he was hearing. He gave his brother a long look, and Hamilton's expression softened. He crossed the small space to join Cole at the table.

"You really didn't, did you?" Hamilton asked, the rage gone from his voice. Cole shook his head, and Hamilton laughed ruefully, shaking his head, too. "Only you, little brother. I don't know how you get yourself into these things."

He patted him on his shoulder. "Go lie down," he told Cole, his voice kinder now. "We'll take care of this. It'll be okay."

As much as Hamilton could be hard on him at times, he was still his older brother, and Cole knew that when things got really, *really* bad—like now—Hamilton had his back. Grateful, he nodded up at him, breathing more easily.

"What's happening to her?" William, a friend of Hamilton's— the one who'd given Caitlyn the washcloth—broke in. He pointed a trembling finger at Caitlyn's inert form. His expression was of pure terror.

Cole turned his attention back to Caitlyn, whose face now looked mottled, as though her capillaries had begun to burst. Worsley bent over her just as the redness in her skin began to form long, jagged cracks that split and leaked until her whole face was covered in fissures and blood. It looked like her face was a mask that had begun to break apart. Cole took a small step back and stumbled. He gripped the wall for support.

"Narxis," Worsley said, straightening up. The room went silent. "I had a professor in West Freecom who talked about it. There were rumors, mostly—no tangible evidence. But this is exactly what he described." Worsley's face was ashen.

"Narxis," Cole repeated, afraid to keep looking but unable to look away. "What's going to happen to her?"

Worsley met his eyes. "If it really is Narxis," he said, "she'll die. There's been no research for treatments. There's no cure. Everyone who gets Narxis will die."

"Die." Cole allowed the word to roll off his tongue and sink into his head. He glanced toward Caitlyn's body, where it lay prone on the floor. Her face was now bleeding so heavily that he could no longer make out her features. He sank to the floor and knelt beside her, wanting to grab her hand but afraid to touch her now.

Hamilton crouched next to Cole and draped his arm around his shoulders. "It'll be okay," he told him. "You were right. You did the right thing, bringing her here." It was what Cole needed to hear. He turned his head, fighting the tears that pooled in the corners of his eyes. A gagging sound came from the corner, and then a splatter; it was William, vomiting into the sink.

"Can't you do anything?" Hamilton asked Worsley, his voice rough. "Can't you at least make her more comfortable?"

"She can't feel anything," Worsley told them. "She's too far gone."

A hacking sound came from the pallet where Caitlyn lay. Blood gurgled from her mouth onto the towel Cole had wadded up next to her. Then a rush of more blood, and then she was still.

"It's over."

Hamilton disappeared and came back moments later with a sheet, their only spare. He draped it over Caitlyn's body, taking pains not to touch her. Cole had been in a hundred fights, but he'd never seen anyone suffer so violently.

"I'm sorry," Hamilton said, gripping Cole's shoulder. Cole knew that was his way of saying he wished he hadn't been so hard on Cole.

"What is . . . Narxis?" Cole asked Worsley.

"It's an infection," he replied. "I haven't ever seen a case myself. It's . . . it's . . . ." He trailed off, shaking his head.

"Tell us," Hamilton said. "Please. I want to know what we're dealing with."

"One of my professors claimed to have treated patients with Narxis," Worsley explained. "But everyone thought Professor Alkem was senile, and he never had any evidence to support his claims. Prior bodies aren't supposed to be vulnerable to anything. But my friend Jensen swore Narxis was a result of all the manipulations Priors do. The experiments. Jensen had met with Professor Alkem, who said denial was an inherent part of the disease. Priors would never be able to recognize the symptoms in time to contain the virus and prevent it from spreading."

"So why haven't we heard of it?" Hamilton wanted to know.

"Politics. The Priors suppressed it. They thought they'd gotten rid of it—ironed out the kinks in the technology. Alkem's findings were never recognized. They were never included in any official diagnostic handbooks."

"What does that mean?" Cole's voice sounded far away, even to himself.

"It means they'll die," Worsley said quietly. "Every one of them."

# ⊰ 5 ⊱

## DAVIS

It was Monday, the day of the PAs, and Davis's dad was late.

"Rock that body, girl," called out Sasha, winking as she passed Davis in the courtyard just outside Excelsior. It was her way of saying good luck.

"Thanks," Davis called out weakly, wishing she could manage a smile.

If Davis didn't qualify for the ballet trials . . . She pushed the thought out of her mind. She would. She had to.

She sat down on the shiny steps of her school's main entrance, adjusting her sunglasses against the afternoon glare, trying to focus her swirling thoughts and steady her shaking hands. She zipped up her light jacket, fiddling with the small pig charm she'd threaded onto Vera's braided leather cuff. Fia had given her the little silver pig that morning, a solemn look on her face as she'd pulled it from a chain of her own. "Pigs are good luck," she'd said before wrapping her arms around Davis's waist.

"You're all the luck I need," Davis had told her, kissing her lightly on the cheek before dashing out to face one of the biggest days of her life. Now she waited, staring at the ground, breathing deeply, hoping that luck would work. Her shadow on the limestone slabs was dwarfed by the imposing stone administration office, its peaked roof supported by pillars as thick as tree trunks. A long iron gate marked the school's circumference, separating it from the rest of the city.

Even trying to count the rungs on the gate, she couldn't keep her mind from buzzing all over the place: The party. The boy. The way he'd kissed her ... Davis had replayed the events of Friday night over and over again pretty much all weekend. She couldn't get him out of her head. Vera had thought there was something weird about him, didn't get a good vibe. Davis winced at the memory of her friend's disapproval. There *was* something different about him ... but for some reason it made Davis's adrenaline spike in a good way. Still, maybe Vera was right that it was just the unexpectedness of it all that had been so exciting. Vera had even offered to hook her up with Oscar's cousin Joaquin, who was going to be home on break from college next month. She knew Vera was probably right that Cole couldn't be trusted. But then why was the memory of it as fresh as if it had happened moments ago? Why did it still, days later, make her weak with excitement? Why were these thoughts interfering with everything she'd done since, from brushing her teeth to making breakfast with Fia to practicing for the PAs?

Five minutes passed. Then ten. Davis felt her toes reflexively curling, flexing, pointing. Curling, flexing, pointing.

*Where was he?*

"Hey," said a male voice, and Davis turned, half expecting to find Frank waiting to escort her to her dad's car.

Davis's heart jumped a little, making her even shorter of breath. Not Frank.

*Him.*

It was the guy from the party. Cole. Like the mere power of thinking of him had brought him to her. He wore a blue button-down and jeans, a silver dog tag decorating his neck. His sleeves were rolled up almost to his elbows. Interesting DirecTalk; Davis hadn't seen the military style before.

"Sorry. Didn't mean to scare you," he said as Davis stood up. His brown eyes, the color of dark wood, bore into Davis's with an unusual intensity.

"I wasn't scared," she replied, instantly feeling something buzz between them—almost as though the kiss Friday night had just happened, like they'd pulled apart only seconds ago. "Just startled," she added, trying not to stare at his lips.

She straightened her shoulders, running one hand through her silky hair in order to tame it. "Are you heading to the PAs, too?" She looked at him then looked away, having trouble meeting his eyes. Was she the only one who thought the kiss was incredible? Maybe it wasn't. Maybe it was just her imagination, tricking her into believing something she wanted to believe. *Why* couldn't she stop thinking about it? Especially now of all days, when focus was more important than ever?

A flicker crossed his eyes, and just as fast, it was gone. "Nah," he said, keeping his voice even. "I'm done with all of that."

So he must be older. Strange how he'd just appeared when she'd been trying so hard not to think of him. Like he had stepped out of her subconscious.

"Are you okay?" Cole asked abruptly, and she couldn't stop herself from blushing. "The other night, it was . . . scary."

"Sure," she told him, pasting a smile on her face. "Absolutely."

"It's just . . ." He reached for her, almost as if he meant to touch her, and then pulled back before he could make contact. He let his hand fall back by his side. "Anyone would be shaken up."

"What happened with Caitlyn after the party?" she asked then. "I called her parents and they said she's fine but they wouldn't let me talk to her. Did you find her house okay? Was *she* okay?"

"Yeah," Cole said, avoiding her eyes. "I mean, I assume so. I dropped her off on, ah, Sherman and rang her doorbell, just like she asked."

Davis nodded, relieved. That was one weight off her shoulders. "I guess it was some optimizer she'd taken . . . I don't know. I guess she's freaked since we're so close to PAs."

Cole nodded, but his brow was furrowed, like there was something he couldn't figure out. Which was understandable. The whole thing was weird, what they'd experienced together. The kiss, then Caitlyn almost OD'ing—at least Davis assumed that's what had happened . . .

An image of Caitlyn at the party flashed through her mind. Blood coming from her mouth. She'd never seen blood like that before. She'd never even really seen anyone get sick before, aside from one time when Fia was a toddler and her temperature had reached dangerous highs. Back then, Terri and her dad had been thrown into a panic. Davis thought she knew now how they must have felt. The terror, an overwhelming rush of helplessness. Feeling out of control. She shuddered.

"I'm glad I saw you," Cole said, looking concerned. "I was a little worried." He stumbled over the last sentence, and Davis felt her face heating.

"Really, I'm fine," she told him again, burning all over from his previous words. Everything he said seemed weighted, like his words held greater significance than they could possibly convey. "I promise. I'm really, really glad you were there to help." It was an understatement.

Even more than that, he'd found her again. She hadn't dared hope to see him again, but she'd wanted it badly. And now he was here, and the space between them was magnetic.

"I'm glad I was there, too." His eyes met hers, burning her with their intensity. Her body filled with the same indescribable heat she'd felt kissing him. Even a look from him rivaled a touch from anyone else she knew in its ability to make her skin react. She wondered if he'd kiss her again. She wondered if he had this same effect on everyone; the thought made her stomach turn, and she took a reflexive step back.

A loud beep interrupted them. Her dad's vintage Rolls-Royce, dating from the first half of the twenty-first century, was just rolling through the gates to the school. Davis took a large step back, praying her dad hadn't seen anything. If he had, there would be an awful lot of questions. *Impeccable timing, Dad.*

"That's my ride," she told Cole, but he was already starting to turn from her. "Hey, Cole?" she called after him. "Wait a sec." He stopped but didn't move any closer. She trotted the few steps between them to close the gap. "Will I . . . see you again?"

"Yeah," he told her, smiling a little. "I'll be around."

Her heart sank. Maybe he hadn't felt what she felt, after all. Maybe he'd just checked up on her as a courtesy, not because he cared. If he'd cared, he would have made plans to see her again, asked for her number . . . or at least her last name. With cold shock, she realized that maybe Vera was right. Maybe he couldn't be trusted, and she'd fallen for something false—based on what? Her own feelings, and that was it.

"Davis!" her dad shouted through an open window. "Hurry up. We're running late."

"Obviously. Whose fault is that?" She muttered it under her breath, but Cole had heard her; he looked back and grinned, and she gave him a small wave, trying hard to smile in return, but failing.

"Wow, Dad," she said, sliding into the backseat next to him. She ran her hand across the car's leather interior. "You really pulled out the big guns for my PA. Sure this isn't a publicity stunt?" She hadn't meant for her words to come out with such bite, but there it was. Her dad never picked her up on a typical day, and she suspected this "special treat" had a hidden agenda.

"I'm here because I care about you," he responded, his voice gruff. "This is what a good father does."

Davis swiveled around to glance out the rear window, but Cole had disappeared. Her stomach clenched again. He didn't want to see her, it seemed clear. So if she happened to run into him again, she'd keep her distance. The dismissal was already too painful, and she barely knew him. She couldn't let her guard down like this again.

She turned back around in her seat and sighed, firmly pushing Cole out of her thoughts as best she could. She refocused her attention on her dad's words: *This is what a good father does.* She knew what a good father did. Her father had always been good. He'd sat through her practices when she was little, wrapped her feet with gauze on the rare occasions her toenails yielded to the pressure of the pointe shoes, made her pancakes for dinner in the years before her stepmother came along, held her when she'd had bad dreams. His whole life had revolved around her and Fia and making them happy.

Even his campaigns—the recent pull on his attention—were motivated by his love for them. At least that's what he'd always told them—that he wanted to make Columbus a better place for them to grow up in.

Even though he'd tried to hide it, before he met Terri, her father had been lonely. She'd seen it in his eyes, in the way he'd stared at the pictures of her mother and a few pieces of her clothing hanging in his closet next to his, as if nothing had changed. She'd seen his pain. Sometimes she still caught it; because you never really get rid of the sadness of loss.

"I'm sorry," she said. "Just nervous, that's all."

"You'll be perfect," he told her, reaching for her hand. For a minute, Davis felt like she was going to cry. She *had* to win the Olympiads. Her dad would be so proud; it would mean so much. She squeezed her eyes shut and swallowed until the feeling passed.

"So," her dad said after a moment. "Who was that boy you were talking to?"

So he'd noticed. Embarrassing. "It was just a friend of Emilie's," she said, turning toward the window. "He was at the party the other night."

"Ah," her dad responded, giving her a sidelong glance. "Someone special?"

"*Dad.* Stop," Davis said, rolling her eyes and trying hard not to blush. "I just met him myself." Her words were deceptively casual; she couldn't believe how convincing they sounded, when inside she was spinning and fluttery at the very thought of him. He derailed her, and she'd only just met him. Davis bit her lip, willing herself to maintain a placid exterior.

There was a long silence, and then her dad squeezed her hand harder. "Just be careful," he told her. "Boys are devils. Particularly around girls like you."

"What are 'girls like me'?" she asked, rolling her eyes.

"Pretty ones," said her dad.

"Oh, whatever." She sighed. "We're all pretty."

"You're *especially* pretty," he responded. "And I don't want you getting hurt."

She swallowed. Sometimes it was hard, knowing how much he cared, how much he worried. She wanted to assure him that she would be fine, that no boy would ever break her heart.

But for the first time, she wasn't sure if that was true.

Outside, Davis heard the muffled sounds of chanting and shouting. She squinted out one of the tinted windows.

"What *is* that?" she asked. "What's going on?" There were crowds of people, some holding signs she couldn't quite make out.

"Protestors," her dad said. Davis pressed her forehead to the window. One of the signs read INTEGRATION MEANS FULL EQUALITY, and they drove by another that someone pressed up right against the car, causing her to shift back in her seat toward her father while the chauffeur drove on. That one said: WE SHARE YOUR STREETS—WE SHOULD SHARE YOUR SCHOOLS.

*What would it be like, to have the Imps at school? Would it be dangerous?* There was talk that Parson Abel wanted to relax current segregation laws; Davis's dad was working hard to make sure that wouldn't happen. Davis had heard that the Imps were unevolved, prone to violence and aggression and unable to control their impulses. It was their carelessness—their lack of attention—that had killed her mother. She knew her dad's stance sometimes seemed a little harsh, but she could understand why. He would never let what happened to her mother happen again, to her, or to Fia, or to anyone. He just wanted a better world, a safer world, for everyone.

With only ten minutes to spare before her evaluation, the glass peaks of the Jenkins Center rose before them like a glittering castle. Davis took in a sharp breath, admiring the way its angles reflected light back into the street and onto the other buildings, creating crystal-rainbow patterns all around it. She'd always loved the Jenkins Center.

"Right up to the front, Gideon," her father instructed the chauffeur. He had unceremoniously replaced Malik, an Imp Davis had known all her life, with Gideon just two months before. Davis had asked why and received no explanation other than that her father felt he was sending a mixed message to the public by allowing Malik to be a part of their lives. Davis had liked Malik, who had always slipped her a special good-luck treat—usually a square of caramel chocolate, her favorite—with a wink and a smile before competitions. She had been sad to see him go—she'd forgotten, in a way, that he was an Imp. Now that she was seeing some of the violence and anger in the streets, she wondered what had happened to him.

She stepped from the car, ducking her head against the sea of cameras that greeted her and her father. With the election looming ever closer, they'd been following him wherever he went. It made her uncomfortable, and even walking no longer felt natural. She wondered if the cameras would pick up on everything she was trying to keep inside. She ducked her head, folding into herself. Her dad pulled her close against him and wrapped one arm around her shoulders rather than ushering her through the crowd as he usually did.

"Smile," he whispered. Davis glanced at him, and his own smile looked painted on. She did her best to straighten and smile anyway. Her dad patted her shoulder, releasing her, and Davis gave him a quick kiss on the cheek.

"Good luck, sweetie," he called out after her as she made her way toward the glass building. "Make your mother proud."

Even though she knew he'd meant them to be encouraging, his words felt heavy on her heart. Not winning meant losing the best shot she'd ever had at making her father happy, at honoring their family and her mother's image. Winning would mean the world to her dad. It would make him smile. It would bring her mother back to life, if only for an instant. And that was everything.

"PA?" a nurse waiting in the lobby asked.

Davis nodded.

"That way," the nurse replied. "On the left down the corridor. They'll give you your number."

Davis walked to the enormous conference room that had been dedicated to this purpose. It, too, was glass, yet somehow she couldn't see the hallways once she was inside. *Double-paned glass,* she thought. *Only the best.* She walked to the registration table and swiped her P-card to record her arrival.

"Please press your thumb to the keypad," an automated voice intoned from her DirecTalk. Davis did as instructed, firmly holding the pad of her thumb to the surface of a small, rectangular device glowing red and mounted to the back of a large computer at the registration desk in front of her.

"All set," said the admin who was perched atop a stool behind the computer. She typed furiously, glancing up at the screen in front of her. "Fifty-two," she said tersely after a few seconds had passed. "That's your group number. Just wait over there," she said, gesturing toward an enormous computer monitor to the left, in front of which dozens of Davis's classmates lingered. "and it'll pop up when they're ready for you."

"Thanks," said Davis.

The wait couldn't have been long, but to Davis it felt interminable. A small part of her wished she were a little kid again, with her dad waiting at her side. She shifted uneasily in her chair, wrapping her fingers around the bottom edge and squeezing tight. Finally, her number appeared on the screen, accompanied by the boom of another monotone automated voice. Davis filed into a smaller room with about a dozen others. There, she spent the next three hours completing a test tablet filled with rigorous questions meant to test her intellectual aptitude: her interpersonal, intrapersonal, linguistic, spatial, musical, existential, and logical-mathematical intelligences. By the time the proctor called, "Styluses down!" in a clipped tone, Davis's brain felt like total mush.

The intellectual aptitude test didn't really matter, though. It was just a formality, a pass/fail system meant to verify a basic standard of brain functioning among qualified athletes. Sometimes it culled those who scored in the top 0.1 percent for recruitment programs, but that wouldn't apply to her. The most important exam was yet to come: a bodily-kinesthetic intelligence test. Physical Aptitude. The PA test would determine whether she would qualify for the Olympiad trials—and from there, the Olympiads themselves. Davis filed out into the hall with the others, craning her neck for a glance at Emilie. But she was nowhere in sight; it was possible the proctors had planned it that way. Maybe they were deliberately mixing the testing groups. She peeled off her outer layers as instructed—the jacket, her black workout pants, and sheer blue top—until only her leotard, tights, and slippers remained.

After a short half-hour stretch break, it was her turn.

"This way, please," one of the proctors said, directing her toward a large white door marked with the number 4. Davis turned back as she went, watching the proctor as she nudged the other athletes from Davis's group into other similarly marked doors according to their respective concentrations.

The gymnasium was large and domed and made of glass. High

above her, Davis saw evidence of artfully concealed observation decks. There wasn't a stage in sight—or even a good surface to dance on—which caused Davis's heart to swell and thud with a pressure so intense she thought it would crack a rib.

*The judges*, Davis realized. The judges were up there. At least the council had made an effort to conceal them behind double-sided mirrors, though their shadows were still detectable. It took just another quick scan of the gym to see what the goal of the event was: the proctors and judges wanted to see how the competitors would perform under pressure.

Inside the massive indoor gymnasium, she faced Emilie, along with other dancers from top-tier dance programs across the New Atlantic territory. They had been reunited with one another for this competition. This should not have been a surprise, Davis realized, even though the format of the PAs varied every year.

But in addition to the expected faces—the dark, magnetic beauty of Alexis Bateman, a superstar from Echo Solar; the willowy Carolina Sheppard; and Leanne Pastor, so pale she appeared ethereal—were the legends. Davis's heart pounded and she tugged nervously at her simple regulation white leotard as her eyes scanned the room.

All the winners of the ballet Olympiads from the last ten years were standing before her, wearing their medals. Davis realized with a wave of new panic that she would be competing against the greats, the women and men who were now globally considered the best.

Davis took a few deep breaths and curled her toes in her pointe shoes. She fought the urge to tear them off, taking a few deep breaths instead. She had to pull it together. This was it. It was her moment. And it didn't matter who else was going to be there, because she'd been training her entire life for this.

"Welcome, contestants," said the proctor. She teetered in high heels next to the athletes who dwarfed her on either side. "This year marks a change in the format of the PAs. As you can see," she continued, gesturing toward the previous Olympiad winners who stood beside her, "for the first time in history, we have invited the dancers of the prestigious New Atlantic Dance Company to attend the trials." She paused then, taking a moment to applaud the athletes and gesturing for the students to do the same. The former athletes weren't there to compete, Davis realized with a rush of relief; they were there to judge. Which was better or maybe worse, depending on how you looked at it.

"We have also changed the nature of the trials. We have modeled our program after the classic training programs of the country's best athletes. The program will gauge not only your capacity for physical excellence, but also your mental acuity and your cognitive-physical faculties. These are all essential qualities for becoming a professional dancer."

As the proctor rattled off the rules for the competition, Davis glanced up at the events roster that flashed via hologram above their heads.

The female dancers were required to do a minimum of seventy-five push-ups in two minutes, though Davis knew the minimum was far below what she'd have to achieve to be competitive. Then they'd complete a hundred sit-ups in two minutes, followed by twenty pull-ups. At the very end, they'd be asked to strip while their body measurements were calculated. Davis could read between the lines. She'd have to beat all of these minimums by a landslide.

"You have been preassigned an athlete judge who will record your performance. It is only once you have achieved the minimum expectation for all of these challenges that you will be given a ten-minute break to rehydrate and a seven-minute opportunity to showcase your improvisational ballet to the music of the judges' choosing," finished the proctor. "These judges will determine whether you are qualified to compete in the Olympiad trials. And of course," she said with a broad smile, "only a few of you will go on from here to the Olympiads. Remember, competitors: your futures start now. Judges, find your students."

Davis's judge was a winner from seven years back, Molly Medina, who came from South Gulf—a territory that hadn't yet produced many winners, as they'd been hit harder and were slower to rebuild after the floods that had consumed major portions of the coastline. Davis remembered watching her in the final rounds; they'd had second-row box seats, which they'd been given by one of her father's friends. Davis had been mesmerized by Molly as a kid. She was still radiant with long blond hair, full lips and striking blue eyes, and her compact frame looked strong as ever. Her shoulders and arms rippled with muscularity and femininity both.

Molly smiled at Davis in a way that seemed meant to convey kindness. "We'll start with the body-resistance exercises and move on to the rest," she told her. Davis hit 140 sit-ups with barely any effort, though push-ups were a little more difficult. She managed to break thirty pull-ups, however; when she finished, Molly was grinning.

"You did almost as well as the boys," Molly told her, smiling full-on then. "So I'd say you did pretty well. Now all you have to do is dance your heart out."

"And get measured," Davis corrected her. She allowed herself a little smile but took another long breath, fighting to keep her excitement in check. She could feel the end, taste it. She could almost see the letter inviting her to compete in the Olympiad trials. All she had to do now was dance.

"What about Emilie?" she asked, knowing Molly would understand what she wanted to know.

"She slipped to sixth," Molly said. *Sixth*. That was so bad, Davis almost felt sorry for her. Only four dancers from their area would advance to the trials, and only two to the Olympiads after that. "You're tied for first," Molly continued.

"With Alexis?"

Molly nodded. "I'm not supposed to say this, Davis, but I've been keeping an eye on you for the past few months. Ever since I found out I'd be judging the PAs. You're a darned good dancer. I was glad to find out this morning that I'd be paired with you. Now go get changed, then get out there and kill it." She handed Davis a smoothie: a cup of green sludge that tasted like chalk and went down thick and sticky. Davis downed it in two gulps.

Spots of sweat were already staining her leotard; she hoped the judges wouldn't take off points for that. For now, though, the stage was obscured by a plasma screen, darkened to a deep shade of gray—almost black—an odd, mottled color that resembled smoke. She couldn't see who was performing behind it. She stood on her toes, flexing her calves in an effort to breathe life back into them.

All she had to do was feel the music, breathe life into a routine, nail it. It was the easiest part of the whole day. So why did she feel so nervous?

A second later, Emilie emerged. Davis tried smiling at her, but Emilie just grimaced, looking super pale. Had she fallen? Emilie was famous for being flawless, almost robotic. Emilie avoided eye contact and pushed past Davis, her pace quickening. Davis's world narrowed a little, dampening at the edges before shifting back into focus.

"Pay attention!" Molly said sharply. She nudged Davis toward the stage, and it was only then that Davis heard her name being called. She walked through the dark barrier onto the cold stone slab, and Molly was gone.

Everything was gone. She was enveloped in a sheet of black. The screen that separated her—and the stage—from the rest of the gymnasium extended in all directions, its surface a disorienting, cloudy black. As a result, the stone stage appeared to float in a chasm of nothingness, as if she were suspended on a tiny island in outer space. Davis couldn't see anyone. From somewhere beyond, music piped and as a result her pulse slowed. It was Stravinsky's *The Rite of Spring*. She'd have known it anywhere. It was lovely, playful, and most important, familiar. She'd danced to this ballet more times than she could remember.

As the opening chords filled the space around her, enveloping her body and working their way into her limbs, Davis felt her body coming alive. The Olympiacs were right in front of her. She felt as though she were stealing them from all the others, as though the trials had been rigged in her favor.

And then it happened: she felt a spasm shake her hands as she completed her jeté. It jolted her entire frame from spine to tailbone. And there was a sharp shudder in her head, as though her brain were sloshing as it tried to keep up with the movements of her body. It must have lasted only a fraction of a second, but when she regained control, her timing was off. The flute and viola worked together in a frenetic pace and she worked to chase them. She felt wave after wave of panic consume her, and her pace became frenzied as she tried to pace her movements against the escaping rhythms.

Then it was over. The music cut out.

Davis fought tears, fought the trembling of her hands. And she curtseyed to a wall of black.

———

The rumors must have spread quickly.

"It's not the end of the world," said the nurse who was taking her body measurements. Her waist-to-hip ratio blazed its red hologram above her, in letters bright enough for whoever was observing to see from above. "Your timing was just a quarter second off," she continued. "You're a favorite, you know." She gave Davis a warm smile. "Your mother was . . . well, she was a dream. Everyone wants to see you follow in her footsteps."

Davis tried to smile but found herself fighting back tears. At least her body measurements were right on target, even closer to perfect than she'd dared hope.

"This won't affect your ability to qualify," the nurse said around the miniature calipers that she gripped between her teeth as she worked a thin wire around Davis's forearm to test her bone mass density. She gave her a reassuring pat on her shoulder. "We hope it won't, anyway. Everyone's rooting for you to make the trials."

*We hope it won't, anyway.* The sentence hit Davis with the force of a boulder. She staggered back, struggling not to give in to another bout of the same overwhelming light-headedness she'd experienced onstage.

"Are you okay?" The nurse gave Davis a concerned look. "I know this kind of thing can be disappointing—maybe you ought to lie down. We're finished now." Now Davis was sure she was attracting attention from the other girls. A brunette with a pixie cut whom she didn't recognize giggled a little, and Davis burned with fury and embarrassment.

"No," she said, stepping away from the nurse. She hopped down from the pillar. "No, I just need to use the bathroom. I'll be right back." She struggled back into the clothes she'd put on that morning and slipped out of the room before anyone could protest.

Once in the bathroom, Davis leaned over the sink and took a

number of deep breaths. How had this happened? Her stomach began to roll. She wasn't supposed to be feeling this way. She was supposed to meet her father for a fancy dinner to celebrate her straight optimals on her PAs. He'd be sick with disappointment. She imagined the look in his eyes when she told him the news—when she told all of them. Fia and Terri had just assumed she'd win—they had all the confidence in the world in her. What would they think when they heard she didn't make it? Would they feel bad for her? Or would they be let down? Nothing, *nothing*, though, would compare to her father's reaction, his face, his dismay. Davis had never felt so miserable. She wished beyond anything that she could turn back the clock, have a second chance.

But instead, she was here, in a public restroom, trying not to be sick. *Sick.* She looked in the mirror. Why was she so pale? Her skin had never looked pasty and translucent like this before. It reminded her of how Emilie had looked in the gymnasium, too. Was there something wrong with the lighting?

Davis blinked and examined herself more closely, and this time she looked fine. Better than fine.

A fit of coughing—followed by a thud came from one of the stalls behind her, making Davis jump; she'd thought she was alone in the bathroom. "Hello?" she called out.

Silence.

She crept closer to the stall door and knocked twice. Receiving no response, she peeked under the bottom of the door and saw a pair of legs splayed at an unusual angle, bent at the knee and tilted sideways, almost as if the girl inside were praying.

"Hello?" she called out again, jiggling the door. A stripe of panic worked its way from her chest to her belly, and in an instant all of her own issues were forgotten. "Who's in there? Are you okay?" She jiggled the door hard this time, and it swung inward.

The girl was lying motionless over the toilet bowl. Her cloud of dark hair spread over the seat and some of it draped in the water, floating on its surface. Davis moved closer and saw several smudges of blood decorating the girl's hands and the porcelain of the bowl where she must have grabbed it.

Davis tilted the girl's head sideways, trying to get a better look at who it was. Memories of Caitlyn at the party flooded back, and her whole being filled with the unmistakable beginnings of panic.

"Emilie," she whispered, holding the girl's head aloft. "Emilie, talk to me." But Emilie was unconscious. Davis's heart raced and she felt tears forming in the corners of her eyes. Then the door to the bathroom swung open, and Sasha walked in.

"You okay?" she asked Davis. Her words expressed concern, but her tone was flat and disaffected. She walked over to the mirror, barely glancing at Emilie as she passed.

"Sasha, get help! Emilie needs a doctor." Sasha glanced in their direction, rolling her eyes when she saw Emilie's body slumped in Davis's arms.

"Please," she said. "That girl's always been melodramatic. Trying to get attention for a little hangover. Pathetic."

Davis's chest tightened. Emilie wasn't even *moving*, and she'd been coughing up blood before she passed out. This wasn't a hangover. Anyone could see that.

"Are you kidding? Look at her. We need to help her." Davis's voice was rising, becoming shriller with each word. She felt woozy and light-headed. Sasha was still standing at the mirror, reapplying lipstick like nothing was the matter while Emilie bled in Davis's arms. What was *wrong* with Sasha?

"Davis, take it down a notch. We'll get a doctor as soon as I'm done here, okay? Will that make you happy?"

"Open your eyes, Sasha!" Davis said it more sharply than she'd ever spoken to anyone. She laid Emilie's body on the floor, turning her on her side just in case she coughed up more blood. Then Davis ran for a proctor.

Ten minutes later, Davis watched as some of the PA attendants—including the one who'd examined her—led Emilie's body out of the bathroom on a stretcher. She stood there long after the stretcher was gone, staring at the blood that decorated the porcelain-tiled floor.

She lingered there, leaning against the doorjamb, even after some Imps went in with mops and buckets of soapy water. "Will she be okay?" she asked no one in particular. "Will she? Will Emilie be okay?"

The Imps ignored her, going about their business as if she weren't there, although she saw the younger one lift his shoulders in an apologetic shrug.

Then nausea overcame her; she felt her knees buckle beneath her, and everything went dark.

# 6

## COLE

Cole needed to think. He sat down on the same steps where he'd found Davis (not so accidentally) a few minutes before. He had wanted to talk to her—really talk. He'd wanted to tell her the truth about Caitlyn—but she'd looked so nervous about her PAs, whatever they were, and then her dad had shown up . . .

He'd barely slept since Worsley had told him about Narxis. He was relieved that Davis didn't seem to be affected, but how long would she remain safe? The thought of her sick, suffering . . . it was almost more than he could take. The idea that it could happen shredded him. There was no reason for this reaction; he barely

knew her at all, but he couldn't get her out of his head. The worst
was the physical ache he'd felt when he saw her—the need to protect her, to wrap his arms around her and pull her to him, where
she'd be safe in his arms. It was a compulsion he'd barely been
able to control. And one he didn't understand, not when she was
a Prior—*a Prior*. Every part of it was horrible. But no matter how
much he told himself to stop feeling for her, he couldn't.

And then there was the whole Caitlyn situation. What had he
gotten himself into? What might happen if someone had seen him
and Davis with Caitlyn? What would happen when Davis found
out that Caitlyn was dead—would she tell someone that Cole had
been the last person to see her alive? He couldn't decide what worried him most—the trouble he'd be in if anyone knew, or the disgust Davis would feel when she found out he had lied. It was
unreasonable—insane—to care what she thought. But he did.

He chewed on one cuticle, already ragged. Parson hadn't told
him to seek out Davis that afternoon. But then, Parson didn't know
what had gone down after the party. Parson would freak, Cole was
sure of it. And if Parson pulled Cole out of the FEUDS . . . what
would Cole's family do then? He took a deep breath and struggled
to calm down. Should he wait for Davis to finish her tests? No—
"bumping into her" again in the same afternoon would be way too
obvious. It occurred to Cole then that maybe Parson was the person he *should* be looking for. If he knew about the disease, maybe
he could do something; he had enough power, money, resources . . .
he was the most powerful person Cole knew—one of the most
powerful people in Columbus, period. He could do something.
Cole *had* to tell him. More than that, Cole wanted out. This, all of
it—his strong aversion to the idea of deceiving Davis, the incident
with Caitlyn—was way more than he'd signed up for, and everything in him knew it was wrong, and it had to stop here.

Cole looked out at the landscape and the taller buildings rising

up maybe a mile beyond the school gates, past the imposing building facade from which Davis's dad's car had spirited her away. He
knew that among those buildings loomed the gray structure of the
factory where his mother had worked for longer than he could
remember—since he was maybe five or six years old. And a few
streets down from Factory Row was the political district and Parson Abel's office. Cole made his decision.

It was roughly a mile, or a fifteen-minute walk, but Cole jog-
walked, quickening his step the closer he got. Anticipation sped
his heart, adrenaline shot through his limbs. Once the decision
was made, it all felt critical. He wanted to get there right away to
tell Parson it was over.

Parson had to do something about Narxis instantly. There was
no time to waste.

He wasn't sure which office was Parson Abel's, only that the
three behemoth, glass-fronted structures that shared a common
entrance near the fountain at the center of town usually housed
offices belonging to politicians. Cole drew in a breath, wondering
for the first time exactly how he was going to manage to get in.
Security in these buildings was extra tight. He hadn't thought it
through at all. He sidled up to the entrance, trying to get an idea
of where to go next while remaining relatively inconspicuous. It
wasn't working; he was drawing looks. Moving toward the lobby
entrance, he noticed a banner hanging above what appeared to be
a conference room inside. It was labeled CAMPAIGN HEADQUAR-
TERS, and adorned with the signature yellow emblem signifying
Parson Abel's political party.

Cole had just edged though the sliding doors and had begun to
shoulder his way through the busy lobby, keeping his head low,
when he heard a commotion at the entrance to the campaign
headquarters. He ducked behind a broad stone pillar as a burly

security guard appeared in the lobby, hustling a lean blond man in a beige suit out of the room. The man's face was twisted in a grimace, as if he'd smelled something bad. His reddish, fancy scarf-thing was flopping out of his suit jacket, and beads of sweat were forming at his temples. Cole's heart sped up and he felt his adrenaline spike.

"Get the hell out of here," the guard was saying in a voice low enough that Cole had to strain to hear it. "If I ever see your face in here again, I'll make sure you leave a little less pretty. Parson Abel can take the first swing. You think he cares who you work for? Hm?" The security guard yanked the man's arms backward a little harder at this, and the man gritted his teeth to avoid crying out. "Here's a piece of advice: he doesn't give a shit who you're with. We don't deal with extortionists here." At that, the guard shoved the man toward the lobby door; the man stumbled a bit, almost toppling over before regaining his balance. Then he looked side to side and straightened the red scarf, hurrying quickly out of the lobby.

Cole kept his eyes focused on the marble floor, careful not to attract his attention as he brushed by. But his heart pounded wildly. If Parson would do that to a well-dressed Prior, what would he do when he saw Cole? Still, Cole ground his teeth and watched the security desk from behind the pillar, waiting until the lobby guard lowered his head and began shuffling through some paperwork. Then he beelined toward the entrance to the conference room. He had no choice. Too much was at stake.

Cole made it inside the headquarters and scanned the room. It was wide and open and contained about two dozen work stations staffed with interns and managers who were working busily. He didn't see Parson anywhere. The good news was that no one was paying him any attention—most of the staff were probably around his age or early college age. He looked down at his jeans and the same button-down shirt Parson had given him to wear to the party the other night—he'd washed it since the night of the party; it was the only nice thing he had, and it helped him blend in. Anyone who hadn't seen him slip in probably thought he was an intern, too.

Cole approached a pretty blonde in a pencil skirt and gray blouse, who was squinting at her tablet, her brows knitted and her face pulled into a frown. He took a deep breath. "Excuse me," he said. "I'm looking for Parson." He smiled broadly, hoping his smile passed for Prior. Hoping the small chip in his tooth from a baseball injury when he was a kid didn't mar his grin too much. Did Priors get chipped teeth? Probably not. And if they did, they'd have it fixed right away.

"He just left," she told him in a bored tone, like it was obvious and Cole was some kind of idiot. "Didn't you hear him make that announcement?" She leaned back in her chair and studied Cole, her expression wary.

"I just walked in," Cole said, improvising. "I work in the . . . satellite office."

"The satellite office." Her tone was suspicious.

"Yeah," Cole told her, affecting an impatient, confident tone. "Are you new or something?" The girl blushed in response, and Cole soldiered forward, hoping desperately that his act would work. "I've got to get back over there," he said, "but can you give him a message for me?" He smiled again, this time throwing in a wink, to warm her up. She looked up at him, her expression softening just a little.

"Sure," she told him. "Shoot."

"Just let him know he needs to meet Cole at the regular place in two hours," Cole said. "I have something to tell him."

"Yeah, okay," the girl said, sounding bored. She scribbled something on a notepad. "That all?"

"That's it," Cole said. "Don't forget." He smiled again, and she smiled back, and he was off, feeling euphoric. He broke into a broader grin as he went, imagining Parson's reaction when he realized Cole had made it into his headquarters, broken through his safe, protected Prior bubble with no trouble at all. He couldn't help feeling self-satisfied at this. It wasn't until he crossed the expanse of the lobby and hopped down the steps bordering the building, though, that he again allowed himself to breathe.

The Swings were at the edge of his neighborhood. Cole had chosen it strategically—first invading Parson's turf, then requesting that he come to Cole's. The question was, would Parson show up?

Here, Cole had the advantage. Cole had always loved the Swings, a big empty lot that he and the other FEUDS fighters used as a makeshift training ground. Even as a kid, he'd looked forward to being old enough to work out with the other guys. It was just a big, open plot of land with a lot of rocks and overgrown weeds, but he'd grown up there.

The smell of rust and sweat and metal gave Cole a sense of nostalgia, the feeling that he was powerful and comfortable and home.

It was mostly empty at this time of day, though. There were just a couple of people working out: another FEUDS contender from a few years ago, Jason, as well as an older guy and a kid about his age whom he didn't recognize. Cole air-high-fived Dustin, the neighborhood kid who was always hanging around the Swings with his ratty gloves on. They were way too big for his small hands, probably inherited from a relative. Dustin grinned in response. The kid was what, maybe six, seven? He worshipped the FEUDS fighters, that much was obvious. But it was weird that he was always alone, no one ever looking out for him. Cole made a mental note to talk to the kid after his workout, see how he was doing.

After changing into regular ratty clothing, Cole lay back on the bench and drew the weighted bar to his chest, bearing ten pounds more than his usual 260. He thought pushing himself—expending his energy this way—would help calm his anxiety. He didn't know how Parson would react when he told him he was out; or even if Parson would show. Here, at least, Parson couldn't hurt him—not overtly. But who knew what he would do when he'd had time to process Cole's decision? Cole shuddered, gritting his teeth and pushing the bar into the air, then lowering it back to shoulder level and repeating. Every muscle in his upper body—even his neck—strained with the effort. But the endorphin rush he was used to didn't come, and his heart beat so fast he thought he might pass out. Even after he'd managed to push the image of the security guard and the blond guy out of his mind, his brain kept ping-ponging back and forth between Caitlyn and Davis.

The kiss flashed through his mind for what seemed like the millionth time. Her lips, searing into his. Her heart, pulsing against his chest. It was so overwhelming a memory that he nearly dropped the bar, nearly passed out from the exertion coupled with emotion. He struggled to replace the bar in its tray. He had to tell Parson, one way or another. He had no choice. The alternative was too awful: if Davis found out the truth—found out why he'd kissed her—she'd be crushed. Telling Parson was the right decision. The only decision.

An hour passed. Ninety minutes. One hundred twenty. It was now more than two hours since Cole had left the campaign center, and his muscles were so limp he could barely lift his body from the weight bench. He headed toward the showers of the nearest public bathroom, which served as a makeshift locker room and was used

almost exclusively by the people who trained at the Swings. A couple
of the guys who'd also been working out in the yard grabbed the
remaining nozzles that lined the open, tiled room.

"... All over the place," one of the guys was saying. "It's sick.
The squatters are moving out 'cause of the smell."

"Jesus," said one of the others in a low tone. "That's some serious shit."

"Yeah. And, like, they're just leaving them there. Not even burying their own goddamn people."

Cole suddenly realized what they were talking about:
*Bodies.*

The guy was railing now, his voice taking on an angry pitch.
Cole's heart stopped.

"Piles of them," another guy added.

"Piles of them," the first guy confirmed. "A dozen, maybe more.
That's what people are saying, at least."

Cole turned up his faucet and ran his hands through his hair,
hoping no one thought it was weird that he was lingering. He needed
to hear more.

The first guy continued: "Lab rats make me sick. We'd never
dump our own people without a burial."

"Hell no," the stocky guy said.

"It was creepy as hell, dude. I heard they had these weird marks
on their faces, covered in dried blood, like their skin split open or
someone took a knife to them or something." He paused, letting
the stocky guy take this in.

Cole's fingertips turned cold. Blood. Split-open skin. It wasn't
just Caitlyn. Was it Narxis? How many others had died from it?
How long had the Priors been keeping it quiet?

"Holy shit." It was all the stocky guy could say. "What the hell
happened to them? Is there some psycho killer running around?"

"No idea," said the first guy. "Some people think it's a strategy. To stop us from spreading."

"Killing off their own people?"

"No, idiot. Throwing the bodies along the river. Keeps us out."

"I don't believe it," the stocky guy said.

"I'm just telling you what I heard. Next thing, they'll shut down the Swings. We're too close to the border." He glanced over and nodded at Cole just as Cole was about to switch off the water, having taken way longer than usual. He'd heard enough to scare him shitless.

"Hey," the guy said. "What's going on? You're using up all the water, man." Everyone knew who Cole was because of Cole's status among the FEUDS fighters, so he knew they weren't going to get too aggressive.

"Sorry," Cole told him, grabbing a dingy towel. "Just heading out."

He was even more wound up now than when he'd first arrived at the Swings. Did Parson Abel know about the bodies? Did Worsley and Hamilton? Had they dumped Caitlyn's body there, too, along with the rest of them? Assuming the other people died the same way Caitlyn had, how fast was this thing spreading? Cole caught himself; a week ago, he realized, he wouldn't have cared. He would have made fun of those lab rats right along with the guys at the gym—would have assumed, like them, that all Priors were the same. But now he'd met one, had gotten to know one. She wasn't at all what he'd expected . . . and he couldn't get her out of his head.

He had just walked out of the bathroom when he saw a suited form in his periphery. Parson Abel's fists were clenched and his stride was long. Even from thirty yards away, Cole could make out his fury by the way his shoulders pressed together and his fists clenched at his sides. Cole stood his ground, letting Parson come to him.

"How dare you?" Parson hissed, the veins in his forehead popping. "You summon *me*? You break into my headquarters? You invade my personal space? Let me remind you," he continued, jabbing one finger into Cole's chest, "you are working for me. Discretion is paramount." He paused, taking a breath, and Cole took the opportunity to break in.

"I'm not doing it," he said, his voice firm. "You think you can make me do your dirty work? There were a few things you left out. As far as I'm concerned, all bets are off. I'm out."

"What are you talking about?" Parson's voice was low, guttural.

"I'm talking about the bodies. About this . . . *disease* that's killing Priors. About the fact that this girl you have me following . . ." Cole's voice nearly cracked at this, but he continued on. "She's not a bad person and she doesn't deserve whatever you are planning. I have a bad feeling about this. I feel like it's gonna get me in trouble, whatever it is you're angling for. I didn't get a picture and I'm not going to. I don't want any part of it."

Parson laughed in Cole's face. "That's what this is all about?" he said, sneering openly. "'She's not a bad person,'" he mimicked, and Cole flushed from embarrassment. "Let me tell you something," Parson said, taking a step toward Cole. "You threaten me again, I'll rip your head off. I'll do it when you least expect it. You better believe I'll destroy you, and your family. You want to see your mother get fired, Cole? This is how to do it. You breathe one more word about this disease, and your mother's job is gone. *Any* job, *anywhere*. Don't even think about it, Cole. Don't go up against me. You need me more than I need you." He stopped, breathing hard, faint spittle building up at the corners of his mouth.

Cole stared at him. He didn't know exactly why Parson Abel had hired him, but it was for a reason that was very, very important to the politician; that much was clear.

"The disease," he tried again. "You can *do* something about it—"

"The disease is bullshit," Parson hissed, leaning in toward him. His eyes were wide, and he was speaking so animatedly that flecks of spit sprayed from his mouth. Cole could sense fear and anxiety radiating from him, and he realized Parson was lying. Cole grew cold with fear—if Parson was hiding the disease, then it *must* be real. It wasn't just Caitlyn. Worsley was right—all the Priors could die. Still, he had the upper hand. "This better be the last I hear of it," Parson said, lowering his voice. "Or all of it: the money, your mom's job, your house—it's gone. All of it."

Cole was quiet. Every nerve in his body was firing, but he had nowhere to go. He so badly wanted to put Parson Abel in his place . . . but he couldn't. Parson was right; he was powerless. He had no alternatives—and Parson, he sensed, though nervous, meant every word of it. He could lift a finger and destroy Cole's life, and he would.

"I didn't get the picture," Cole said in a dull voice.

"So go after it again," Parson snapped. "Get me what I need, Cole. And be grateful that you're getting *any* of the FEUDS winnings at all. *If* you win."

Cole snapped to attention, and Parson smirked, taking obvious pleasure in his confusion. "You didn't hear?" Parson asked, his eyes widening in faux concern. "Oh, poor Cole. Your old friend Noah Gibson's rejoined the fight. Bets are split. Actually," he corrected himself. "Bets are against you. Noah's back from South Gulf, Cole. All he's done for months is train. You better pull yourself together, boy, or you're going to get the beating of your life. So get the photo of you with the girl, and get training."

"It'll take me a little while," Cole replied. "I'll do it," he said, stalling. He'd agree for now, but only to buy himself some time. "I'm just going to need a few days at least."

"Fine," Parson agreed, running one hand over the stubble on his chin. "Fine. I don't care. Just get me the damn photo." Then he swiveled on his heel and strode away, through the fence that bordered the Swings, back toward the motie that would take him to the city center. Cole stood by the weight bench for several minutes, waiting for his heart rate to return to normal. He'd figure this thing out. He just needed time. One thing Parson was right about: winning FEUDS was his only shot at freedom. He needed that prize money. He needed to get out of this mess.

# 7

## DAVIS

On Tuesday, Davis set out for the studio at five in the morning, eager to fit in a good workout before school. The letters announcing PA results would be mailed out the following Monday, along with a list of the athletes who had qualified for the Olympiad trials. Davis had a sinking feeling in the pit of her stomach every time she thought about that letter and the news it would bring. She couldn't help replaying her misstep in front of the judges in her mind, her mortification over it sweeping back in. When she'd voiced her concerns to Vera over DirecTalk, Vera had assumed she was being overly anxious. But she'd offered to take her out for froyo anyway, and when Davis refused, she'd ordered her a subscription to her favorite tablet tabloid. Davis was too anxious to finish even one article, though. Ballet training was the only thing keeping her sane as she waited.

But when she arrived at the monorail, she saw it wasn't working. She stood for a minute, staring at it stupidly. Never in her life had the monorail been shut down. She knew the strikes had been escalating, after halfheartedly listening to her dad and Frank, his campaign manager, bicker about it for days. But she'd definitely had no idea what it would be like or how far-reaching the consequences would be.

She set off to walk the mile and a half to the studio, which would leave her only about twenty minutes to practice, but she didn't feel like asking for a ride and then waiting around for the car to be brought out of the garage. Her father wouldn't approve, but Davis relished the chance. It was so seldom she went anywhere alone.

The city was quieter than usual, and bits of paper and other trash swirled in the wind over the empty sidewalks, settling in little piles like debris after a hurricane. Davis had never seen the city so unpolished; the streets were typically sparkling and pristine, though there was only so much you could do about the million footprints left behind on their sleek surfaces every day. Now dusty footprints and litter crowded the limestone sidewalks.

She passed a dozen shuttered storefronts, looking ghostly in the dawn light, their entrances blocked by glaring metal teeth. A train sat stalled on the metro track, as if waiting. One door was wedged open, and Davis could make out the figure of an old man curled up in its interior. She quickened her pace.

When she reached the studio, the doors were closed and bolted.

PLEASE EXCUSE THE INCONVENIENCE, read the sign that was tacked to the door. MEYER STUDIO WILL BE CLOSED UNTIL FURTHER NOTICE DUE TO THE LABOR DISPUTES.

"Excuse me," Davis said to a woman who was walking by. The woman kept pace, didn't even bother to answer her. But Davis was determined. "Excuse me!" she said louder, jogging to catch up. She placed a hand on the woman's arm and the woman spun, nervous.

"What?" she said.

"Do you know how long everything's going to be shut down?" Davis asked.

The woman peered at Davis in disbelief. "Haven't you been keeping up with the news?" she asked her. "Half the city buildings are shut down because there's no staff. I have no idea how long it's going to last. It'll last 'til they get hungry enough to work again." Then she hurried on, as though she couldn't be bothered to say more.

The city was eerie without the Imps. Cold. Deserted.

Plastic bags and scraps of receipts and other trash floated across the street, carried by a light but not unpleasant breeze. It seemed like a thin coating of dust had already settled over the sidewalks and building surfaces. Windows that had once been immaculate—glossy enough to double as mirrors—were now smudged and flecked with bits of sediment.

Davis walked home with her arms hugged tightly across her chest. It was becoming more and more obvious how much the Imps were a part of things, how they kept everything running. She didn't like being dependent on the same people she was supposed to pity. It was one thing to screw up the PAs; it was another not to have access to the place she considered a refuge. Her heart sped up, and she fought to control the ever-encroaching sense of dread that had threatened her since the night of Emilie's party—and even more so since the PAs. Without dance . . . she didn't know what she'd do. She'd probably fall apart. She needed it, the same way other people needed sleep. It was such a part of her that the thought of ripping it away felt like a version of death.

The only comfort was the thought of Cole. Their kiss still wrapped around her like a warm blanket every time she thought of it. Somehow, it hadn't decreased in intensity; it held her as tightly in its grip as it had the night it happened. But even if she were brave enough, she had no way of contacting him. Even Vera didn't know how to get in touch with him, and she knew everybody. She had promised to ask around, and that had been days ago. Everything about him was a mystery.

Davis's unease only worsened when she got to school an hour later and saw that Emilie was absent. Davis's own attendance record was near-perfect, marred only by that one time when her father gave a major campaign speech and had required her to be there. Ninety percent of the other students at Excelsior could say the same. But in Advanced World History, no one even glanced at the empty seat, third from the back in aisle two.

Mrs. Marrick's voice droned on about the dark period after the last of the ice caps melted, when floods and hurricanes devastated the United States economy; Kensington's alliance with India; the eventual treaties between Old Canada and the Old United States; the forming of the New Americas and its division into territories, including New Atlantic; blah blah, stuff that felt so irrelevant. Davis glanced at Emilie's empty chair.

Emilie's absence gave Davis a notch up on the victory scale— assuming Emilie missed a few days of practice, Davis would be at a huge advantage—yet she couldn't muster the excitement she knew she ought to feel. She just kept picturing how pale Emilie had looked on the bathroom floor, passed out . . . It had been so eerily similar to how Caitlyn had looked. And even though her parents had said Caitlyn was fine, she hadn't come back to school, either.

Could it have been a coincidence? And why did no one else seem to think there was anything wrong? Was she overreacting? It was possible. Davis knew she was more sensitive than she should be.

And somewhere mixed in with the huge whorl of stress was the image of Cole smirking slightly on the school steps yesterday. He had to have asked around to find out she went to Excelsior. Did that mean he was into her? She'd had the distinct impression he'd been about to open up to her, tell her something important, but then her dad had arrived and ruined the moment. But then . . . if he was into her, why hadn't he gotten her number or made plans to see her again? Was popping in and out of her life his MO? It was so frustrating, the way he seemed totally fine with leaving things up to chance. It was so hot and cold . . . maybe he wasn't that into her. Maybe it was just the same game he played on everyone. Davis hated the thought of it, but couldn't help wondering if it might be true—if Cole was just a player who was toying with her, seeing if she'd take the bait.

When the bell rang, she shot to her feet and folded her tablet, shoving it into her school tote, a rare leather number she'd found wedged in the back of the storage closet at home. It was probably worth a ton of money. She liked to imagine that her mom had once used it for the same purpose when she was in school, though there weren't any pictures left to confirm it. Not since Terri had taken over. Davis gathered her things and caught up with Vera near the front of the room. They always walked to lunch together, but today Davis wanted to check in with Chloe, Emilie's cousin.

"Can I catch up with you in there?" she asked Vera, who furrowed her brow in response. "I just need to call my dad really quick," Davis clarified, feeling a pang of guilt over the lie.

"Yeah, totally," Vera said. "But did you catch the way Reagan cut me off a minute ago? I swear," she whispered, pulling Davis close, "she's *still* holding out for Oscar. It's driving me insane." Davis nodded distractedly: Chloe was making her way out of the room, and she was in the later lunch period. It was now or never.

"She's the worst," Davis agreed. "The living worst. Catch up with you in a second?" Vera nodded, frowning a little, but she perked up when Davis tugged her hair and smiled. "I'll spit on her vegan muffin for you," she teased, giving her friend a wink. "I'll be right there." Vera picked her way toward the cafeteria and Davis dashed down the hall in the opposite direction, barely catching up with Chloe. Chloe was wearing enormous wedge heels and yet somehow speed-walking in the direction of the swimming pool, shouldering unsuspecting victims out of her way as she went.

"Hey," Davis said, breathless. "Chloe. Wait up." Chloe stopped but didn't turn right away, instead cocking her head in a gesture of impatience as she waited for Davis to talk.

"Hey," Davis said again.

"Yes?" She sighed and turned to face Davis. Chloe was nasty to everyone, but she was generally civil to Davis because of who Davis's dad was.

"How's Emilie?" Davis asked.

"What do you mean?" Chloe snapped, but Davis thought she saw a flicker of something—discomfort?—cross her face before it again turned impassive.

"Have you heard from her? At the PAs yesterday . . ." Davis

trailed off, confused. She'd thought the news would have at least made its rounds, even if Chloe hadn't heard it straight from Emilie.

"We had a call from her mom," Chloe said. "She said Emilie has been exhausted from practicing extra and that I should pass on her homework today. But she didn't mention anything else. Why? Did something happen?"

"She was just . . . sick." Davis hesitated, stumbling over the word. It was completely unfamiliar on her tongue—but how else to put it? "At the PAs, I mean," she clarified, shrugging off the squeamish sensation the word *sick* had produced.

Chloe rolled her eyes. "Listen," she told her. "I know you and Emilie have your thing. Your dance rivalry and all. But if you're trying some weird mental tactic to freak her out, you're wasting your time. She's probably at home saving up her energy to kick your ass."

Davis knew she should back off—it really wasn't her problem. If Chloe wasn't worried, then she didn't have reason to be, either. But then . . .

Davis thought back again to when Sofia was sick as a toddler. It was a fluke, a rare infection that had temporarily paralyzed Sofia's immune responses. Fia had always been small—they called her the runt of the litter because she was the youngest, but also because of her slight frame—and it had the effect of making them fawn over her all the more. Terri had brought her cold cloths and she'd even stayed one night in a hospital, one of only two that existed in Columbus, alone in the cavernous facility but for one other little girl who'd suffered a terrible burn. Their father's face had been creased with concern for three days straight, his eyebrows wrinkled and his expression set. The whole time, he never took his blue-gray eyes off Fia's own—but Fia's were bright and glassy with fever. Davis remembered Fia asking for Terri, and Davis wanting more than anything for her own mother to be there. She remembered feeling a pang of jealousy at the sight of Terri's thin frame cradling Fia's, their identical curly, dark hair blending into one enormous mass of waves. And she remembered being afraid her little sister was going to die—because that's what the sweat, the flush across her face, and the tears had implied. She'd never seen those things before.

It wasn't supposed to happen. Not to Priors.

The TV was droning on when Davis walked into their flat later that day, its picture splayed across their living room wall. Parson Abel's unmistakable face filled up the screen: the broad grin that never seemed to reach his eyes, and the dimple that sank half an inch into his chin. Her stomach rolled at the sight of him. She was sure her father would win the election, but it would be a relief once it was over, that was for sure.

"Oh hi, honey!" Terri greeted her, looking up from the aquarium tank where she was feeding her fish. "How are you? How was school? Can I make you a snack?"

Behind her the face of a newscaster on the TV droned. ". . . was the daughter of Glen and Tatiana Brooks, esteemed professors at Columbus University. Both parents have declined to comment on the grim tragedy of their daughter's death, but neighbors have speculated that the young Ms. Brooks consorted freely with Gens . . ."

Davis inhaled sharply. Terri gave her a concerned look, and her brown eyes widened even more dramatically than usual. "Are you okay, honey?" she asked.

"I'm fine," Davis choked out. The pictures that flashed across the news screen were of a couple walking briskly to the metro, the woman covering her face with her handbag, her husband's arm wrapped around her waist. And then they flashed a picture of the daughter. A beautiful redhead with a glowing smile.

It was the girl from the party. Caitlyn.

"The cause of death is as yet undetermined. According to a neighbor, the young Ms. Brooks may have been involved in illicit dealings in the Gen community." Davis felt nauseous. So Caitlyn wasn't fine. Her parents had lied. *Cole* had lied. Or maybe not. Maybe she'd been fine and then worsened. *Or maybe . . .* The thought caused her stomach to turn . . . *Did Cole have something to do with it?*

She couldn't, wouldn't believe he'd had something to do with it. He'd seemed so concerned, so gentle when he was taking care of her outside the party. Maybe Caitlyn had been on drugs, after all.

And then images of the Slants began to flash across the screen. There were mangy dogs with dust-flecked fur. There were children playing barefoot outside in filthy puddles. Their housing structures were flimsy and apparently made of tin—little shingled buildings on wheels with maybe one or two bedrooms. Some were so small that the entire house could fit inside Davis's bedroom, and they all looked like they could blow away if the wind picked up. These structures could house anywhere from two to six Imps, according to the newscaster.

She turned from the TV. Her stomach turned, giving way to something deeper and hot and intense. Davis gripped her hands into fists, feeling her nails digging half-moons in her palms.

Terri abruptly shut off the TV. "Disgusting," she said with a sigh, her long eyelashes fluttering as she blinked. "Isn't it?" She wrapped an arm around Davis, pulling her close. "Don't worry, sweetie," she said. "When your dad's elected, he's going to make sure Priors never have exposure to any of that. We both love you and your sister so much. You'll never have to worry about anything like that."

Davis couldn't answer. Without responding, she fled to her bedroom and slammed the door, flopping onto her bed. Her sunshade was settling into a deep green. It was meant to soothe her, but she couldn't get the news broadcast out of her mind. Terri's words had soothed her more than she could have known. Davis had nearly cried in front of her; the emotion she felt—gratitude and fear and relief combined—was overwhelming. She wanted to ask her dad what was happening, but she didn't want to bother him. As the election loomed, he was becoming increasingly stressed out. It was like his whole identity was consumed by what used to be just a job. Her questions would probably just weigh on him further. She didn't want to distract him when he was so close to achieving his dream; and besides, his dream was all for her and Fia. After he was elected, she hoped, there'd be more time for questions . . . for the kind of conversations they used to have.

But for now, if Davis was going to get any answers, she'd have to find them herself. She sat up and grabbed her tablet from her schoolbag. She powered it on and typed in the code that allowed it to connect to her flatscreen. Then she logged into her e-mail and settled back against the mountain of purple and green throw pillows that decorated her bed while a list of messages loaded up on the wall facing her. A couple of fashion adverts, nothing of interest. No personal e-mails, which was unusual, aside from an announcement from the studio regarding reduced Saturday hours. Next she switched to Community, the social site everyone posted on. Maybe Emilie would be online.

A newsfeed of her friends' video-streams greeted her, but she skipped the updates and went straight to Emilie's page. Emilie's smiling face shone out from her profile, but she hadn't posted a vid in days. Davis scrolled down, checking for information.

UserHunnyBea16 posted a message @ 2:15 p.m. yesterday.

Davis clicked the link, and Beatrice Castellin's face popped up, framed by curly auburn hair. "Feel better, lady!" she chirped from the screen, chewing a wad of gum as she spoke. Davis shuddered. She was making little chomping sounds as she spoke. "I'll come sneak you chocolate so you don't have to deal with that gross hospital food." She made a gagging face before concluding her message with "Love you lots, Em! Muah!"

So Emilie was at the hospital. A surge of panic overwhelmed Davis. Caitlyn was dead, and Emilie was in the hospital, but no one was talking about the seriousness of it. She felt her fingers shaking as she typed the exit command and returned to her home screen, a picture of her and Fia on her sister's last birthday. In it, Fia's dark curls and skin pressed up against Davis's lighter, looser hair and creamy complexion. The two didn't even look like sisters in the picture, except for their shared noses: slim and straight and little. Button noses, their dad had always said. Davis made a sudden decision.

She'd go. She'd go see Emilie, and she'd get some answers. Davis threw on her jacket and shoes and was out the door before Fia or Terri could ask her any questions.

She could hear the chanting and shouting as she rounded the corner toward the hospital, only to find a hundred or so protestors holding signs and banners. She walked closer, morbidly curious to hear what it was they were saying. Her heart raced out of control as she thought about how angry her dad would be if he knew she was willingly approaching Imp rioters.

She walked up the sidewalk in the midst of the crowd, which was pushing and moving in a unified mass. "Higher wages, give us rights," seemed to be the current chant.

She turned, trying to make her way toward the side entrance, but the crowd had grown and now there were protestors on every side. She felt her body being pushed in the mass, bumped back and forth until her feet were lifted from the ground and she couldn't see beyond the moving bodies around her. Then the shoving became more violent, and all the chanting whirred around her like dark music, and someone screamed. Davis became panicked; she needed to get to Emilie, but there was no way she could fight through this crowd.

She craned her neck and saw two men, one dressed in an expensive-looking tailored suit and the other in rumpled jeans and a T-shirt, shoving each other. Others in the crowd around her got involved until the person next to her punched the person next to him. Davis looked down and saw that her shirt was spattered with blood, and yet the two guys kept at it.

It all happened so fast, then. The blond one hit the dark-haired one and he stumbled back into Davis, knocking her down.

She hit the ground sideways, landing on her hip and her right arm. She tried to stand up, but there were bodies all around her, knocking into her. She yelped as someone stepped on her hair. She had the sudden, terrifying thought that she'd be trampled to death. Panic took over and she wrapped her arms over her head, unable to struggle against the crowd or get up.

Then she felt hands under her shoulders lifting her up and forcing her forward through the crowd. She was shaking and tears blurred her eyes and she could barely tell where she was going or how she was moving at all. Someone was guiding her.

When they broke through she was exhausted, sweating, and crying and not sure where her tears stopped and the dirt-streaked sweat began. She turned to see who had helped her, and gasped.

It was Cole. Cole, who had been nowhere all her life and was suddenly everywhere all at once.

"What are you doing here?" she blurted out. It was the wrong thing to say. She should've said *Thanks for saving me*. But she was still completely shaken from being practically stampeded.

He didn't answer, just scanned her body as if checking for wounds. "Shit. You've got blood all over you." He reached out as if to touch her and she took a slight step back from him. "Are you okay?"

"I think so," she said, measuring her words. "It's not mine. It was just . . ."

"Out of control," Cole finished, moving toward her again.

"Yeah," she said. "It was." She wiped her eyes quickly, hoping he hadn't noticed she'd been crying.

"Where are you headed? Can I walk you?"

Davis hesitated, struggling to gain control of herself. "I was going to find my friend Emilie. She's in there, but . . ." She trailed off, breathing deeply. She realized her hands were trembling, that she was feeling a little light-headed. There was a shooting pain in her right shoulder, and she was having trouble articulating her thoughts.

"You have a friend in the hospital?" Cole sounded surprised, and his eyebrows knitted in concern. "What happened?"

"I'm not really sure," Davis started. "She collapsed at the PAs. I haven't heard anything about her since." A look of worry flickered over Cole's face; his eyebrows knitted together and his already dark eyes deepened to black. He laid a protective hand on Davis's arm. "You can't go in there now. And not like that," Cole told her in a soft voice, gesturing to the streaks of blood and dirt on her shirt. "Do you want to sit down somewhere for a second? Get some water, maybe? You can see her once this has all calmed down. I can walk you there, if you want—help you make sure she's all right." His words struck her as concerned, almost tender, and when her eyes darted to his, his face mirrored his tone. Davis felt her heart twinge, a different feeling from the one she'd gotten when she'd kissed him.

She thought maybe it was okay to hang out with Cole. She *wanted* it to be okay. But after seeing the news about Caitlyn, she wasn't sure if she could trust him. What had he been doing there at the hospital? The familiar anxiety moved through her, drawing her to him at the same time it propelled her in the opposite direction. If only she could trust him; she wanted to trust him. Every part of her reached out to him naturally, wanting him to open up to her, to give her something firm about himself that she could cling to. But he was still elusive, and every time he held back, it felt like a tiny needle prodding her heart. She wanted him too much. Sometimes she felt like she was standing on the edge of a chasm, a hairbreadth from hurtling over its edge. Her shoulder tensed again, sending a shooting pain down the back of her left arm, and she winced.

"Are you okay?" Cole asked, his forehead creased with worry.

"Fine," Davis told him, but when she rolled her shoulder back, the pain recurred, and she winced again.

"Davis. If you're hurt, we should see someone." His voice was urgent. "We should go to the hospital."

"No!" Her voice was sharp. "No," she said again more quietly. "Please. I don't want any attention. I'll be okay."

"Let's go somewhere to sit at least," he pressed.

"Okay," she said, relenting. She didn't want to be alone right now. And if she called her dad to get her, it would take at least half an hour before he arrived, and then another half an hour of lectures once he got there.

Cole put one hand against her back as though he thought it could shield her from the horde. She scooted ahead to avoid his touch. The electricity between them was distracting—it messed with her head. She had questions she needed to ask him, like why he was always around all of a sudden. And why he'd lied—*if* he'd lied—about Caitlyn being okay.

They turned a corner away from the commercial center of town and headed toward the restaurant district. Davis leaned against the cool brick of the alleyway, grateful for a chance to catch her breath.

"Cole," she said. "What really happened to Caitlyn?" She forced herself to look at him.

His face flushed. "What—what do you mean?" he asked.

"I saw it on the news. They're saying Imps did it. You told me you got her home safe, that she was fine. I don't know what to believe." Her voice had risen several octaves, and the look on his face did nothing to calm her.

"I did get her home," he said. "She *was* fine. At least, I thought she would be. Believe me, Davis, I had no idea what would happen. If I'd known . . ." He trailed off, and she noticed he had unconsciously squeezed his hands into fists.

His words reassured her a little—what had she been thinking? That he'd somehow known Caitlyn would die? He probably felt just as horrible as she did to have been one of the last to see Caitlyn.

He moved forward, taking her hands in his. There was a strange quality to them—a roughness that was unfamiliar and yet weirdly comforting.

"Look at me," he told her. She lifted her eyes to his. "I promise you, if I could have done anything to save her life, I would have." The way he said it was firm, heated. He held her gaze for a long time without looking away. He *wanted* her to trust him, she realized. He cared what she thought.

"Okay," she said, wanting to believe him. Trying hard to feel as certain as she sounded. "Okay. I'm sorry. I guess I was scared. I mean, it's crazy. I'm having trouble believing she's really dead."

"Me, too," he said quietly. Then: "I don't know why she died. But things are bad out there. Dangerous."

He must have been talking about how dangerous the Imps were, and trying to warn her. Obviously he hadn't hurt Caitlyn; she was sure of it now. He was just as concerned as Davis was. "Yeah, I know. I hear about it all the time from my dad," she replied. "He's super protective of me."

"I like the sound of this guy," Cole said, cracking a smile.

Davis smiled, kind of loving the fact that Cole clearly didn't know who her dad was. He had to be totally out of it. But it was so refreshing not to just be seen as Robert Morrow's perfect little daughter.

"Where are we going?" she asked, remembering herself. Her arm was really aching now—it felt like maybe a pulled muscle; she hoped nothing worse.

Cole scanned their surroundings, his eyes resting on an ambulance parked nearby, half on the side of the road and half on the curb, its doors left wide open and its lights off. There was no one inside. "There's our hospital," Cole said, taking her hand. She flushed at his touch but allowed him to guide her to the abandoned vehicle. He hoisted her into the backseat and followed her, pulling himself in afterward and sitting opposite her.

"What if someone comes back for it?" she asked, feeling nervous. She didn't like breaking into someone's car. It felt illicit. She was suddenly aware of how small the space felt, how close Cole was, how her body was reacting against her will. She felt warmer, and the space closed in on her, making her feel like the outside world had ceased to exist.

"If someone comes," Cole told her, his voice somehow soft and strong, "I'll tell them you're a girl who needs medical attention. And that's what I'm giving you. This is, after all, the best place for supplies. It couldn't be more perfect, wouldn't you say?"

She smiled. "I would," she agreed. He motioned for her to turn, and he placed his hands on her shoulder, prodding gently. She shivered involuntarily under his touch.

"Did that hurt?" Cole asked. Davis bit her lip, shaking her head. She leaned into his hands. It did hurt, a little . . . but it also sent shivers down her spine in a good way. He seemed so strong, so self-assured; she wondered why and how he knew what he was doing.

"Years of fighting," he answered her, without her having to ask. "Lots of dislocated shoulders. Fighting with my brother," he amended, averting his eyes. "Just normal kid stuff." He looked off into space, feeling the area around her left shoulder blade. "Yours is in place," he told her, "but there's some swelling. You'll need some anti-inflammatories."

"You have a brother," she said, hoping he wouldn't clam up as he had in the past. "What's he like?"

"Hamilton?" Cole laughed, his expression wry. "He's . . . well, he's his own breed. I guess we're a little alike." He reached for a first-aid kit that lay open on the front seat, rummaged through it, held up a packet of pills and examined them, then discarded them in favor of another. He tore the packet open with his teeth, and she shivered. He was incredibly sexy, but it was almost accidental. It wasn't like how Oscar was, always so sure of himself, aware of every action, every word he ever uttered, most of which were predictable. Nothing about Cole was predictable.

"How are you alike?" she pressed. She held her breath, afraid he wouldn't continue. But he smiled up at her, offering a tablet and a bottle of water. "Take this," he said. "I'm going to look for some sort of topical ointment, too. You've got a huge scratch there." She felt for her sweater and realized it had torn, slipping down her shoulder and exposing a bloody scrape. He rummaged again in the box, producing a disinfectant. "I guess we're alike because we're both really strong-willed," he said. "Just about different things. Growing up, Hamilton always had to win. He was super competitive. I was all about challenging myself, beating me. I liked to set records—how far I could run, how long I could hold my breath, that kind of thing—and beat that. Unfortunately he liked to beat me, too. He loved proving me wrong." Cole paused, obviously thinking back. He laughed at the memory, and Davis's heart swelled. She wanted him to keep talking forever. It was the first time he'd opened up. "Like I said, we fought a lot. It's how I learned to be strong. But if anyone else messed with me, watch out."

"What would he do?" Her question was tentative, searching. He seemed not to notice, lost in his memories. He rubbed ointment on his hands and placed his fingers on her shoulder, massaging a little to rub in the antiseptic. Davis's breath caught. Audibly, she thought. Her eyes darted to his, but he didn't look up. He was staring at her shoulder, concentrating. He bit his lip. Breathed. They both breathed. His eyes met hers. He seemed to wrestle with something inwardly, his mouth opening like he was about to talk, only to clamp shut again. He moved away, lifting his fingers from her back. She felt the loss, her body cold where just a second ago it had burned at his touch.

"You?" he said, the word forced. "Do you have brothers?"

"A sister," she said quietly. "Fia. Sofia. She's . . ." She trailed off, smiling. Unsure how exactly to describe Sofia. "She's dynamic," she continued. "Talented. Brilliant. A reader, an artist, everything." She laughed. "I feel pretty inadequate in comparison. I wasn't like her at that age. I just danced all the time. I wasn't curious like she is."

"You say 'just,'" he said, looking at her intently. "But there's no 'just' about what you do. I can just tell you're passionate. You devote your life to something. You . . . God," he said. He shook his head.

"What?" Her skin felt electric. He was so close, leaning toward her. So close. Just a little bit more, and they'd be close enough to kiss. "What?" she said again, whispering. He leaned toward her, so near that she felt his breath heat her cheek.

But then he stopped. She saw him close off as quickly as she might turn off her sunshade. He almost seemed to dim, a wall dropping between them. His posture became stiffer. He leaned away, like she'd done something wrong. She fought a swell of frustration, but it threatened to overcome her. He was so hot and cold. So mixed. So confusing.

"You're all set," he said, reaching for the handle of the door. "I'll help you get home."

"It's not far," she told him. "You've done so much." She expected him to protest, to offer to walk her home, but he just nodded.

"Okay." He helped her out of the vehicle, and they stood there, not quite meeting eyes. The moment was awkward—thick and clunky. Davis's whole body ached from the loss of him, the disappointment of a second kiss not realized.

"Well," he said.

"Why don't we hang out sometime?" she said, unsure where the courage was coming from. Maybe the painkillers were having some side effects, because she was never so bold. "I mean," she amended. "I don't know." She racked her brain for some way to make the moment less awkward. "There's a roofing party on Friday," she replied, hoping it was the right thing to say. Relieved she remembered. "Why don't you meet me there? It'll be some of the same people from the last party."

"What's a roofing party?" He frowned a little.

"You're kidding," said Davis. "You've never been to one?" She smiled at Cole, but he didn't smile back. "You're going to love it," she finished, less confident than before. She hoped he would. At least her friends would be around so she'd have a little moral support.

"I'd love to go," he told her. "Just tell me what time."

"Sure. I'll call you."

Cole nodded and pulled out his phone. But he seemed awkward, uncertain. Maybe he was nervous? Davis shrugged off the uneasy feeling and commanded her DirecTalk to project her keypad in the air. She selected the option to add a new entry and gestured to him, trying not to be bothered that Cole was taking so long to enter his number, or that he gave her his number without taking hers.

"I'll see you on Friday," he said. "I've got to get going now, though. Get home safe, okay?"

Davis nodded. "Thank you," she said simply. Cole nodded, then walked away, disappearing into the crowd without so much as a glance back in her direction.

Davis felt as if a hollow had opened in her chest. What was with his fast exit? And why was it so awkward? Had she imagined that there'd been a spark between them in the ambulance? Or was it all in her head? Had she said something wrong? She'd probably bored him half to death with her talk about Fia. She was such an idiot. Or was he just trying to play it cool? She'd never been so confused in her life.

She would do better on Friday. She would be perfect.

# 8

## COLE

The walk home was interminable. Cole was reluctant to leave
Davis. Even though he'd known where to look for her—even though
Parson had given him the rundown on everywhere Davis ever hung
out, including her ballet studio, school, apartment, friends' apart-
ments, favorite froyo place, and boutique—he'd still had a moment
of panic at the riots when he thought he wouldn't be able to locate
her in the throngs. And then his guilt—guilt at following her in
the first place—had changed to panic. He'd been *glad* he'd followed her—glad despite how wrong he knew it was—because if

he hadn't been there, she could have been badly hurt. No one was looking after Davis in all this madness. No one but him.

Still, it wasn't enough to rationalize the deception Parson was forcing him to enact. He wasn't going to get Parson that photo. No way. But he had to buy time. Going on a date with her, that would buy time, would make him look like he was invested in this thing he was doing for Parson Abel. He had to at least look like he was trying. But he wasn't going to get a photo. He'd hold Parson off without one for as long as he could. He could follow her because maybe in some small way that would keep her safe. But he could never expose her.

The thought of it made him want to punch something. Anything. The thought of anyone else exposing her made him want to scream, to rage, to hurt anyone with any intentions of hurting her. Going on this date would be okay; it would keep Parson at bay for a little longer. If she found out the truth, she'd never forgive him . . . but he had no choice, for now. And besides . . . he'd be lying if he tried to tell himself every single part of him wasn't leaping at the chance to see her again.

But he'd have to watch himself. In the ambulance . . . he'd almost opened up. Another minute, and he would have told her everything.

Cole spotted his own familiar gray trailer among the others that lined the back of his housing lot in the Slants. From fifty feet away, he could already hear that Hamilton and his friends were at it again. Cole pushed open the door, ducking a little to clear the threshold. Hamilton and his friends clammed up the second they saw him.

"Relax," Cole said. "I can hear everything you're saying through the wall anyway."

"Where are you going?" Hamilton wanted to know.

"Don't worry about it," Cole said.

Cole could see impatience working its way up Hamilton's neck in the form of a red flush. His brother had been after him to join the cause for years. But Cole was more about making things better right *then*. Hamilton was brilliant—but when would something come of all that planning?

Hamilton spoke up again, his voice hard. "When are you going to grow up, Cole?"

Cole had heard it a million times. He felt a tightness beneath his rib cage. "When are *you* going to back off?" Cole fired back, and pushed out the door.

He was tired—physically exhausted—by all the talk. He knew his brother's heart was in the right place. But he was sick of talk. Cole was all about action. Winning the FEUDS was the way out. It was what he'd always wanted, dreamed of. Cole had always thought he wasn't going to stick around the Slants once he won, like Tom had—getting a top-level education at some fancy research facility full of Priors, courtesy of his FEUDS earnings— then running right back home, back to where he'd started. His whole life, ever since he'd started fighting, Cole had planned to win and get outta there, bringing his family with him. He'd dreamed of moving to a faraway continent—Africa or Australia, maybe— where there was no such thing as segregation. It was a next-to-impossible dream, he'd always known . . . at least without the FEUDS money. He'd need a bank account with enough cash inside to prove he could support himself—and that was just to qualify for an application. He'd need sponsorship, someone to vouch for him, and even then, even with all the prereqs satisfied, he'd heard it could take months for the paperwork to go through. But he'd always been certain he could find a way. Now, though, the fantasy of finding a place where he could live free of Prior rule didn't bring him the same pleasure it used to. He still wanted to live on his own terms . . . but he didn't want to leave. Not unless Davis was with him.

What if she came with him? The thought was silly, impossible—a fleeting fantasy he'd let himself dwell on in the moments post-kiss and pre-sleep, moments when his defenses were down. He'd even let himself wish he could somehow enter the Prior world forever, not just as Parson's hired errand boy—but as someone who could live the way Davis lived, right there with her, in her world.

It was ridiculous. It was impossible.

Freedom was one thing. It was remote, but still possible, maybe, if he could win FEUDS. With enough ambition, hard work, and drive.

But a freedom in which he and Davis were together? Impossible.

And freedom without her took on a different meaning. It felt like just another set of trappings.

He was tempted to hit the Swings, but he wasn't in the mood for training. It was late, and training would just leave him alone with his thoughts, and his thoughts would lead him back to Davis, and how much he felt for her, and how awful he felt deceiving her. He'd known something was different about Davis. The way he was with her . . . *he* was different. Happier, more open, more alive than he'd ever been. The thought of seeing her at the roofing party made him feel weightless, charged. And because of it, he felt even worse for what he was doing.

He *liked* her. He didn't want to like her. It was crazy. First there were the obvious dangers: if anyone in the city found out he wasn't a Prior and that he'd even been flirting with her—let alone that he'd kissed her—he'd get locked up, or even killed. Worse, she was ignorant, like the rest of the Priors. He hated how she called Gens *Imps* so casually, like it was their proper term. If she knew what he was, she'd probably be disgusted by him. It was what she was conditioned to think. She liked him for what she *thought* he was—not what he really was. And yet, he couldn't deny it: he liked her anyway. It wasn't just that she was hot. There was something in her eyes—some spark he'd felt instantly, even before they kissed—that made him want to be around her, know more about her. And it made it that much harder for him to use her.

But he didn't have a choice.

Cole was antsy, fired up from the conversation with Hamilton. Screw the Swings. He'd just go to Brent's. Brent was one of his oldest friends, though what with the FEUDS occupying so much of Cole's time lately—and now Davis—it had been weeks since they'd hung out.

"Hey, man," Brent said when Cole knocked on the door. "Long time, no see."

"Going out?" Cole asked him, though it was obvious he was. Brent was already drinking from a flask he apparently planned to keep on hand that night. He offered some to Cole, and Cole took a long swig. It was half-filled with Brent's dad's homemade liquor. Cole tried not to gag. Then he took another gulp. It tasted better on the second sip, even better on the third and fourth.

"Nice," Brent said, slapping him on the back. "Glad to have you back."

"Where are we headed?" Cole asked, wiping his mouth with the back of his hand.

"The mines," Brent said. "But not for another few hours. We're hanging here first. Matt and Pearson and Hunter should be over in half an hour. You up for a long night?"

Cole avoided his eyes. "I'm counting on it," Cole told him, reaching again for the flask.

———

By the time they got to the mines, Cole was drunk. But not as drunk as the other guys, who were sloppy and loud, whistling and calling out to the girls they'd been with and the ones they wished they'd been with. Cole wanted just one girl—and he couldn't have her.

They stepped onto the elevator, which resembled one of the metal fighting cages Cole was so familiar with, and descended into the shafts. Cole reached out, touching the crumbling wall as the elevator descended, and bits of gravel loosened beneath his fingertips.

"Whoa," Hunter said. "Lay off the walls, man."

Brent started laughing long and hard, his hands resting on his knees, and accidentally snorted some alcohol out of his nose. That made Cole start laughing, too. It felt good to be back with the guys, ribbing each other, not taking anything too seriously.

When the elevator gate opened, the bass was so loud Cole could swear he saw the walls shake. Old gilded mirrors and other ornate Prior trash-turned-treasure—stuff that had been stolen, like antique chairs and even a chandelier—were propped next to and around them and hung from the ceiling above. Kids from all over leaned up against the filthy walls, and others danced in the center of the room to the hip-hop playing around them, blasting from vintage speakers—the whole party powered by electricity diverted from generators on the surface. Cole headed for the makeshift bar that was set up in the corner, offering booze stolen from parents' collections, made in friends' houses, and pilfered with fake IDs. He grabbed a beer. When he turned around, he saw his friends had already been swallowed by the crowd. He wasn't too worried. He knew almost everybody here.

It took less than five minutes for Michelle to find him . . . as he'd known, deep down, would happen. Had he been hoping for it or dreading it? She had always said she was just like him, that she wasn't looking for a relationship, either. But lately, Cole had gotten the sense that she wanted more, and he knew he'd have to address it sooner or later. He liked her a lot, but he didn't like the guilt that wormed its way through his stomach lately.

Now he felt her wrap her arms around him from behind and press her face against his neck.

"Hey, Cole," she said, and as he circled around to face her, she started moving against him to the beat of the music.

"Hey," he said back, stepping away to create a bit of distance between them. She was hot, one of the hottest girls he knew. Nearly as perfect as a Prior. But he couldn't think of her that way; he'd known her forever, and she was as familiar to him as a sister. Lately, though, he'd started realizing that the affection she felt for him was different. More intense and far less . . . comfortable than what he felt for her. Before he met Davis, Cole had tried to like Michelle. He'd tried to conjure up the right kind of feelings. She was beautiful, and they'd always been close. But there was something missing for him.

Even through the haze of booze, the pounding of the music, and the swaying of Michelle's hips against his, he couldn't stop thinking about Davis.

He took Michelle's face in his hands and leaned his forehead against hers. She leaned back into him, responding to his touch. Michelle would be such a simple choice. But when it came down to it, Davis was there when he closed his eyes. Michelle would never be more than just a friend. Even though he had to admit he was lonely, isolated, aching . . . and all he wanted to do was surround himself with those closest to him, he *had* to put more distance between him and Michelle, before she got hurt.

He stepped back from her.

"What?" she said. "What's the matter?"

"Nothing. I just . . . need another drink." It wasn't what he needed at all, but he wanted to get Davis out of his mind and thoughts. He gritted his teeth and grabbed a shot glass, downing two in a row. He was in serious trouble.

It wasn't until he tried to make his way back into the crowd that he realized he'd gone from drunk to trashed. The room seemed to be swimming under a red haze, and all of the music was muffled, as though he were hearing it from under water. Faces leered at him, people were shouting, punching his arm, wanting to know about the FEUDS.

And all of a sudden, he knew he was going to be sick.

He fought his way to the rickety old elevator and went up to the entrance to the mine, feeling the air grow clearer as the music retreated below him. He just wanted some air.

He sat on the gravel and leaned back against a fence surrounding the mine, putting his head between his knees and taking long, deep breaths until he felt better. Eventually, his head stopped spinning and he leaned back. It was a clear night; a thousand stars decorated the sky, and he could hear music pouring from neighboring homes as well as thumping below him from the party. He closed his eyes.

Then the elevator door ground open, its rusty wheels making a long creaking noise as the gate lifted. He didn't turn. But he knew it would be her.

Michelle plopped down next to him, leaning her head against his shoulder and looping her right arm through his left. He wrapped his arm around her. Michelle wasn't Davis, but that wasn't her fault. She was a good girl.

He opened his eyes then, gazing up at the dazzling beauty of the stars overhead. It was the best spot in the entire city to look at them: free from the blaze of buildings and removed enough from the Slants to feel like he was alone with just the night sky.

"I don't get you, Cole," Michelle mumbled, nestling her head deeper against his neck. "I don't get what you want."

"Yeah," he told her, finding her hand with his, and thinking of Davis's enormous eyes, the way she bit her lip, the smell of her. Like lilacs. *A Prior.* "That makes two of us."

# ❦ 9 ❧

## DAVIS

Normally on the day of a roofing party, Davis felt a combination of excitement and dread. But this Friday both emotions were in double dose. And it was obvious why.

*Cole.*

She knew the city was bracing itself for the next round of continued Imp protests, that she was just three days away from receiving the results from the PAs, and that she should be concerned that Emilie had never reappeared at school that week. But all she could worry about during her classes on Friday—and then the long walk home after school (the monorails were still down)—

was whether Cole would really show up that night. Even the thought of him standing her up made her stomach drop the emotional equivalent of ten stories.

All of this worrying was making her dizzy, and her stomach felt a little twisty and weird. So when she got home from school, she decided to paint her nails gold—as much to steady her hands and nerves as to beautify. She was missing Sofia, who was away at a birthday party that evening. Every now and then, Fia's hovering annoyed her, but usually she loved having her little sis around to chat with—it had almost become integral to her pre-party routine. Davis's room felt uncustomarily empty without her, despite the music she was blaring.

She dialed Vera on her DirecTalk, hoping for a distraction. Her friend picked up on the third ring. *"Hey,"* Vera said. *"Are you as excited as I am for tonight?"*

Davis smiled. They were almost always on the same wavelength. *"I am,"* she said. *"I love roofing."* She hesitated; she hadn't yet told Vera that Cole was coming.

*"What's up?"* Vera asked. *"You're being awfully quiet for one who's purportedly so excited...."*

*"I invited Cole. The guy from Emilie's."* Davis held her breath, unsure how Vera would respond.

*"That's good, right?"* Vera said finally. *"Where did you say he went to school again?"*

Davis bit back a rush of irritation. Vera had asked the most difficult question, the one she couldn't answer. Okay, there were practically none she *could* answer, but still. *"I'm not sure; he never mentioned it."*

*"Okay, well. He was definitely cute."* Vera's voice was hesitant.

*"But?"* Davis braced herself.

*"Nothing,"* Vera said. *"Really. I get why you're into him. I just ... we don't know anything about this guy. Just be careful."*

"*That's the whole reason he's coming roofing,*" Davis told her. "*Because it's a group thing. I didn't want to suggest doing something alone, not so soon.*"

"*You suggested it? He didn't ask you out?*"

Davis felt heat flooding her face. She didn't know why this conversation was making her so uncomfortable. It was never like this with Vera. "*It wasn't like that,*" she said. "*It's fine.*"

"*What's his last name?*" Vera wanted to know. "*Maybe I can see if anyone can vouch for him.*"

"*What is this? You can save the interrogation. I can handle it.*" The second the words escaped her lips, Davis regretted them. She'd sounded way more snappish than she'd intended, but the truth was, Vera was just voicing all the concerns she already had.

"*I should go,*" Vera told her.

"*Vera—*"

"*I'm not mad. I'm just worried about you.*"

"*I know. Really. I'm sorry I snapped. I just think we need to give him a chance. Just because we haven't known him all our lives doesn't make him a bad guy.*"

"*You're right,*" Vera said. "*We'll get to know him as it comes. I'm excited for tonight.*"

"*Me, too.*" They said their good-byes and Davis commanded her DirectTalk to enter "Do Not Disturb" mode. She needed time to think. No matter how much she reassured herself, repeating the same phrase she'd said to Vera, Vera's questions ran in circles through her head. She *didn't* know much about Cole. He'd opened up a fraction of an inch and it had felt like he was giving her the world. Why was he so secretive? It just wasn't normal. Davis swallowed back her discomfort, but her hand shook.

A few coats of mostly-within-the-lines glitter nail polish later, and she'd made her decision. She was going to spend three hours instead of two at practice before the party. She was going to beat those nerves to a pulp. And then she was going to show up fashionably late to the party and have fun like a normal teenager, Cole or no Cole. She deserved a break from the craziness and stress of the past week.

By seven o'clock—after one of the more intense workouts of her life in her building's substandard studio, since the real studio was still closed, maybe indefinitely—she was decked out in her cutest running pants (the spandex dark gray ones with the neon-pink piping) and a sheer, loose-fitting tank top layered over a hot pink sports bra. She felt cute, and a new excitement was buzzing through her.

She was good at roofing. The leaps, the flexibility—it was what a ballerina was made for. She flushed at the thought of how Cole might see her, what he'd think. Davis felt more *alive* at roofing parties than almost anywhere else except the dance floor.

She kissed her mom's Olympiad medal on her way out the door. It hung right next to a picture of her parents from the night they met—her dad was gazing at her mom with the cutest smile on his face while her mom laughed with a friend. It was the only picture of the two of them that remained. "First place, just like you," Davis whispered at the medal, yanking the door open as she said it.

"Watch it!" she cried out, jumping a little. Frank was standing right outside her door in a tight-fitting, tailor-made beige linen suit, his signature red silk cravat tied around his neck and an old-fashioned pocket square completing the look. His blond hair was parted on the side and slicked back with who knows what goop he'd slathered on. Davis shuddered before she could stop herself. It was almost as if he'd been *listening*. Or as if he'd wanted to startle her, one of the two. She'd never trusted Frank—in fact she never trusted *any* man who used hair gel—and he'd been up her butt about her father's election campaign. "Excuse me," she said, trying to shoulder her way past him. She was never going to get used to all the campaign managers—*intruders*—crowding their house.

"I was just coming to get you," Frank told her, smiling wide enough to produce dimples in both cheeks. "Terri wants you downstairs—she needs your help getting ready for the fund-raiser. But I see you have other plans." His gaze moved over Davis's body, lingering a little too long on her chest and legs. She squared her shoulders and stared back at him, forcing him to meet her gaze. "Are you sure that outfit is . . . appropriate?" he said. She didn't miss the lewd tone in his voice. "You look more like an Imp than the daughter of the city's next prime minister."

Davis felt her cheeks burn. Why did Frank assume he had the run of the house? Who did he think he was, coming up to the second floor, where all the bedroom suites were? And why the heck did he think her wardrobe was his business, anyway? Davis gritted her teeth, trying hard to conceal her frustration. She didn't want him to have the satisfaction.

"I'm already late," she fired back. "I'm not going to change now. And I'm not sure it's *appropriate* for you to be looking." She pushed past him roughly. Terri emerged from the stairwell just as Davis was about to descend. Terri took one look at Davis's face and put a hand on her shoulder, glancing from Davis to Frank and back again.

"Frank, don't tell me you're giving her trouble again," Terri said. "What's wrong, sweetie?"

"I was just telling her to reevaluate her wardrobe," Frank said, his voice stiff. "She doesn't quite fit the image of the daughter of a prime minister candidate, wouldn't you agree?"

"I wouldn't," Terri informed him. "And we've never been a family that bought into someone else's idea of perfection." She smiled warmly at Davis, and Davis gave her a grateful look. "Go on," she told her. "Have fun with your friends."

Davis gave Terri an awkward peck on the cheek and hurried down the stairs and out the front door. She'd never been more grateful for Terri; sometimes it was like her stepmom had a sixth sense. Fia had some of it, too, an innate empathy that never failed to touch Davis's heart. Times like these, when Terri stood up for her against Frank—she felt like they were a real family, that she didn't need anything else. That there wasn't something missing.

It was a ten-minute walk from Davis's house to the Lights Zone, the grouping of public high-rises where the roofing was scheduled to start. No monorail required, thankfully. Who knew when they'd be back in operation. Besides, she was starting to like walking around on her own. At night it was especially exciting; she felt a thrill of adrenaline work its way up her spine as she turned another dark corner to pass through a narrow alley.

She was high-energy from her afternoon workout and in a good mood, so she broke into a moderate jog to warm up her muscles. The dark helped push her forward. She emerged from the passages behind her neighborhood and ran ahead onto the limestone surfaces of the downtown area, loving the way her shoes gripped the panels beneath her. She couldn't make out her reflection in the stone anymore, though, given its newfound grimy quality, courtesy of the strikes.

Cole hadn't yet arrived at BKC Tower 2. She swiped her P-card and rode the elevator to the top. There were about thirty or so kids from her school up there already. Davis saw Vera and Oscar gathered on one corner of the roof, along with Max and Desiree, a couple of other third-years from Excelsior.

Vera gave her a hug, but Oscar ignored her, looking irritated.

He took a quick gulp from the flask he was holding in his left hand—his parents never noticed when he swiped from their liquor cabinet, despite that he drank more than they did.

"Have you seen him?" she asked Vera quietly, pulling her aside, feeling a sudden flurry of nerves. What if he flaked? What if he stood her up?

"Cole?" Vera asked, a concerned look immediately spreading across her face.

"He said he'd be here," Davis said, growing more and more concerned that he was bailing.

Vera reached out and hugged her, reassuring Davis, "He wouldn't do that to you," but she could tell Vera was worried for her.

Davis nodded, trying to smile. But she felt a knot of anxiety in her stomach. What if he didn't show? "Where's Nadya?" she asked Vera, trying to change the subject. Nadya, another ballerina, hadn't been at studio for a couple of days—but that was nothing new. Nadya ditched practice sometimes. Ballet was only one of at least five extracurriculars she did, and her real talent lay in tennis. She was notorious for skipping out on dance. Roofing, however, she did not typically miss.

"I don't know," Vera said, her forehead wrinkling as she thought. "Maybe she'll show up later. Stop worrying so much."

Davis nodded, turning her attention to the more pressing issue: *Where was Cole?* She'd never been stood up before. Vera gave her another sympathetic pat on the back. "Only an idiot would miss a chance to hang out with you," Vera told her. Davis smiled gratefully at her friend. Vera was biased, yes, but Davis still appreciated her words. She turned a full circle, looking for Cole in the crowd. Why was he so unpredictable? It was starting to make her mad—starting to seem more rude than attractive.

"Maybe we should start without him," Vera whispered, keeping her voice low.

Davis nodded again, her eyes burning. She was wrong to fall for him; Vera had been right. She felt impossibly naïve. She hoped it wasn't obvious to everyone else that she'd been ditched.

And then, with a huge wave of relief and excitement blotting out all her former worries, she spotted him. Moving through the crowd toward her, tall, taller than she'd even remembered. He was smiling. He was beautiful, even though *beautiful* wasn't a word you were supposed to use with guys.

"You're here," she blurted out, and then regretted it; that made it sound like she'd been worried.

"I am," he said back, but his own expression was unreadable. Why was he so hard to read? He had his hands stuffed in his pockets and he was wearing dark jeans, slim cut, a bad choice for roofing. Maybe he was just that confident that he wouldn't wipe out on the rough cement. His wardrobe choice was like a dare—or a taunt—to everyone else. Davis admired his confidence. A happy glow filled her up, making her realize for the first time just how worried she'd been that he wasn't going to show. "How's your friend?" he asked, taking a step closer, narrowing the gap between them.

"Emilie?" Davis's heart dropped as she felt worry overcome her at the thought of her friend, but it was sweet of Cole to remember, to ask. "She's okay, I think," she told him. "I talked to her cousin about it. Well, twice, actually. She's not exactly the most forthcoming . . ."

"Is she still in the hospital, though?" Cole pressed.

"Chloe said she's out, but doesn't really feel like seeing anybody. She did mention that she's probably coming back to the studio next week, so I think it's all fine. I mean, I'm sure it is," she corrected herself. Cole nodded, but he frowned a little at the same time. He opened his mouth as if about to ask something more, but Vera appeared at Davis's side.

"Hi," she said. "I'm Vera. We met the other night." She held out her hand, and Davis braced herself for the questions she was sure would follow. She was half nervous, half glad Vera was the prying type. Before she could say anything, though, Oscar wrapped his arm around Vera's tiny frame, lifting her high in the air. She kicked her legs and threw back her head as she yelped, clearly enjoying being teased.

"I want to get started! Let's do it," Oscar shouted out, getting the attention of everyone on the BKC2 deck. "We've been waiting around long enough." He directed a pointed look at Davis.

"I'm only two minutes late!" she protested. She noticed Oscar barely glanced at Cole.

"Right. Not as late as usual," Oscar said. "But still late." Davis rolled her eyes. Oscar was absurdly punctual. And since most people were afraid of Oscar, most people showed up on time for things.

"Cheer up, baby," said Vera, jumping on his back. He wrapped his arms around her legs and shifted her up a little higher in a perfect piggyback position. "We're going ROOFING!" she shouted, raising her fist, and some of the others joined in, cheering along with her. "How about I start?" Vera said, her voice faltering so subtly that Davis was sure she was the only one who noticed. Vera skipped over to her and bent, retying her running shoes. "I'll start the inquisition later," she said under her breath, so only Davis could hear. Davis laughed, and Vera winked. Then she straightened, readying herself for the first leap.

Davis felt adrenaline course through her; all her senses were alert. She was charged, ready to go. She watched as Vera accepted a little white pill from Sierra, tossing it back with Oscar's flask. All around, her other friends were doing the same. She glanced up at Cole, wondering if he'd want one of the black-market enhancers, but he didn't say anything. Maybe he was too polite to ask—or maybe, like her, he already had a powerful natural high.

The night was cool, crisp; the sun was almost all the way down now, and it left a purple haze with fading hints of red in its wake. From way up here, it was impossible to see the streets beyond the soaring peaks of the buildings. For a moment, it was like none of the tumultuous stuff she'd been dealing with—Caitlyn, the riots, the Olympiads, her father's campaign—existed. It was like it was something awful she'd dreamed up.

"Ready, set . . ." Oscar nodded to Vera. Then Vera blew a gold whistle that hung around her neck—a birthday gift from Davis the year before—and the first pair of runners started, leaping over the ten-foot gap between the BKC2 and BKC3 towers with ease.

"Hey," Cole whispered, making Davis jump. Their hands brushed against each other and she felt another bolt of adrenaline—more powerful than the last—travel up her shoulder to her spine. "I didn't realize . . . I mean." He stopped and took a breath. "Remember, I've never done this before," he blurted out. "I didn't realize *this* was roofing."

"Seriously?" Davis looked at him, eyes wide. "Nobody roofed at your school?" Cole shook his head and Davis laughed. "You're in for an awesome rush. The first time is always the best." She blushed, realizing she'd just set him up for a lewd joke.

But he didn't seem to notice. He was staring at the gap, which almost all of her friends had already cleared.

"It's easy," Davis told him, afraid she was insulting him by saying it. *Of course it was easy.* Most guys loved roofing for the chance it gave them to show off: be big, testosterone-laden men, that kind of thing.

Cole sucked in a deep breath.

"Okay," he said. "So what are we waiting for? Let's do it."

Davis found herself laughing as she ran. She vaulted off the edge of the building, and for one second was suspended in the air,

wind rushing in her ears, and the streets like dark canyons far below her. Then she landed neatly on the next building. Cole landed a
second after her, breathless.

"See? Isn't it great?" she said. But she didn't wait for him to answer. She took off running again.

Both of them cleared the first three buildings without any
trouble, but that was the point; the gaps grew wider and the buildings were staggered in varying heights, so toward the end they'd
find themselves jumping higher and farther. Davis relished the
challenge. She picked up the pace, eager to catch up to the rest of
the group. Cole fell back, several paces behind her.

Davis's body was on fire, and it took a lot of control to slow down
to wait for him. She wondered why he was hanging back—even if
this was his first time, he couldn't possibly have been intimidated
or nervous. He was so strong and fit, she could tell just by looking
at him that roofing should come easily to him.

But then another thought crossed her mind. Could he be slow-
ing down because he wanted to get her alone? Maybe he wanted
another kiss as much as she did.

Still, she kept running, looking back occasionally to make eye
contact with him. If he *was* trying to get her alone, she wouldn't
give him the satisfaction just yet. Besides, her nerves were fully
aware, her entire body responding to the sensation of her muscle
power, the lift and momentum she required to clear one gap after
another. She leaped the buildings like she'd leap around the dance
floor: gracefully, as though flying. Once you got going, it was like
your body didn't even have to work anymore. You just moved with
the momentum, like skiing or skydiving, giving yourself over
to the velocity. Aside from dance, it was the only time Davis ever
felt this way.

On their sixth rooftop, Cole stumbled. The rest of the group was already well ahead of them by then. Davis noticed Cole's mistake even as they leaped; he didn't jump high enough. Davis landed and spun only to see him desperately trying to pull himself up over the ledge of the next building. Then he lost his grip altogether and plummeted.

Davis shrieked.

She ran to the edge of the building, her heart threatening to split her rib cage wide open. She stared down.

But she did not see Cole's body hurtling toward the pavement seventy stories below.

"I'm fine," Cole said from the fire escape two stories down, where he'd landed. "Totally fine." Davis breathed a sigh of relief, but her body was still weak from the shock. She swayed a little, taking a step back to catch her balance.

"Are you *trying* to freak me out?" she shouted down at him, trembling from anger and relief.

Cole shook his head. "I'm sorry, I—" he started.

"I'll come down," she interrupted.

By then, Vera had crossed back to their rooftop. "What's up?" she asked, giving Davis a questioning look.

"You guys go on," Davis said. Now she felt like an idiot for screaming. "We'll catch up in a minute."

"Sure you don't mind?" Vera asked, raising her eyebrows.

"I'm fine," Davis said. Her fear had evaporated. It was obvious— Cole *did* want to get her alone. He had clearly orchestrated the whole thing. "Really." She shot Vera a look.

"Call me when you get home," she told her. "I want to hear everything."

"I wouldn't dream of *not* calling you the second I get back," Davis said. Vera giggled and blew her a kiss before she dashed off to where Oscar was waiting a couple of buildings ahead.

Davis swung down onto the fire escape and climbed down to where Cole was sitting.

"You weren't even close," she told him in a teasing voice. She reached for his hand and tugged it, trying to bring him to his feet, but he jerked it away, wincing.

Davis drew back, confused. Was he actually *hurt?* She'd never once seen anyone get hurt roofing. She knew in theory it was dangerous—that's what made it so fun—but even the least athletic Priors she knew could handle the physical demands of roofing. Really little kids did it sometimes. Davis had started when she was twelve.

And yet, here Cole was, refusing to get up. Looking, in fact, like he might be injured.

"Wait," Cole said, and for the first time, Davis realized he was out of breath, too. "Let's just sit here for a second."

If this was an act, it was an elaborate one. She had no idea what to think. But Davis sat next to him on the fire escape anyway, staring out at the city below them. It was luminous, its lights creating a starry landscape that stretched for miles.

"It's so beautiful," she said. "Just like a million stars."

"The real thing's better," he told her. "Stars, I mean. You wouldn't believe what the sky looks like from outside the city." He stopped abruptly, as though he didn't want to say anything more.

"Like in the other places you lived?" Davis prompted. She was desperate to know more about where Cole had been. She had never, not once, been out of Columbus, and had always fantasized about seeing Old New York, now mostly underwater, from above.

Cole hesitated. "Yeah," he said, but nothing more.

Davis wrapped her arms around her knees and shivered. There was a wind up here, and it was colder than usual.

"The sky makes me feel close to my mom," she said, almost to herself. "I feel like she's up there somewhere, watching me." There was a brief silence, and she began to feel silly for saying anything. She'd never expected anyone else to get it.

"What happened to her?" Cole asked softly.

"She died giving birth to me," Davis told him. "The hospital messed something up. Something simple." *It was the Imps' fault,* she thought. She remembered hearing her father say that many years later to Terri when he thought Davis wasn't listening. *It was the Imps' fault.* She cleared her throat. "My dad doesn't like to talk about it."

"I'm so sorry—" Cole said, but she cut him off. It was as if she couldn't stop talking now that the initial words had forced their way out.

"My mom was, like, this perfect ballerina. A better version of me, I guess you could say. She's what I want to be someday. We still have all the old recordings from her competitions . . . she was the best ballerina in the world, at one point. She was famous. When I was a kid, I'd watch them all the time. I still put them on sometimes . . . they help me fall asleep. She was so beautiful." Davis stopped, a little out of breath. It was the most she'd ever said about her mom to anyone, even Vera. "When she got pregnant with me, she was at the height of her career. She could have done anything. My dad never said so, but I'm sure I was a mistake. I wasn't supposed to happen in the first place, and then she died, and she could have been touring the world, doing what she loved best. That's why I dance. I guess I want to make it up to her. I mean, sure, I love to dance, too—I really do. But I wonder sometimes if I would care so much about it if she hadn't died."

"You would," Cole said, taking her hand in his. "I can tell by the way you talk about it. You have passion." The words seemed difficult for him to say. But his hand felt warm and solid in hers. It made her feel like she could say anything.

"When I was little," Davis started again, "I used to climb out the escape hatch onto the roof of our building. I'd take the elevator to the top floor and access it from there. It was easy, although if my dad had known, he would have killed me." She let out a laugh. "But he never noticed. Sometimes I'd—I'd shut the floodlight on and off. On and off. Making signs to her. Hoping she would make a sign back. Hoping *anyone* would," she finished, trying not to let her voice falter, even though his thumb was now tracing semicircles on the inside of her palm. "Sometimes I like to explore the old churches." It was her deepest secret; she had never told anyone. "I know God isn't real, but . . ." She paused, trying to find words for what she wanted to express. "When I'm there, I can't help but wonder . . . I don't know. I don't know how to explain."

"Try," Cole said softly.

She sucked in a deep breath. "I just think of all the people who were there before, all the hope and prayers poured into those places. And I feel . . . safe. But still surrounded by something bigger. And that makes me feel better. If I didn't *know* souls were made up, I . . . I think I'd believe." She laughed, blinking back tears. "I know. It's stupid," she said, sneaking a look at Cole.

"I don't think it's stupid," he said. She stared at him, waiting for him to crack a smile, but his face remained serious. She broke eye contact then and cleared her throat. "My dad died, too," he said suddenly. Davis felt herself turning to him again, her eyes meeting his. His were full of pain. "I know what you mean. About looking for someone you've lost. I—I don't like to talk about it." He cleared his throat. His expression was solemn. "I almost never do. But I look for him in things all the time." Davis squeezed his hand tight, her heart expanding, reaching out to his.

"Want to see my favorite?" She stood up, and he stood with

her, still holding on to her hand. She leaned out over the fire escape, squinting.

"Which is it?" he asked. But he was looking at her, not out toward the roofs at all. She lifted their hands, still clasped together, and pointed out toward the lights in the distance.

"That one's my house," she said. "See the building with the tower that's lit up red? Now look left. All the way down, toward the street. See the big cross?" He nodded, smiling. "There. That's where I go. Don't tell anyone that, okay?" She shook her head, anxious. "My dad would kill me."

"I won't tell a soul," Cole said. Before she could register what he'd said, he wrapped his arms behind her back, pulling her hips ever so slightly closer to his. Her heart pounded and her whole body felt light, like it was floating up into the sky and over to the church roof all by itself. Their faces were only a couple of inches apart. They were so close, so close to what she'd been wanting ever since the last time. His eyes locked on hers.

And then there was no space between them at all; he was pulling her toward him and pressing his lips to hers with the kind of passion that she hadn't even felt the last time, a passion that made her reel until she wasn't sure whether she was standing up anymore or floating out through the sky. But then she felt the cold metal of the rail pressing up against her back and everything came back in a whoosh: the urgency of his hands on her skin where they pushed up underneath her tank and hoodie, the faint noise of the traffic far below them and the more immediate noise of the wind brushing them with its night-cold fingertips.

He kissed her neck and she tilted her head back, her eyes closed, breathing along with the sensation of chills traveling up and down her left side. His mouth was warm on her but the rest of her body was freezing cold—from the nerves, the sensation, his presence, she thought. His lips made a trail up her neck toward her earlobe, then to her forehead and back to her lips, where they pressed more firmly, his tongue moving as if it knew exactly what it was looking for while his hands cupped her face. She thought all of a sudden that she could fall, plummet backward all seventy stories. Then she thought he could push her . . . but she could pull him, too, so they were even: both needing to trust each other. And even if they fell together, it wouldn't be much different from the rushing and soaring she was feeling right then.

"Cole," she started, pulling back slightly so she could look into his eyes and catch her breath. "This is crazy."

"I know," he said, breathing heavily. "But it's so . . ."

"Right," she filled in as he leaned closer and began kissing her neck again.

"More than right," he whispered, and she knew: whatever it was, this force between them, drawing them together . . . he was feeling it, too.

His hands made her feel like he knew her. All of her, her body and her heart. And their touch, eager but gentle, told her that everything he knew, he adored. The best part was, she wasn't hiding a thing. She reached for his hair, grabbing a handful of it and feeling it sift through her fingers.

But then Cole was yanking his arms from hers, taking an abrupt step back. She moved toward him, but he held out one hand to block her.

"What?" she asked, panicked. "What is it?"

"We can't—" he started.

"What?" She was alarmed, afraid she'd done something wrong. She could feel herself begin to shake, starting with her hands again—it was probably a response to all the sensations that had just wrapped themselves around her.

He was breathing hard. "This—it isn't right," he said. "We can't do this." And then he took another step away, starting down the fire escape.

"Cole!" she shouted. "Cole, what are you doing? Are you insane?"

But he ignored her—and soon, he was disappearing into the dark.

# 10

## COLE

Cole's running shoes barely touched the rough metal steps. He moved so fast it felt like he was free-falling down the sixty-eight flights of fire escape stairs. *Free-falling.* It was the same feeling he'd had when he'd kissed Davis. The second his lips had met hers, everything he'd been afraid of had been confirmed. He'd done the very thing he'd promised himself he wouldn't: he'd fallen for her. He hadn't expected her to be the way she was. He'd expected frigid lips and stiffness instead of the way her body leaned into his, soft and pliable. She was strong, obviously—she had the strength only hours of ballet training could provide—but there was this quality of vulnerability that he could detect every time his hands touched her shoulders and the small of her back. It was the way she yielded to him—she so clearly trusted him. And the way she'd opened up about her mother . . . He and Davis were similar in a way he hadn't expected. He felt like he understood her. She was everything Cole *hadn't* thought Priors were—kind, relatable, warm.

And yet, they were still so different in other ways.

She was intelligent and sophisticated. She knew things he didn't about art and history and literature, and she wasn't afraid to be smart. She had the best laugh he'd ever heard. She could laugh openly and without reservation. She had a million different smiles that betrayed all of her complex thoughts, and he felt like every single one was exciting to discover. The kiss shouldn't have happened. But it had, and all he wanted was for it to happen over and over again. More than that: he needed it, with a physical craving more intense than any FEUDS adrenaline he'd ever felt. Half of him wished it had never happened, because the mere fact that it had was making him crazy. The other half realized he hadn't lived, not really, until he'd felt her lips against his. Now, however, he was in over his head. What tightrope was he walking? Worse, what game was Parson Abel playing? Davis and he were both being used, Cole was sure of it. But how high were the stakes, and how could he come out on top without knowing the answer?

Never in his life had he felt so out of control. His heart pounded with the exertion of running—or maybe from the kiss—but his lungs felt clear and strong. Still, panic worked its way through his veins in the jolting form of adrenaline. Cole pushed through the dark alleyways of the city, careful to stick to the shadows rather than the lit glare of the streetlamps. A neon sign for a cosmetics company flashed over him as he turned toward the waterfront, its red lettering casting an eerie glow over the street.

Cole was a two-minute sprint from the dock where he knew the motie would be waiting when he heard the squeal of tires behind him. Then he saw the red flashing light that signaled a cop car; it had been obscured by the neon pall of the street. He ducked under a low awning for coverage, his heart thudding. He'd reached the industrial vicinity of Columbus, and the buildings were fewer and spread farther apart as the landscape transitioned into the Slants. The car slammed on its brakes a mere ten yards from where Cole stood, partially concealed by the abandoned storefront's foyer. He leaned against the door and it moved inward—it was already ajar—and he slipped inside as quietly as possible.

*They couldn't be after him.*

Could they? Did Parson know what he was up to with Davis? Was Parson going to blow the whole thing? Or had Davis figured it out and called the cops on him? His heart pounded, and it was all Cole could do to hold himself together. It occurred to him: he might lose her. It was a blow that left him nauseated, weak. He was startled by the intensity of his emotions, more startled, too, by how it impacted him on a physical level—his whole body was tensed, poised in fight mode. He would do anything not to let it happen, he realized. Another car sped around the corner, its wheels screeching as it pulled up next to the first. Cole's heart was in overdrive, his palms slick with sweat and his T-shirt clinging to his frame. Two Prior patrolmen, one burly and the other taller but slighter, stepped out of their vehicles. One spoke low into his DirecTalk, and Cole strained to hear.

"Reinforcement to zone six," the man said into the device. "Gen suspect in sight. Sanction extra units. Over." Cole felt a flash of panic. Had they already spotted him? He pressed up against the inside of the building, holding his body motionless. There was quiet; an interlude in which he tried to get a quick glance out the window. Then a spark of neon flashed in Cole's periphery, and a bedraggled-looking man from the building across the street darted behind the patrolmen, his movements irregular. The man was stumbling, clutching his face as he ran. From the look of his well-worn clothing and his diminutive height, he was a Gen. Cole let his breath out in a whoosh. It wasn't him. They weren't after him at all. The taller policeman turned fast, his flashlight cutting patterns across the dark. Its beam narrowly missed Cole's frame. Cole could see a trail of blood dotting the pavement in the man's wake.

"Gen suspect spotted!" shouted the shorter patrolman into his DirecTalk, confirming Cole's suspicions. "Units pursuing westward down Lynden. Send backup to Lynden and March." Then they were in their cars and off, tires squealing and dust forming a cloud behind them.

For a second, all Cole felt was residual relief. He was in the clear. He'd come so close to getting caught. And getting caught meant losing her. But for now, everything was okay. It was going to be okay. His heart rate slowed, and feeling began to work its way back into his hands, which tingled from the rush of fear. He wondered what the man had done—and why he was bleeding. Then he realized he didn't have time to speculate.

Cole dashed down the street. He reached the dock in a matter of minutes.

"Back so soon?" The same motie he'd used that morning grinned wide at Cole, but his eyes were empty, and he was missing almost all his teeth. Cole shivered. This dude freaked him out, and yet he couldn't help feeling a little bad for him. His shirt was off and a trickle of sweat made its way down the ridges of his bony rib cage. Scars, both old and a fresher pink, crisscrossed his skinny frame.

Some were old and gnarled, but some had the pinker hue of fresh abuse. Cole ignored the question and slapped some change into the guy's palm, signaling for him to get moving. The motie fired up the engine but kept his eyes trained on Cole, scanning him from head to toe.

"You good, man?" Cole felt sorry for the motie, who'd obviously been through some harsh stuff in his day, but he also didn't like the way the guy was looking at him—like he wanted something more. The motie merely cackled and gunned it toward shore. Cole reached into his pocket as they went, extracting the tiny camera Parson had given him. This was his chance to get rid of it for good, to make sure there was never any proof of his near-betrayal. Cole clutched the camera in his palm, bringing it to the side of the vessel. He let his fingertips trail over the water. And then he let go. Cole didn't realize he'd been holding his breath until he'd released the camera from his grasp, felt it drift away from him under the water. He had to do it; he cared too much about her to risk destroying her. And if she found out, she'd be devastated. There would be no going back. When they touched down on Gen territory three minutes later, he found himself gasping for air.

The air was cold but it smelled complex—different from the air in Columbus—in a good way, Cole thought. He could smell the algae from the water and light traces of the wildflowers that grew along its bank. A musky odor rose from the dirt as his feet sank into the damp soil that lined the shore. The air in Columbus smelled empty; that was it. Maybe that's why Davis's skin had been so intoxicating. Against the nothingness of the city air, she'd been tangy and forbidden. The memory of her skin and what it had felt like under his lips—her neck rising in goose bumps under his tongue—made him shiver. Whatever the risks, he wanted more.

But for now, he had to get home. Cole took a direct path rather than circling through the outskirts of the Slants as he usually did. As he neared the center of town, he heard voices rising and falling. It was strange for the late hour, even for a weekend. But sometimes his friends liked to gather near the well to drink and hang out, and every now and then an impromptu party broke out. Cole quickened his pace, wondering if any of his friends were around. He could use the distraction. Anything to keep his mind off Davis, really. After the night he'd had, a couple of beers might be in order.

As he neared the well, though, he could tell something wasn't right. Someone brushed past him at a jog, knocking his shoulder from behind—Cole turned to see Griff, the guy who owned the Drowned Rat, a dive bar in the most decrepit section of the Slants, hurrying past.

"Watch it," Cole muttered in Griff's general direction. But Griff didn't even turn, and the voices ahead were rising in volume by the minute. Cole knew he wasn't imagining angry tones. A couple of crashing sounds drifted back—shattering glass?—and Cole broke into a jog behind Griff. What had happened in his absence? Griff wouldn't have left the bar unless something serious was going on. Cole felt a shiver of dread work its way through his body, followed almost instantly by a wave of exhaustion. All he wanted to do was go home and sleep. But he had to know.

He burst past the row of trailers that bordered the old downtown to find the field in a state of absolute chaos. Worsley was heading up what looked like a demonstration, standing on the edge of the covered well. He was already so tall at over six feet that the ledge made him look larger than life. There was Jason, looking freaked out, his face mottled as he yelled something in Worsley's direction. Michelle was sitting on an overturned garbage bin, straining to see over the crowds. Her face was tight and she was biting her lower lip like she always did when she was nervous. Cole couldn't make out what Worsley was saying. He edged closer, following the path Griff was clearing as he shoved through. A bunch of Prior patrolmen fought their way toward the center of the crowd from the opposite side; Cole's nerves shot to high alert.

Hamilton and his buddies were on the opposite side of the masses. Hamilton was talking heatedly to Leroy Beauchamp, his lanky form dwarfed by an oversized cotton shirt. He looked almost excited, not scared, his brown eyes lit from within—the opposite of the other 90 percent of the crowd, from what Cole could see. There were probably sixty or eighty people shoved into the small space among the trailers. Others were camped out on the flimsy front stoops that marked their properties. One guy was banging his window with his fist from inside his trailer. The ground was littered with garbage where Dumpsters had been overturned, and Cole had to step carefully around a pile of broken glass as he shouldered his way closer to Worsley and the well, which was apparently serving as a makeshift stage. A guy knocked into him hard from behind, and Cole swore as he struggled to regain his footing.

The general din of what appeared to be the makings of a riot began to distinguish itself in words and phrases. Worsley's face was taut, his sinewy muscles tense and rippling; and Cole could see the sweat trickling down his forehead as he struggled to maintain order over a bunch of men who were twice his age. At twenty-three, Worsley was still basically a kid himself in these guys' eyes, despite his education.

"Please, everyone, calm down," he shouted. "You're not in danger. Gens are not going to be affected by the disease. This is a Prior disease. It is a Prior genetic condition." He repeated the phrase two or three times but it seemed to have an adverse effect. By the last time, the voices had risen to a roar and his words were entirely drowned out. Cole strained to hear and pushed in front of a guy in a gray sweater—an athlete he recognized from the Swings—in an attempt to get closer to Hamilton. Hamilton was still a good fifteen feet away, but Cole caught his eye and gestured him forward. The sound of more glass breaking echoed from a trailer on the border of the crowd, and Cole saw a gaping hole with a few daggerlike shards where a window had been. A child wandered in front of the trailer, crying. He raised his muddy, tear-streaked face, and Cole could see that it was Dustin, his little buddy from the Swings. Cole rarely saw the kid other than when his face was pressed up against the chain-link fence that surrounding the makeshift gymnasium, watching in awe—a future FEUDS champion in the making. Cole hadn't even known he lived around here.

Cole began to move toward Dustin when he felt a hand at his elbow.

"It's insane, right?" shouted Hamilton over the din, the tendons in his neck straining from the effort to be heard.

"That's one word for it," Cole shouted back. "What's going on?"

"The disease," Hamilton said. "Eight more bodies were found outside the city limits. All the same signs. Cracked skin, blood, the whole thing. It's out of control, Cole. People want to know what the hell's going on."

"Can't Worsley do something?" Cole's pulse accelerated at the thought of Davis. Was she okay? Were her friends okay? Not knowing was torture. He had to find out. Cole squinted toward the well, but Worsley was no longer there. In his place were two or three guys Cole's age—guys he didn't recognize—their faces contorted in expressions of fury. "This is looking pretty bad," he said. "This is really fucked up. It's got the makings of a riot."

"It *is* a riot," Hamilton told him before shoving back toward his friends and disappearing into the crowd.

Cole watched as a handful of armed Prior patrolmen struggled to keep order against the teeming masses. From the look of it, they didn't stand a chance against the railing community. One of the patrolmen lashed out, punching a guy square in the jaw. A couple of the guy's friends swung back; Cole eased toward the interior circle of the crowd, trying to locate Worsley.

"It's contagious!" he heard a voice shout from somewhere in the crowd. "You just have to touch one of them!"

"I got her blood on me!" another voice rang out.

"The blood's tainted," came a cry from Cole's left. "It'll get in our water supply if we bury them!"

"Please, everyone, just calm down. You're not in any danger!" That came from Worsley, whom Cole had finally spotted—his dark head bobbing over the rest—near the west side of the well. By then no one was paying attention, though. A few people were clustered around the guy who claimed he'd touched a corpse and was feeling symptoms already. The patrolmen were struggling to maintain order all around, but more people were flooding in from the outer radius of the Slants, and at least two fistfights had broken out in front of a blue-sided trailer near the alley that led to Cole's house. Several women were crying and Dustin was still wandering wide-eyed and terrified underfoot. He was likely to be crushed if Cole didn't help him.

Cole fought his way to the child and picked him up, throwing him over his shoulder and walking him toward a relatively calm area shielded by the frames of two houses. A sharp thud sounded by his foot, and a metal object nicked the side of his shoe so hard Cole almost fell over. He looked down and saw the unmistakable label of a gas canister.

"Crap," he muttered, setting Dustin down. He looked into the child's eyes and spoke calmly and slowly. "I need you to run in that direction," he told the boy, whose eyes were shiny with tears. "Run down by the river and don't come back until the yelling stops, okay?" The kid nodded but didn't move. "And if you get nervous," Cole said, "just feint left and throw a couple of those sick punches I showed you." He forced himself to crack a smile and ruffle Dustin's hair, and Dustin gave him a half-grin in response. "It's just like a game," Cole said. "You gotta be the faster, smarter one. Now go," Cole said, giving him a nudge. Then he heard a yell from the crowd and turned; the yell had sounded like Hamilton.

"Burn them!" Someone shouted from the crowd. "Burn the bodies!"

"Burn the bodies!" some other voices shouted, until they were all chanting it and Cole could no longer distinguish one voice from the next. Heart thudding, he made his way back toward the nucleus of the mob.

But it was Tom Worsley, not Hamilton, whom he glimpsed on the ground a few feet in. Tom was groaning in pain and clutching his side. His dark, floppy hair was slick with sweat. It draped over his forehead, covering his glasses, but he made no attempt to move it. A line of dirt streaked over his right arm, and beneath it, Cole could see that the skin was rubbed raw. Cole watched helplessly from a few feet away, bound by the crowds, as an older man stepped into Worsley's thigh. Tom seemed unable to stand, and from the glimpses Cole caught, his face was contorted in an expression of agony. Cole had never seen Worsley, a fighter himself, betray such weakness. He could die if someone didn't help him. Cole fought his way forward, nerves and fear propelling him along.

Then he heard the shriek.

It was long and high and unmistakably feminine.

This time, there was no questioning whom the voice belonged to. Cole turned toward its source and found himself staring directly into Davis's eyes through the crowd. Panic shot through him with the force of jet fuel. He blinked, questioning whether she was an illusion, a product of his own insanity. But her long, chestnut waves and wide green eyes were unmistakable, even ten yards away. They were focused directly on the pile of Prior bodies that were mounting atop the back of an old truck. The smell of rot filled the air. Cole watched Davis's reaction as several Gens shook gasoline from a canister over the bodies. Then someone lit a match.

The blaze was furious. The smell worsened.

Davis's face changed from terrified to pale to sick. She coughed in hard, hacking gasps; she was so rarely exposed to unfiltered air. A few people turned to stare. Cole saw them take in her face with its porcelain skin, invisible pores, and even features. Her long, lithe legs with their perfect muscle definition. Her silky hair, looking glamorous even disheveled. She looked back at them, and he could only imagine what she saw: pockmarked skin from years of untreated acne, disproportionate bodies, thinning hair, and large noses. To her, in a big group like that—and in that context—they probably looked like monsters.

She'd followed him there. She must have. Cole forgot about Worsley and ran to her, but before he could reach her, she screamed again. This time, others noticed.

*Morrow.* The whispers surrounded him like a bad dream. Some Gens about his age lunged at her.

"It's Morrow's kid," shouted a middle-aged man with a firm, round stomach and a chest full of hair. "Robert Morrow sent his kid out to check on the *Imps.*" He sneered. "You like what you see, sweetheart?" He moved toward Davis. Cole was only a few feet away now.

"How about we send a body back to Columbus, see how they like it?" jeered his friend.

Cole felt a blast of panic quicken his heart. She'd followed him. He had to get her out of here *now*. If something happened to her, it would be his fault. The Gens were worked up, thirsty for blood. They'd want to do something symbolic and huge to hurt the Priors, and this was their chance. His heart sped up, and every protective instinct in his body began to fire. Cole fought to push closer to Davis, every muscle in his body tensed in anticipation of one goal: protecting her. If anything happened to her, he knew in that instant, he'd never forgive himself. He'd never survive it.

Cole watched as the two men rounded on her, and he knew what he had to do.

Cole landed a punch to the left side of the leering man's head just as the man reached out to touch Davis. The other guy turned on him, but Cole was on top of him before the guy had time to move. Davis's face was barely registering recognition when Cole screamed at her.

"Run!" he shouted, even as two more Gens hurled themselves in his direction. He could hold them back only for another few seconds. She stared for a long second into his eyes, her own green orbs projecting the shock and horror she surely felt. And then she ran, graceful like a deer but strong and limber like something much more powerful, a panther, maybe. Cole caught his breath as she neared some debris, freshly broken from a nearby building; her eyes were trained straight ahead and he wasn't sure she'd seen it. But she cleared the splintered wooden beams easily, jumping higher and longer than any Gen ever could.

*Morrow*, they'd said. The significance of the name hit him only then, as he watched her back recede. And all of a sudden it was clear. Parson wanted to ruin her father. He wanted to tear apart her family and destroy her father's reputation at the expense of her own. And he wanted to use Cole to do it. It was all for the election.

Cole had been so stupid not to see it sooner. Now Davis was in real danger, and everything was falling apart. All he'd wanted was to do the right thing, to help the people he loved. Instead, he'd screwed everything up, and potentially hurt this girl, this person he'd begun to cherish. But Davis Morrow wasn't just the daughter of Parson's enemy. She was the daughter of *the* enemy. Robert Morrow was responsible for everything the Gens stood against.

In a sense, *Davis* was the enemy. But he'd fallen for her like a fool, and now she was in danger because of him. He would do anything—even if it meant sacrificing his own life—to protect her.

# ⊰ I I ⊱

## DAVIS

He was one of *them*. Davis clutched her pillow to her chest, folding her body around it like she used to when she as a child. She thought what had happened would haunt her forever. She squeezed her eyes shut, hoping to quiet her brain. Hoping the familiarity of her room would restore some sense of safety. But the images she'd seen were seared inside of her head with such clarity that she might as well have been staring at a projection screen. She couldn't shut out the blank eyes and gaping mouths and melting skin. Davis's stomach clenched again and again, and she struggled to think of something else, anything. But the only image that came to mind in the brief seconds where she could force the bodies to disappear was Cole's face when he realized what she knew.

Everything she thought he was—wanted to believe he was— had turned out to be an elaborately crafted persona designed to . . . *to what?* Why had he wanted to manipulate her in the first place? Was she just some random girl he'd chosen, the first one he'd spotted at Emilie's party that first night? Had she just been any other challenge to him? She shuddered, sick that she'd been used so easily, despite everything Vera had cautioned her against. Even her dad, growing up, had always warned her that some guys would just want to use her—that she had to be careful. They were both right. She'd been the blind one. She couldn't shake the horrible, teeming panic in her stomach. It rose up toward her heart, threatening to spill over. She'd trusted Cole, and Cole had lied to her. A wave of dizziness washed over her, and her hands began to tremble from the panic she felt. She hadn't known heartbreak could be like this—could make her physically ill. But there she was, trembling and sweating, all because she'd fallen for the wrong person. She was so stupid. She felt so sick and stupid and unable to trust anyone ever again.

Davis curled onto her side, but she couldn't get comfortable. The mirror lining her closet wall showed her everything; her eyes were streaked black from sweat, dirt, and mascara. Unfamiliar bulges puffed out just between her lower eyelids and cheekbones. She didn't look like herself at all; no one would believe she was Robert Morrow's daughter. Her face looked wan and her skin tone was yellowish. She looked identical to how Emilie had looked at the PAs.

Davis ran to her adjoining bathroom—or maybe stumbled; she suddenly felt weak, like nothing more than a puppet—and splashed some water on her face. She grabbed her toothbrush and scrubbed hard at her teeth, but her hand trembled as she did, and she lost her grip. The brush flew across the sink and onto the floor. She left it there, feeling cold panic work its way from her feet to her hands. Her hands. She looked down at them—their light trembling had worsened to something that looked like full-blown tremors. In the mirror, her image was flickering, almost like her vision was cutting in and out at a rapid pace. Davis's heart pounded wildly.

She closed her eyes and breathed in and out for five beats, trying hard not to lose control. A little of her strength seemed to be returning—she felt a fraction steadier and clearer-headed. It must have been the anxiety after all, or the shock of the whole night: Cole and his betrayal, then her mad dash to get home before she was discovered. Finally she allowed herself to open her eyes and assess her complexion in the mirror.

Her bright green irises contrasted against stark whites. Her eyes were nestled against creamy, almost porcelain skin and lips that boasted a natural rosy hue. Perfect. She was perfect, as always.

She returned to bed and squeezed her eyes shut, but the images wouldn't disappear: the bodies, twisted and burning; Prior skin melting as the corpses caught fire. The Imps and the fury and fear in their eyes. Cole's eyes when he looked at her and realized she knew the truth. When she'd taken a motie the first time, she'd assumed it was okay, because she'd watched Cole hop into one. Now she knew better, and a wave of embarrassment overcame her. Davis held back a sob but allowed tears to stream down and dampen the pillowcase beneath her.

Everything made sense to her now: why he'd never been roofing before, why he fell in the first place. Why he acted so goofy and awkward about his DirecTalk. She was an idiot not to have seen through his lies sooner. The pain of it overwhelmed her, and she gasped deeply to avoid throwing up for a second time. He was the only person she'd ever wanted to be with . . . the only person she'd ever craved and felt herself slipping toward unstoppably. She'd wanted it. She'd wanted to give herself to him fully. She *still* wanted it: to feel his body next to hers, to trace the contour of his jaw and place her lips on his familiar collarbone and lean her head against his chest as he wrapped his arms around her back in a promise to protect her. She knew it was impossible, but deep inside her there existed a mad, desperate hope that this was all some kind of mistake.

Davis used the remote control at her bedside to flip on her wall unit. Its screen lit up with images that seemed too bright, too colorful to be real. She switched the channels through all the major news stations, searching for a breaking news report detailing what she'd seen. But there was nothing. There was coverage of the recent development plans in the lot that used to house a community playground. There was a quick segment on the campaign. She flipped more rapidly, passing through images of a new department store and a state-of-the-art irrigation system. No bodies. No horror. Just smiles, eerie in their bright frankness. It was enough to make her think she'd dreamed it all up.

Davis had never felt more isolated or more terrified. It was as though her heart had picked up a new speed, running twice as fast as before, and she was almost getting accustomed to the low-level nausea that had settled in the pit of her stomach. Everywhere she looked, a thin but impenetrable barrier existed between her and the people around her. She was walking in the same world as before, but she had the sense that no one would hear her if she shouted, and she'd no longer understand any of them.

She was so, so scared. Scared of what she'd seen in the mirror, scared of what could happen to her dad if he knew what she'd done with Cole, scared of the stacks of Prior bodies back in the Slants, scared of the Imps she was now certain had killed them, and scared of the way her heart was breaking. The thoughts tangled together until their edges blurred and faded into one messy lump of bad feelings, a steady swell of sadness that finally lulled her to sleep.

She woke to her intercom crackling to life. Fia's voice sang through it, offering a welcome reprieve from her twisty nightmares. "Where are you? Are you still sleeping? Mom made gluten-free cookies and they're not that gross, come out!"

"Give me a minute! I was just reading." Davis hoped her voice sounded more convincing filtered through the intercom than it did to her own ears. She sighed and pulled herself into a sitting position, checking her DirecTalk for missed calls. Four messages from Vera about some party at the House of Mirrors later on—but nothing from Cole. Not that that should surprise her. She didn't know how he'd had access to a DirecTalk in the first place. She shook her head, angry with herself for thinking about him and—worse—for caring. He was an Imp. He'd probably stolen it. He didn't care about the rules, or her for that matter.

Davis wanted to crawl back under her covers and sleep forever. She wanted to skip right past this unbearable thing her life had become and move forward to some future, better time. The fact that she was even having these thoughts at all freaked her out a little. It was all within her control; it had to be. She'd been perfect before, and she could have it all back if she worked hard enough and focused and wiped her mind clean of the past week. It was all Cole. The kiss on the roof had been . . . it had been ecstasy.

And that simple fact made her stomach twist in horror. His body pressing against her, feeling like its rough edges and soft spots were produced specifically for hers—all of that, it was an illusion. A sick, twisted lie. His skin against hers, the way his hands cradled her face so carefully. The way he'd whispered that he'd take care of her—she'd believed it all. She'd fallen for it, and she'd fallen for him, and now she had to face it: he had betrayed her, played her, used her.

A single clear thought found its way into her head, giving her something to focus on beyond the pain in her limbs: she had to turn Cole in. She didn't have a choice. She was jeopardizing everything—her reputation, her father's campaign—if she didn't. Because if she didn't and someone found out, she'd seem complicit. Her life would be over.

Davis showered quickly, indulging for only the briefest minute in the soothing feeling of the water pelting down on her aching shoulders. She threw on a pair of jeans and a button-down, feeling energized from her resolve. She sprayed her face with the barest mist of tinted sunscreen and swiped on a thin coating of lipstick. Her hand trembled a little, but that was just from her exhaustion; it had to be. She switched on her vitals monitor then—she tried to remember to get a read at least once per week, but it had been a while. She centered her body in front of the tablet, so the device could get an accurate reading. Maybe she wasn't eating enough. The machine would tell her which nutrient supplements to load up on. The machine emanated a shifting red beam that scanned twice over the length of her body. Then the red light disappeared and a soft thrumming sound indicated that her report was about to be generated.

Just then, the intercom blared to life from the bedroom. Davis heard the squeal of Fia's tinny, little-girl voice blaring out of it; she hit *cancel* on the report and moved quickly into the bedroom to see what her sister wanted.

"They're, like, almost gone," Fia was saying. "Davissss. Daaaaaavis. Hurry up!" Davis rolled her eyes but couldn't help smiling a little; Fia was so bubbly and full of life. No matter what else was going on, she never failed to make Davis feel a little lighter.

"Hold one hostage for me," she said into the device. "I'll be right there." Davis smoothed her shirt with her hands and took a few steadying breaths. Seeing Fia and her father would calm her. It would make her feel more like herself. Confessing would relieve the enormous burden she was carrying, wrap her back in the safety of their protective net. She would do it.

She glanced at the vitals monitor, wondering if she should generate a new report. She hesitated, about to step back on—but pulled back. Davis dashed out of her bedroom, heading toward the sound of voices coming from the living room. She was almost to the threshold when Frank materialized, blocking the only entrance to the room with his hulking frame.

"I don't have time, Frank," she hissed under her breath. "I need to talk to my dad."

"Your dad's busy," Frank told her. "He's in a meeting."

"He's always in a meeting," Davis snapped. "He can take two minutes to talk to me." She shoved into Frank, harder than she meant to, and he moved out of her way, looking surprised. Davis stepped into the living room. There was her dad with a camera crew and . . . was that Wes Hollinder of the *Hollinder Hour*? It was. Davis felt her heart sink; the *Hollinder Hour* was one of the most watched programs in all of New Atlantic. Apparently she was interrupting something big, after all.

"Dad?" Davis said, taking in the scene. Her face flushed as three sets of eyes—the cameraman's, her father's, and Wes Hollinder's—

turned to meet her own. Her dad stopped in midsentence and the cameraman yelled, "Cut." Then her father moved toward her, and a look of concern passed over his features.

"Davis, sweetheart," he started. "Is everything okay? Didn't Frank tell you we were in here?"

"He did," Davis said, her heart hammering. "I'm sorry. We can talk later." She backed out of the room and hurried into the hall, shaking.

"Davis, wait," her father called after her. "Just a second," she heard him tell the other two men. "This won't take long." He met her in the hallway, his brow furrowed. "Honey," he said. "What is it? You look upset." Davis stopped, surprised that he'd hit pause on what was apparently a huge interview to listen to what she had to say.

"You'd talk now?" she asked. "In the middle of an interview?"

"Of course," her dad replied. "If it's important. You must know by now that you're my first priority." Davis's heart swelled and she struggled to blink back tears. Her dad truly loved her; that much was clear, despite the campaign and everything else going on. He loved her, and she knew in that instant that she couldn't bear to let him down. There was no way she could tell him about Cole and devastate a career he'd been building as long as she could remember. She saw that now. He tried, he really did. It couldn't have been easy. She had to support him—she couldn't ruin his life. She wouldn't come clean. Instead, she'd pretend Cole had never existed. She'd return to her normal life, to being the perfect daughter she'd always been before. She had no choice.

"Mr. Morrow?" The cameraman poked his head out from the living room. "I'm sorry to interrupt you, sir, but I wanted to remind you that we're on a tight schedule. Mr. Hollinder is putting in an appearance at a charity event in just over an hour."

"Just give me a minute," her father told the cameraman. "I'm with my daughter." The cameraman nodded, looking uncertain, and retreated back to the living room.

"Davis, you're shaking." Her dad put his arms around her, trying to draw her close. She shrugged him off.

"No," she said, backing away. "I'm totally fine, Dad." She pasted a smile on her face, hoping it looked natural. "I'm so sorry to interrupt you. Really. I was just a little stressed about dance," she said, fumbling for an excuse, "but I never would have gone in there if I'd known you were in the middle of an interview. Frank just said it was a meeting. I should have known better—I'm sorry."

He held her eyes with his own, his brow furrowed. She maintained her smile, waiting for him to continue. He ran a palm over his jawline, which was freshly shaven for the interview. "I checked in on you around noon and you were asleep," her dad said. "I know how much strain you've been under with the Olympiads coming up. I was happy to see you get some rest, noodle."

"Noodle? Seriously Dad, you haven't called me that in forever." She frowned at him, pretending to be annoyed, though the use of her old nickname almost made her cry, it was so sweet. "And I did get some rest," she assured him. "I'm fine now, I swear. You should get back in there." For some reason, though, her dad wasn't leaving. It made her feel even guiltier to know that he would take time out of this important interview to talk to her, even though she really didn't have anything to talk about—at least as far as he was concerned.

Her father sighed and rubbed his temples, and the gesture made him look somehow older. For the first time, Davis noticed a few gray streaks in his sideburns, and she wondered when they had appeared. He'd never looked anything but distinguished and handsome to her; she so rarely saw him with his guard down. "The thing is, honey," he continued, "you're always in the spotlight. Everyone's following your Olympiads progress. I know how hard it's been for you. And I want you to know that you make me incredibly proud. I couldn't be prouder. You've already helped me so much during this election. It hasn't been easy on you—or Terri, or your sister. I'm aware of that. And I'm so grateful to you for being the way you are."

So much of her had wanted to tell him the truth only moments before. She had badly wanted to be relieved of the burden, to have someone else handle it for her. But she knew she never could. Even the knowledge that she'd done something that could potentially hurt her father threatened to rip her apart. Even if he never found out—and he couldn't—she'd always know. She'd always carry that burden. The only way out of this was to return to as normal a life as possible, as quickly as possible.

"Come here," her dad said, pulling her into a bear hug. "What is it, Davis? Is it really just practice that's bothering you?"

She shook her head quickly, pulling away. "I'm fine. Really. Really, Dad. Just get back to the interview. Time is money, right?" She smiled again. "I'm late for meeting Vera, anyway. That's where I was headed before—I was on my way out." The second she said it, she was glad she had. Seeing Vera—hearing her gossip and helping her weave elaborate braids through Davis's dark hair and brainstorming Vera prospects for the orchestra—all those normal things they always did together were the quickest way to feel normal again, she was sure of it. It was what she needed more than anything just then, she realized. Even thinking about it lifted her, just a little.

"I'll see you later on, okay?" she persisted.

"Okay," he told her. "Don't stay out too late."

"I won't."

Her dad moved back in the direction of the living room, then paused, one hand resting on the doorframe. "Davis?" he called after her.

"Yeah?"

"I meant what I said about being proud of you before. I couldn't wish for a better daughter." The pang that crept up her chest was almost as crushing as the one she'd felt at Cole's betrayal.

It was only when she was well outside, halfway to Vera's, that she remembered Fia and the cookies. She massaged her temples, suddenly feeling even more stressed. It had been so long since she'd spent time with her little sister. She'd make it up to Fia later. Later, always later. But she would, she swore it. She pulled up her tablet keypad and typed out a quick message to her sister.

"Sorry, Fi-Fi," she wrote, adding in a wink face to show she was teasing—Fia hated that particular derivation of her nickname— "Didn't mean to skip out on cookies. Let's do something just you and me this wknd? Froyo and park? Love you. xo." She hoped mentioning the park would show Fia she really was sorry . . . that she meant it. Froyo at the park downtown had been their tradition when Fia was really little. Davis wasn't sure when it had stopped, but she made a firm resolution to bring it back. Davis made the promise and put it out of her mind, eager to get as far from home as she could.

Five hours and countless wardrobe options later, she and Vera were on their way to the House of Mirrors. Davis's pulse was in her ears; she was high on the adrenaline of anticipation, glad to be out with her friend. *This* was what she needed to distract her from the turbulence that had marred the rest of her life lately.

"I'm so glad you suggested this," she remarked as they climbed aboard the monorail, sliding easily through security and past its chrome doors. Prior volunteers had replaced the Imp workers on strike, so the monorails were running again.

"Duh," Vera replied easily. "Don't you remember talking about it last week? I also left you like four messages about it. Here, try these ones. The brown doesn't stand out enough against your hair." Vera removed a dangly earring from her own ear and pressed it into Davis's hand as the monorail whizzed past the East Sector toward the House of Mirrors. "You're sure you still want to go?" Vera's eyes were bright with concern. She would never pry, always wait until Davis was ready; it was the way she'd always been.

Davis offered her what she hoped was a reassuring smile, nodding. She rested her head on her best friend's shoulder, trying not to look out the window or think of what stretched beyond. What she'd seen earlier had started to feel like a distant memory, and she wanted it to stay that way. Instead, she focused on the earring: the feeling of its sharp prong in her palm, the flash of sparkle from the rhinestones. Normal images. Images that would repeat themselves in the form of dancing and music and everything she knew and loved, all through the rest of the night, until what she'd seen before faded entirely.

The club was in a totally sketchy industrial district in a gutted-out factory that had, in old-time Columbus, supposedly been used to manufacture steel. But Davis loved it. It was safely nestled far away from the Slants, and it bordered the river where there were no neighborhoods, just wilderness. Typically that kind of wild inspired fear in her, but for some reason this patch of the city was beautiful—at least from where she sat in her sanitized, Prior-designated monorail car. Its fields stretched for what seemed like eternity, and at this hour of the night, the stars twinkled patterns that weren't too dissimilar from Vera's gold silk top. Davis absently took the earrings from her friend and swapped them out with the gold and tiger's-eye pair she'd been wearing. Her whole outfit—the sequined minidress and razor-sharp, strappy stilettos—screamed "Vera," with its obvious glamour. It was a far cry from the understated, sleek looks Davis usually favored. That was because she'd run out of her apartment totally underdressed and unprepared for the House of Mirrors. Anyway, it was nice to wear something un-Davis for a change. Maybe it could help her leave all the other parts of her life behind, at least for the night. For Vera's part, it was hard not to notice how petite she was in her own black patent pumps, tiny leather shorts, and gold halter. She made up for her diminutive size with bold apparel.

"No one's going to care what's in your ears," Oscar said in a bored tone from where he sat next to Vera. He cocked his chin, revealing lazy blue eyes from under the shock of blond hair that was perpetually crossing his forehead. "We care what's here," he said, brushing one hand against the side of Vera's chest, ". . . and here." He finished by moving it down to her butt. Vera swatted his hand away and rolled her eyes.

"Don't be crude," she told him, looking annoyed. "Sorry," she mouthed at Davis.

Davis smile gratefully . . . Oscar could be tough to be around, and tonight she wasn't in the mood. Vera seemed to understand that intuitively. Davis blinked back the emotion welling within her. Thank God Vera was around; the Olympiads and PAs might have distracted them, taking the focus away from their friendship for a while . . . but that was the beauty of a friend like Vera. When someone's known you your whole life, the bond was strong enough to withstand just about anything.

Oscar pawed at Vera next to her, and for a second, Davis's thoughts flashed to Cole's face, and his hands. The way he'd touched her had never seemed anything but caring. Sexy, yes. But in a very good way, a way that made her feel like he'd only ever touch *her* like that.

Then again, Cole was a lie. Vera and Oscar were not.

Vera squinted out into the night as the monorail pulled into the platform. "Why are so many people walking back this way?" she wondered aloud. "It's super early still."

"Maybe the band sucks," Oscar offered.

Vera giggled and punched Oscar in the arm.

"Doubtful." Vera linked arms with Davis and pulled her in the direction of the club. "Don't worry," she whispered, so only Davis could hear her. "Tonight will cheer you up."

Davis forced a smile and gripped her friend's arm tighter. She missed Vera. She missed the closeness they used to have, the way they used to stay up all night talking. She missed the million times as kids they'd snuck snacks from the pantry at Vera's house in the middle of the night, and played MASH until the early hours of the morning, giggling, legs intertwined at the ankle. And the times later, as they started to grow up: sneaking into movies without paying by flirting their way past the ticket guy; then later, Davis sitting in the front row of Vera's cello competitions, biting her nails to the quick as Vera made it into the final rounds—and crying actual tears of joy when her friend won first place, moving into the top echelon of young cellists in the Columbus orchestra. She needed this night with her friend. She needed her old life back.

The closer they got to the club, the more obvious it was that something was up. Throngs of kids their age were exiting instead of entering, and doormen were standing in front of the sliding doors, which were usually drawn apart by now for the opening acts. Oscar grabbed one of the kids' arms, stopping him as he walked past.

"Hey man, what's the deal?" he asked.

"Show's off," the kid said, shaking his head. "Hope you didn't buy your ticket in advance, dude. They're not doing refunds."

"Off? Why?" Vera's brow was furrowed, her pretty hair highlighting her look of confusion. "It's been set for months."

"One of the drummers never showed up," the kid said with a shrug. "They had to cancel the whole thing."

"Oh no," Vera said. "What are we supposed to do now? We're way out of the city."

"I know a place," Oscar told them. "It's just one stop back toward the city on the monorail. It's a divey kind of place. I've been there with the guys. Our IDs should work just fine."

"Great!" Vera clapped her hands, grinning at Davis. "You on board?"

"Sure." Davis tried to match her enthusiasm, but she sounded a little down in the dumps even to her.

"Cheer up," Oscar said, slinging one arm around her shoulders and the other around Vera. "I don't know what's up your ass, but I'm a happy guy tonight. Cheap booze, two hot girls . . ."

"Shut up, dirtbag," Vera told him, swatting his shoulder, but she was laughing as she said it, and even Davis felt a small swell of affection toward Oscar. He'd been a part of her life for years . . . almost as much as Vera had. They'd known him forever, even before he and Vera had started dating. He was a constant in her life, and although he could be super annoying, Davis liked how loyal he was to Vera. She liked the consistency of the three of them together.

They followed the throngs back on the monorail and stepped off a few minutes later in front of a low-lying, shabby-chic "shack"-style bar of the variety that had become popular in the outskirts of town. It was designed to look run-down when in reality, its sound system was state of the art. Davis saw as much right away, after flashing her fake ID at a bouncer, who barely glanced at it before waving her inside.

Oscar slid over to the Community DJ, lining up a few songs on the queue. Vera and Davis lip-synced to Lady Fire; then Vera grabbed Davis's hands, spinning her up from the bench where she'd been sitting and pulling her into the center of the room.

"Remember when we used to do this all the time?" she asked, smiling brightly, her dark hair whirling around her petite frame as she spun.

"God. We were such exhibitionists. Remember the dance parties on my roof?" Davis laughed at the memory, at their attempts at choreographing dance routines for their parents, forcing any adult in the vicinity to listen to their karaoke. She pulled her friend into a big hug, still swaying to the music. "I love you so much," she said into Vera's hair.

"Love you, too, D," Vera said back. "See? Told you tonight would be fun." It was. It was amazing to laugh and dance and be with the people she'd known forever. Still, something was nagging at her. Something she couldn't quite place.

"All right, all right, cut the love fest," Oscar said, returning from the Community DJ with three beers in hand. "Or let me join in. Your choice."

"Gotta go," Vera mouthed to them, motioning vaguely behind her. "I'm going to grab another drink. You kids behave yourselves."

"Cheers," Oscar said, clinking Davis's bottle with his. She took a long sip, pulling herself up on a bar stool next to his.

"It's a good place," she said, indicating the space around them. "Nice find."

"Right?" he agreed. "Like I said, I came here with the boys once. Usually there's a pool table over there." He indicated a corner of the room. "Not sure where it went."

Davis nodded, and they lapsed into silence. Sometimes when Vera wasn't there, it was a little awkward with Oscar. Hard to make conversation. She wondered what he and Vera talked about all the time.

"Hey, Oscar?" Davis remembered what had been bothering her. "Do you think it's weird that the drummer backed out? That he disappeared and all?"

Oscar snorted. "Way to be dramatic. He didn't *disappear*. He just didn't show. God."

"It's just . . . it was such a hyped concert. It's been in the works for months. It's really weird."

Oscar shook his head. "What, is that guy rubbing off on you or something?"

Davis tensed. "What guy? Cole?"

"Yeah. Ver said he was trying to get to you, was saying something bogus about a disease killing off Priors. She obviously wasn't going to tell you, because it's crazy. Just don't tell me you're buying into it, too."

"Wait, what? Cole was trying to get in touch with me?" Davis's face heated. She straightened, turning toward Oscar. "What else did he say?"

"I don't know, man," Oscar told her. "I'm over it. Way too much drama."

"Oscar, you have to tell me." Davis's hand was so tight around her bottle, she was afraid she might break it. Oscar raised his eyebrows.

"Vera's right," he said. "That guy's no good. But you really want to know what a nut job he is? He apparently called Vera, said Priors are dying, and that this disease is a result of our genetic enhancements or something. He wanted to meet you at Dempsey Street. Tonight. Like I said, totally crazy."

"He wanted to meet me," Davis repeated. "Did he say why?"

"Vera didn't say. You're not going, though." He raised his eyebrows, looking closely at Davis. She avoided his gaze. Her heart was thudding. Her mind was consumed by visions of Emilie, and Caitlyn, and now this band member who hadn't shown up. Could Cole be right? He might have lied to her . . . but he wouldn't lie to her about this. She was sure of it. Especially if he was trying to get in touch, to warn her. No one else was talking about the other people who disappeared. Only Cole. And if he'd tried to reach out to her . . . maybe he cared.

"Shit. Davis. Tell me you're not really going."

Davis was already standing up, gathering her coat. "Did he say what time?" she asked Oscar, who ran a hand through his hair, looking disgusted.

"No. What am I supposed to tell Vera?"

"Tell her I'll catch up with her later," Davis said, and quickly fled before Vera could return and stop her.

Once outside the bar, Davis walked a few blocks north and turned down an alleyway to make sure, if Vera came after her, that she wouldn't be able to find her right away. She whipped out her DirecTalk and activated the navigation device.

*Dempsey Street.*

A map of the territory projected in front of her, and she keyed in her location. It targeted her with a flashing red orb and highlighted the streets in the nearby vicinity. It would be a ten-minute walk to the next monorail stop, located just past Dempsey Street on Ballard. Her pulse was in her throat, and she quickened her steps, feeling the urgency of getting to Dempsey Street as soon as possible. What if she showed up and Cole was no longer there? She checked her DirecTalk for the time: it was 11:54. It was so late. Who knew how long he'd be there, waiting for her? She needed to see him; every second counted. Cole was the only one with answers. The only one willing to talk about what was happening around them. Everyone else was blind. His eyes were open, and he cared. Most of all, he was brave enough to search for the truth. And they needed the truth, especially if more Priors were getting sick, going missing. Time was running out.

Thankfully, the streets were mostly empty except for a few stragglers from the concert, and they were well lit. The buildings themselves, though, were decrepit monsters: they gaped at her through broken windows, and she couldn't help shuddering. Davis stayed along the sidewalk bordering the monorail tracks. Despite the creepy atmosphere, she was already feeling stronger—every step that took her closer to answers seemed to breathe vitality back into her limbs.

A minute later, a graffitied sign for Dempsey Street appeared— she was lucky to be able to read it through the scrawls that criss-crossed its surface. The street was darker than Ballard, which was broader and seemed like the "main street" from way back when, but she proceeded down it anyway. Another ten yards and she could make out the forms of a bunch of people crowded in front of what looked like an old playhouse or maybe a movie theater. Despite herself, she was interested. She'd always thought old entertainment centers sounded kind of romantic—watching films on a big screen in a room full of strangers instead of the three-dimensional optic technology most homes were equipped with now. She heard the bellowing of cheers and saw the people outside begin to react to something inside—yelling catcalls and stomping their feet. She moved closer, her pulse quickening. Was it some kind of throwback film festival? That seemed off. Why had Cole wanted her to meet him here? She was so close to seeing him. She was furious with him. But she *had* to see him. But what was awaiting her there?

Davis tried to push back the memory of their kisses, tried with all her being not to let it affect her. *Focus.* She needed to focus on the questions she planned to ask him. On the disease. Still, she could almost feel his lips on hers. Her hair brushed against her neck and she shivered, for the briefest second remembering his fingers on her neck, her shoulders. . . .

She was nearly in front of the theater before she started to pick out faces she knew in the crowd. They were standing in a roped-off area drinking flutes of champagne and glasses of whiskey. She recognized a minor celebrity—someone from a sitcom that had been popular a few years ago—and one of the execs who'd guest-lectured for her business class. There was Edward Peterson, a friend of her dad's. She had no idea what they were looking at, but it appeared to be some sort of adults-only, restricted thing, and they were all drunk, and she was pretty sure her dad wouldn't want to hear about her being there.

She reached for the hood of the silk jacket she'd swiped from Vera and tugged it high around her face, letting her hair down as she did, so it would shield her features. She wished desperately that she hadn't worn such an attention-getting outfit or high shoes, but there wasn't a lot she could do about it. If she kept her head down, she should be okay. She walked toward the entrance, palms moist.

"Hey, princess," came a voice from her left. "Come to bet on some hard bodies? FEUDS isn't a place for little girls, not even little girls with an Imp fetish." He let out a loud laugh, and the hair on the back of her neck rose, but Davis resisted the urge to turn. She approached the bouncer, who eyed her up and down and finally nodded.

"No free passes for women," he told her. "Thirty bucks, plus your betting slips." Davis hesitated. She opened her purse and pretended to rummage around while deciding whether she wanted to charge this to her P-card. Her dad didn't usually check to see where her purchases were made, but she suspected that if he did, this wasn't the type of venue he'd want to see on her bank statement.

"I've got the girl," the obnoxious guy from behind her said, extending his own P-card toward the bouncer. "You can thank me later, honey." The bouncer nodded and Davis moved forward without bothering to acknowledge the guy who'd paid, too worried about being recognized as Morrow's daughter.

"I wish more girls would come to this thing," she heard another man mutter. "It's a total sausage fest in here."

"Plenty of Imp girls to go around," Davis heard before allowing the crowd to carry her all the way into the main arena. She cringed, her whole body reacting. Was this really how adult men—friends of her dad's, even—talked when they were hanging out? Because it was crude. And creepy. She shivered, despite the heat radiating from the crush of bodies. Every accidental touch held a threat. What *was* this place? Everything about it was unfamiliar, threatening.

Then she was in, and she got a good look at the arena. A half-dozen floor-to-ceiling, metal cages rose up in front of her, showcasing girls in tiny skirts and tasseled bikini tops. The girls twisted and gyrated in ways Davis would never dare. Every single movement breathed sex. She'd never seen anything like their dancing, which was uninhibited and unchoreographed and wild. She wondered if her own body could move like that, but everything she'd ever learned was about precision and training and a certain studied grace. This looser, more primal swaying made her envious. But her eyes stayed trained on their cages for only a fraction of a minute, because a larger, more imposing cage that rose from the center of the room drew her attention. Beyond the cage was a sign painted in scrawling black lettering. WELCOME TO THE FEUDS, it said. And inside the cage, holding taped fists aloft—half-clothed, covered in sweat, and facing a human monster—was Cole.

# ⊰12⊱

## COLE

The buzzer rang. The cage doors were flung open. Several men grabbed Cole and hoisted him onto their shoulders. Brutus was left half-conscious on the floor of the cage, awash in his own sweat and the dregs of spectators' leftover beer. Cole watched one drunk man spit on him and dump the contents of his cup all over Brutus's chest. The FEUDS was no place for losers. A girl rushed to Brutus's side and began to wipe at his wounds, her face creased with worry and dampened by tears. Cole felt a rush of relief at this, relief he couldn't explain.

Then he spotted Davis retreating out the door, and he jumped down from the guys' shoulders, rushing after her. He had no time to celebrate. He had to see her. He hadn't even been sure whether she would actually show. She was nearly gone by the time he managed to fend off the throngs of admirers. He sprinted to the end of Dempsey and caught her arm just before she entered the monorail turnstile.

"Nice fight," she said in a bitter voice, trying to shake him off. So she had seen the whole thing. "I'd like to go home now, if you don't mind."

"Davis," he said. "Stop. Please, let me talk to you."

"You got what you wanted," she said. "I get it. You were right all along. We're monsters, too."

"Too?"

"You should have seen yourself, Cole. They were bad, the Priors. All my dad's friends. Throwing things at you, shouting, wanting blood. But you? You were just as bad. You fought out there like you *wanted* to hurt that guy. Like you enjoyed it." She was blinking back tears in a clear struggle to maintain composure. Her green eyes were so bright, they burned a hole straight into his heart. Her hair was disheveled but beautiful in its wildness. He wanted to reach out, bury his fingers in it, pull her close to him, and kiss away her tears. "I just can't believe I trusted you. Congratulations. You won your fight and you opened my eyes. Now leave me alone." She moved toward the turnstile.

"Davis, please." Cole reached for her, moving to grab her arm, but then he stumbled. For a second he thought he was going to fall. He was overwhelmed by fatigue from the fight, and his muscles were beginning to stiffen and his reflexes were slow. He managed to catch himself, but not before he noticed Davis hesitate and take a step toward him as if to help. His heart lifted at the small gesture.

"Just let me say this one thing," he continued. "I only do it for the money. For my family. I hate being out there. I hate being that person, the kind of guy who will hurt someone else just for entertainment. For me, it's something else. Please believe that. I would never do this in a million years if I didn't think it was my ticket out. If I win, my mom won't have to work. I can get her medicine for her arthritis. Maybe . . . maybe we can get away from here. Or I can get them away from here. My family can have a different life. You don't know what it's like," he finished, his eyes pleading with her, every part of him hoping she'd understand. She hesitated. She still wasn't looking at him, but she was listening. She wasn't leaving.

He wanted her to feel everything he felt pouring from his body, through his touch. "I care about you so much," he told her softly. "I'm an idiot, and I've fucked up, but I care. I can't lose you. I want to protect you. Please, please let me make it better." He moved forward, reaching out to her; she let him for a brief second, but then she moved a palm to his chest and pushed him firmly away. Her expression was blank.

"Please let me protect you," he whispered. "You don't have to like me back. You just have to let me keep you safe. I'll tell you everything I know. This disease, Narxis . . . It's killing Priors. It doesn't come from the Gens. It's killing Priors because it sprang up from all those crazy treatments you guys get in utero. It's highly contagious, but only for Priors. Something about your genetic enhancements—or at least the process of being enhanced—made you vulnerable to the virus, and now that it's manifest, it's spreading fast. The bodies, there are more every day. Priors are dumping them outside the city, in the Slants, where I live. It's happening so quickly, Davis. You need to get help. I think maybe I could help you. We still have time. My friend, Tom, he—"

"I have to go." She cut him off suddenly, her tone firm even as her body shook. She wiped the tears from her eyes and straight-ened her shoulders, taking a step backward. "I'm sorry. I need to go home now." She turned and entered the turnstile without look-ing back, and Cole felt all the energy he'd had from the fight, and from seeing her, leave his body. He didn't have a P-card or any other way of following her.

"I didn't mean for any of this to happen," he called after her. "Please don't go." Physical exhaustion hit him so hard that he felt on the verge of collapse. But Davis stopped, turning back to him. His heart lifted. He moved toward her, intent on drawing her to him. But her eyes were focused on something else—something just behind him. Cole turned.

There, several feet behind him, stood Michelle, her arms wrapped around her torso, shoulders slumped. She wore only a sequined bra and jeans, but she didn't seem cold, only wilted. Her eyes were bright and her usual confidence had disappeared. Hurt and fear radiated from her body in waves. She turned from him and ran down the dark street. She'd seen everything.

"Michelle!" he shouted. But she didn't respond, and he knew he wouldn't follow. He heard the sound of her footsteps retreating down the road in the direction of the Slants. He'd be fooling him-self to think she hadn't seen everything. Now she knew. Now one more person could potentially ruin him if she wanted. The fear he felt was muted; it blended itself with everything else he was think-ing and feeling until he couldn't separate his emotions. This thing had spiraled so far out of his control. It should have been one of the best nights of his life—every step he made toward winning FEUDS should have been—but it was turning into one of the worst.

Davis didn't say anything, but her eyes were wide, asking all the questions she couldn't voice. "You're not safe," Cole told her, grabbing her hands in his. "Go home now. Go fast. You could be caught. Michelle . . ." He glanced back in the direction Michelle had gone. "She could tell someone you're here. Go back and I'll find a way of contacting you. I promise you, I'll make this right." Davis nodded, and Cole's heart nearly broke at the sight of her eyes welling with tears. She turned, pulling her hands from his.

"Bye, Cole," she said.

"I'll find a way to fix this," he said to her.

He watched her retreating form until he could no longer see her in the dark. Watching her go, wanting with his entire being to run after her, to keep her with him always, he knew—Davis was inside of him now, deeply rooted in his heart. He'd never be without her—it was too late. He couldn't lose her; it would destroy him.

Cole walked back to the arena, not even bothering to quicken his pace. Maybe Parson Abel would still be there, maybe he wouldn't. He was done trying to get what he wanted from that guy. Whatever happened now happened, as far as he was concerned. When he reached the entrance to the old movie theater, he was beginning to feel chills, and his side hurt like hell from where Brutus had broken his rib. But Parson was waiting for him outside, his face stretched into a wide grin, his chin dimpling against it.

"Nice fight," he said, clapping Cole on the back. "Thought I'd lost you there for a minute, but you sure pulled through." Cole grunted in response, waiting for Parson to finish whatever speech he wanted to give this time. "Brutus is in pretty bad shape, but man, you've nailed that rare ability for kicking the living shit out of a guy without leaving him for dead. The crowd loves that. Makes you look like a real golden child." He paused, waiting for Cole's response. Cole stared back at him, gritting his jaw. He didn't want to say anything he'd regret, and he didn't know yet what Parson knew about him and Davis.

"Actually," Parson continued in a calmer tone, "I should con-
gratulate you on two jobs well done."

"What are you talking about?" Cole hated himself for taking
the bait. "I don't have anything for you." Cole braced himself, waiting for Parson to lash out at him. He forged ahead, squaring his
shoulders and staring Parson directly in the eye. "I didn't get your
pictures," he said, the challenge in his voice clear. "And I'm not going to. I would never betray her like that. I don't care what you do
to me. Just don't hurt Davis." Cole knew he was betraying himself
with his words—giving away the truth of his feelings for Davis—
but he didn't see any other way. Parson stared at him for a second.
Then he burst into laughter.

"I knew you couldn't be trusted not to fall for her. And I knew
you were a wild card. Which is why I took extra precautions to be
sure you didn't screw everything up."

"What are you talking about?" Cole's hands tightened into
fists. He didn't like the smirk on Parson's face. He should have
been furious; instead, he was enjoying this.

"I'm talking about this," he said, pulling a thin envelope from
his briefcase. He leaned toward Cole, his breath reeking of whiskey. "Go on, take a look." Cole accepted the envelope with hesitation, then opened it and pulled out several printed photographs.
Davis and him kissing on the fire escape. The two of them talking
inside the ambulance. His hand touching the small of her back at
Emilie's party. Them making out at Emilie's party. It was all there,
their entire history.

"What are you going to do with these?" he hissed. He suppressed the urge to rip them up, to spit on them—simply because
he knew Parson would have more, and he knew that reaction was
what Parson wanted. Cole breathed hard, trying to keep his fury
and panic in check.

Parson smiled broadly, reclaiming the envelope. "Wouldn't you like to know?" he said. Cole couldn't help himself—he lunged at him. Parson put out one hand to stop him, his face revealing his displeasure. "It's all over now, kid. We're in the home stretch. These babies," he told Cole, waving the photos in the air, "are just icing on the cake. Keep control of yourself. Keep your eye on the prize. Finals are next. Wouldn't want everything to blow up in our faces now, would you?"

"You set me up," Cole spit out, barely containing his anger.

"I'm on your side, Cole," Parson replied, his eyes narrowing even as his mouth turned up in a smile. "What's wrong? Don't you trust me?"

# 13

## DAVIS

The morning after she saw Cole at the FEUDS, all Davis wanted to do was get back to training. Hard training. Something to distract her from the way she wanted him still, despite everything she'd seen—and the raw brutality he was capable of. His strength terrified her; and yet, it could protect her, and she felt that he wanted to. She wanted him wrapped around her. Something inside her told her he'd never touch her like he'd touched the guy in the cage . . . but the fact that he'd done what he'd done at all was enough to send chills down her spine.

She had to dance to take her mind off it. Preferably with her fellow ballerinas, with whom she always felt grounded. She been off her game for the last few days, and she could feel it all over her body—her muscles slackening and some tightening up, the calluses on her feet softening. It was probably all in her head, but still. She needed her body back. When she was dancing, she felt her clearest and best.

There was a group drop-in session—"open floor"—scheduled at nine that morning, and thinking about it made Davis feel good, normal. Usually the most dedicated ballerinas went to the optional sessions; Davis loved being surrounded by the girls who loved to dance as much as she did. Sure, there was that edge of competition—but there was also an element of innate understanding among them. They got what it was like to work hard, to jump higher, to stretch farther. She needed those primal feelings now, and she needed to be surrounded by the others, to reenter her old routine. Getting her routine back would make her feel like herself again.

Moreover, Emilie was one of those serious ballerinas, and she almost never missed an optional practice. Surely she'd be back by now. Chloe had said so, in her usual irritated way, when Davis had last asked. Once she saw Emilie, everything would be back to normal. It would mean Cole had been mistaken, there was no disease. It was just coincidental, a few people getting sick at the same time. Davis could picture the sense of relief she'd feel, and suddenly she was desperate to have it—to see Emilie and know everything was okay.

It was eight o'clock, far later than she usually departed for the studio—she liked to get there before the other girls to mentally gear up, get in the zone—but she'd allowed herself to sleep in after the shock of the night before. The river sparkled diamond patterns, and the familiar Slants shanties stretched beyond them from

Davis's perch in her monorail car, high above the city. Normally the sight would have seemed beautiful to her, but today it made her shudder. Then again, so did the sanitation checkpoint she passed as she made her way off the monorail. Prior guards were patting Imps roughly, like they were objects rather than humans. One caught Davis looking and smiled at her, but she cast her eyes downward rather than returning his greeting. Every gesture, every mannerism—Imp and Prior alike—felt false now.

Once in the studio, Davis tossed her ballet bag on the floor next to the grand piano. She instinctively reached for her DirecTalk—which she always removed during practice—and groaned when she remembered it was gone. It had disappeared sometime the night before, when she was at the FEUDS. She should have had that chain replaced months ago; all of that data would be lost, and she had no easy way of getting in touch with anyone now. But there was nothing to be done about it just then.

She turned back toward the piano, flexing her toes. She wished a pianist were there now. Sometimes during practice, students who were studying to become classical musicians—pianists who played in the orchestra with Vera, for example—came to play for the dancers. Davis loved the quality of the live music versus the sounds piped through the state-of-the-art, surround-sound system the studio boasted. It would have been a nice distraction just then from her fears and worries and thoughts of Cole—and her anxious desire to see Emilie—which ran through her head like a song on repeat.

Emilie wasn't in yet, but she'd be in soon, Davis was certain. Chloe had told her "in a day or two" when they last spoke several days ago. Three other ballerinas—one who was very young in a purple leotard and matching tutu, and two Davis recognized from neighboring territories—were warming up on the opposite side of the room. It was good to have other people around. Good to have the distraction, something to keep her out of her own head.

Davis began some shoulder alignment stretches, then slid into à la seconde position for hip rotation. Her back ached and still she turned as far as she could toward the right, fighting through the pain. She breathed deeply once, then again. Normally stretching and its associated pain—and ensuing relief—were enough to wipe her mind clean of any distractions, but this time, things were different. She couldn't quit thinking of Cole and the way he'd hit that other guy, that hulking monster named Brutus. *Not a monster, just another kid.*

But she couldn't feel afraid of Cole, even though she felt she ought to. The way it had looked . . . he'd been fighting *for* something, not against his opponent. He'd told her himself: everything he'd told her had been about something bigger—a future for his family. He'd been fighting because he had to. It had been so clear, watching the crowd—the way they'd jeered and thrown things into the cage—that Cole had had little control over the role he played. Even the way the cage was set up: with a huge chain lock preventing the fighters from leaving. The way Cole had slammed up against the bars during that first round, facing outward toward the crowd, his face pressed against the metal ridges of the enclosure and his eyes full of terror. Davis's heart had nearly halved in that moment, she'd been so afraid. It had been like he was pleading for escape in that instant, before Brutus had jerked him back into the fight. She wasn't supposed to love Cole, but she did. She'd known it then by the panic she'd felt at the thought of anything bad happening to him.

And the Priors watching—they'd soaked up the violence with obvious glee. The Imps had loved it, too, but it was the Prior reaction that sickened her, because she'd never thought people like her—educated, intelligent, cultured, *superior*—could give in to such depravity. The weird thing was, it didn't make her less afraid of Imps. It just made her more afraid of Priors. It made her equally afraid of everyone.

It was ironic, really, Davis thought as she began a series of pliés, then jetés, warming up her muscles. They were all finally equal . . . but a very, very bad kind of equal. There were no pedestals anymore. They were all finally knocked down and crumpled like papier-mâché, she realized as she moved in a pirouette. So where did that leave her and Cole among the mess? Did that make each of them good or bad or both or something else altogether? Everything Davis had grown up believing in had been exposed as one enormous lie, and it left her feeling lost, like she couldn't even be sure of who she was anymore or where she stood in the world around her. It was like she had no home, no truth. Like she had to start all over with no one to guide her.

Davis whirled faster, willing the thoughts to go away. It was easier when she didn't know, didn't think about anything but ballet and the Olympiads and helping her dad win his campaign and watching her little sister blossom into a genius physicist. Everything was easier when it was all about her: her immediate life and the little stumbling blocks within it that she could so easily overcome. When the rest of the world was involved, it got messy. And it was encroaching. She could no longer hold it back.

She realized all of a sudden that she no longer *wanted* to. It was everywhere: in the jealousy she felt when she'd watched the Imp girls dance, their sexiness thrumming from their bodies without effort . . . it had made ballet look like a stiff farce. It was in the anger she felt at the fact that something like the FEUDS—reducing humans to toys designed for brutality—could exist. It was all a sick, twisted, convoluted mess of things she couldn't control. Why was everyone else okay with it all? Why was she apparently the only Prior who felt too frustrated to let things exist as they always had? Cole had been right about everything. And her world—her life—meant nothing anymore without knowing the truth.

Davis caught sight of herself in the mirrors that lined the room and felt disgusted by the stiff perfection of her movements. She stopped, took a breath, and instead of moving into another series of jetés, she lifted her arms over her head, dipped her chin toward her chest, and swiveled her hips as if they were independent from her spine. She stared at herself in the mirror through lowered lashes. She stopped watching herself and tilted her head back, moving her body to the memory of Cole. Their beautiful moment together on the fire escape during the roofing party—with the wind at her back, his hands in her hair, on her neck; just the two of them alone up there, with everything else falling away—it moved her. She let it move her body in ways that were unfamiliar but felt right. She tried to let her shoulders and hips move without her brain communicating anything but the sounds and memories of Cole's touch on her body, his voice in her ears, out there in the chill of the night air. The two of them leaning together. Davis moved faster, until she was dizzy and felt feverish in her movements. She stumbled, catching herself against a young girl, maybe fifteen. The girl glared at her.

"Sorry," Davis said, gasping for air. "I wasn't paying attention."

"Maybe you should practice somewhere else, then," said the girl, frowning. "This studio is for serious ballerinas."

Davis felt a bubble of laughter rising in her throat—she tried to choke it back, but it surfaced anyway, pushing its way out. Its uncontrollable abandon felt something like hysteria. Tears welled in her eyes and a lump formed in the back of her throat. She was weak and trembling, and she couldn't hide it any longer. The girl gave her a freaked-out look and turned back toward her friend, whispering something in her ear. The girl had no idea who Davis was, which was a relief. She clamped her hand over her mouth and grabbed her bag from the corner, untying her slippers and pulling on her flats in their place. What had made her want to be a ballerina? It was her mother—but her mother wasn't there anymore, and the futility of being an artist when the world was falling apart—and she with it—hit her with a force that left her breathless.

Davis slipped out of the room and headed for the reception area. Behind her, as the door was still swinging shut, she heard a loud crashing sound and turned just in time to see a piece of metal—a street sign?—ricocheting off a window inside the studio. One of the littler ballerinas let out a frightened cry.

"Focus, Cecile!" An adult, maybe the girl's mother, clapped her hands sharply. Through the frosted glass of the now-closed studio door, Davis saw the little ballerina resume her positions. Davis shivered and continued toward reception. Emilie still hadn't showed nearly forty-five minutes after open floor started, which wasn't like her. She needed to know what was going on. She approached the broad information desk, where a perky blonde in a blue strappy tank top sat, fielding calls.

"Can I help you?" she asked when she was done, looking up at Davis through semiglazed blue eyes.

"I was just wondering if Emilie Rhoads reserved a locker for today," Davis said. "Could you check for me in the system?"

"Just a sec," said the girl, turning to her mounted tablet. She peered closely, then murmured into her DirecTalk: "*Emilie Rhoads, Record Locator.*" Davis heard the tablet scrolling through records, and then a long beep indicated that it had retrieved results. "Nope," the girl said. "She hasn't been in lately."

"Nothing for today? Nothing coming up?" Davis felt panic rising in her throat, but she tried to tell herself it wasn't that weird. It really wasn't; often she booked her lockers day-of. That was kind of the nature of open floor. "Well, thanks anyway," she started, turning to leave.

"Wait," said the receptionist. Davis turned back to see her squinting at the screen. "Oh," she said. "Right."

"What?" Davis was impatient. She moved closer to the desk.

"There's a note here. I forgot. Membership canceled."

"Canceled?" Davis's throat tightened. "Why? Does it say why?" The receptionist raised carefully groomed eyebrows, frowning slightly.

"No," she said slowly, her ponytail swishing as she shook her head. "And even if it did, I'm not authorized to give out that information."

"But did they say anything when they called?" Davis pressed. "Look, I'm her friend. I'm not trying to be intrusive. I'm just worried." The receptionist's expression softened.

"Look," she said, "I have no idea what the reason is. I'd tell you. Maybe. Her parents just called and said she wouldn't be in anymore, and that they'd like to settle up."

"Okay." Still, Davis was reluctant to leave. She felt nauseated. Her pulse was fluttering, a feeling she was almost growing used to. "Okay, sure." She turned to leave, then whirled back, desperate.

"Can you check on one more for me?" she asked. "Nadya Benedict?"

"*Nadya Benedict, Record Locator*," the girl said into the machine. When it beeped a second later, she leaned closer, narrowing her eyes. "No locker sign-up today," she said curtly, frowning again.

"Tomorrow?" Davis pressed.

"Look," the receptionist said, avoiding Davis's eyes. "I've already given you enough information, okay? I'm really not supposed to reveal records. Confidentiality and all. You get it." Her voice was firm, and Davis knew she'd pushed as far as possible.

"Thanks for your help."

The heavy glass doors slid open to the manic, harried sidewalk scene that she felt certain she'd never get used to.

If Cole was right about the Priors and their brutality, couldn't he also be right about why they were all dying? Maybe it wasn't Imp rioting and violence and murders at all. Maybe they really *were* just getting sick. Maybe none of it was a coincidence.

*Her trembling hands.*

*Her dizziness.*

*Her wan complexion.*

*Her* fear.

Nadya was missing and Emilie had been absent from school for a week. Davis knew she had to find out the truth. She hopped back on the monorail, but exited two stops sooner than she normally would have if she were heading home. Emilie lived on Temple Street, among the fanciest high-rises in all of Columbus. Still, as Davis registered her P-card at the entrance and stepped onto the imposing elevator within Emilie's building, she couldn't help reflecting on how different the atmosphere felt compared to the night of the party.

The building was eerie and cold rather than glamorous. Davis's footsteps echoed loudly in the marble-and-glass corridor as she exited the elevator at the penthouse floor—not the rooftop, this time—and walked toward Emilie's family's unit. A large indoor courtyard rose up just beyond an iron gate that bordered the corridor, and it spanned the distance between the elevator and the penthouse door. It boasted a tree house, a small pond, three willow trees lining the pond, and a variety of flowers bordering a grassy expanse with benches to recline on. Sunlight streamed through the glass ceiling above, and butterflies even fluttered around, alighting on hydrangeas. Despite its impressiveness, it looked so different now, in the light, as opposed to the night of the party. It was empty; where her friends had been, now there was no one. No Cole. She felt his absence as painfully as she might a physical blow. Every part of her wanted another kiss like the one they'd had that night. She'd replayed the memory so many times that it was almost as if she could conjure the actual feelings of his lips on her cheek, her jaw, her throat. But it wasn't quite enough; she needed more.

There was something eerie in the memory of the party, in the way she could practically picture everyone milling about. The night of the party, she realized, was the last time she felt oblivious, safe, and comfortable. She couldn't believe the worries that had occupied her thoughts that night—her outfit, her jealousy, her insecurity. It all seemed so trivial now.

It was too quiet in the courtyard. Frighteningly quiet.

Emilie's parents were involved in film and finance, and they were one of the most prominent families in Columbus. Davis had never been to their home without encountering a bustle of staff: cinematographers, personal assistants, trainers, chefs, maids. But now, as she rang the doorbell, the ringing sound wasn't covered by the din of chatter and business like usual. It was eerily silent. So silent that Davis thought maybe they'd gone on vacation, and she was flooded with relief for a brief second. That would explain everything. She felt her heart lifting and turned to leave, angling back toward the elevator through the courtyard rather than the marble path.

"Hey," a tiny voice said just as she was passing the tree house. Davis looked around without seeing anyone; then a little girl dropped down from the tree house, bypassing the ladder altogether.

"Hi," Davis said. "You must be Kira." She'd heard Emilie talk about her little sister, but she'd never met her before now. Kira nodded in response, a solemn expression crossing her pretty features.

"Who are you? Are you my mom's new assistant?"

"No," Davis said. "I'm a friend of Emilie's. Is she here?" Davis was confused—clearly the family wasn't on vacation, because they'd never have left Kira. So where was everyone?

"No," Kira told her, looking at the ground. She looked like she was about to say more, but then she clamped her mouth shut.

"Well . . . what about your parents? Are they here? Do you know when Emilie will be back?" Davis could sense from the little girl's reluctance to talk that she knew *something*, and she was determined to figure out exactly what that something was.

"My dad's at work," Kira said. "Mommy's resting. We're supposed to be quiet."

"And Emilie?"

"She's . . . gone," Kira said, then turned back toward the tree, putting one foot on the bottom rung of the ladder. A jolt of familiar panic clawed its way up Davis's chest. *Gone where?*

"Wait!" she said, more sharply than she'd intended. The little girl turned back toward her, her braids flopping from her shoulders to her back. Her face read both sadness and fear, two emotions Davis had never seen combined in a kid so young. Davis took a step toward Kira and knelt next to her, smiling. The girl reminded her a little bit of Fia, and Davis found herself tugging on one of her braids the way she might have with her sister. Kira smiled a little, but it wasn't enough to cover up her worried expression.

"Can you tell me where she went?" she asked. "Is she okay?"

"Mommy says I'm not supposed to talk about it," the girl replied. She shook her head hard. "I've got to go. I'm not allowed to talk to you." Then she clambered back up the ladder.

"Kira!" Davis called out again, but the little girl disappeared into the wooden structure. The front door to the penthouse cracked open at the same time.

"Kira, who's there?" a female voice called out, sounding strained. Davis didn't wait to hear Kira's answer. She strode toward the elevator bank and jabbed at the *down* button with her index finger. The doors slid open immediately and she stepped in, fighting a wave of dizziness as the elevator descended. She had to go to Nadya's next. She had to know that Nadya was okay.

The Benedicts lived about two and a half miles from Temple Street, and Davis ran the whole way there. When she arrived, she was sweaty and out of breath. It was the second time that day she'd felt out of breath, and it wasn't fun. She wasn't used to feeling that way—she was in perfect cardiovascular condition. She berated herself for not doing regular workouts that week. She'd obviously fallen out of shape. She'd just have to work harder. She was fine. She'd be perfect after a few extra workouts . . . at least she hoped. She wasn't certain of anything anymore. Nothing about her life resembled the way it had been just a few weeks ago . . . and everyone seemed to be ignoring that. The disappearances were happening, things were falling apart. If only she could dance, maybe she could hold everything together. She wiped the sweat from her forehead with her sleeve and retrieved a lip gloss from her ballet bag. She wanted to look presentable when approaching the house—not like some straggler from the streets. She slicked on some gloss and squared her shoulders, making her way toward the small gatehouse that was positioned at the end of the driveway of the modest, three-story house.

The Benedicts, both lawyers, lived in one of the historic neighborhoods in Columbus—on an actual tree-lined street with houses that were considered quaint but generally not highly sought after because they lacked staff and some of the more modern comforts of the luxury towers.

The house was small but pretty, fashioned in a British bungalow style, with a front balcony running across the perimeter of the second story. Davis knew where the security gate was from all the times she'd ridden home with Nadya when they were kids—playing in the backyard after ballet and eating snacks that her mom made for them. The guard on duty was an Imp. She stopped in her tracks, an automatic wave of fear rushing through her. Then she took a breath and kept going; he hadn't noticed.

"Hi," Davis said to him in an even tone through the speaker unit on the side of the guardhouse. "I'm here to see Nadya Benedict, please. I'm Davis Morrow."

"Ms. Benedict isn't available," the guard said without looking up.

"Is she ill?" Davis asked. "I'd really like to see her." Thinking fast, she added, "Her mother asked me to drop off the ballet slippers she left at the studio." She gestured toward her ballet bag with what she hoped was a convincing manner.

"Ms. Benedict is not accepting visitors," the guard said, his voice terser this time. "And I highly doubt she'll need whatever's in that bag," he muttered to himself.

"Why is that?" Davis asked, challenging him. The guard looked up, meeting her eyes for the first time since they'd begun speaking. His eyes were blank, expressionless.

"Because she won't be coming back to ballet," he said. Then he reached up and flipped a switch that turned off the microphone system. The tinted glass window turned a murky black, cutting off Davis entirely.

She walked back to the monorail in a daze. *She won't be coming back*, he'd told her. *I'm not supposed to talk about it*, Kira had said. Davis pictured the bodies she'd seen only a couple of days before. She pictured those bodies with Nadya's and Emilie's faces. She felt nausea roll through her, but she swallowed a few times and willed it to pass.

The monorail was bustling. The usual checkpoints were still being monitored by Prior volunteers, since most of the Imps were on strike. It hadn't been a problem that morning, when the crowds were thin—Davis had barely noticed—but now the Priors' lack of expertise was obvious, and people were getting impatient. Cars were coming in and out of the station half-full and the lines were mounting, since the volunteers were slower and less adept than the usual employees.

As the monorail wended its way past the river toward her neighborhood, she couldn't shake the feeling that a *lot* of gazes were directed at her. Some were curious, some derisive. A couple looked flat-out disgusted. Davis gripped the pole tighter, eager to get off. Maybe it was because she was sweating through her clothes? When she finally reached her stop at Columbus Avenue, Davis stepped from the monorail and started toward her apartment. It was a little chilly, and although she usually didn't feel affected by the chill, this time she had goose bumps. She also felt a bit weak and realized she hadn't eaten in hours. As she passed a newsstand kiosk, she noticed that a crowd had gathered around it. One person looked back and, noticing her, nudged his companion. The other guy turned and openly sneered. A mother walking by with her little boy quickened her pace. Everyone suddenly looked hostile, like an enemy. Like she was the only one on the outside of a secret. She felt herself giving in to the grips of terror, her palms cold and sweaty and her body lighter somehow, less grounded. Had Cole been right about the Priors? What were they hiding? How bad *was* it?

She was overcome by a mounting sense of dread. She edged closer to the newsstand in an effort to scan the digital images that were projected across the front of the counter. Something had to be going on. Was it something with her dad? Had something gone wrong with the campaign? She squinted, craning her neck around a few people in front of her. Then she saw it: her face and Cole's, in profile, as they were locked in an obvious embrace.

Half a dozen images of the same scene were plastered across every single one of the tabloid screens. Some of the images were of them hugging, some worse.

*CPM Candidate's Daughter and the Imp*, read one headline.

*Lady and the Tramp*, read another.

*CPM's "Family Values"?, Prime Minister Candidate a Sham, CPM Candidate's Daughter Rocks Community.* Each of the headlines was more salacious and inflammatory than the last. Davis felt her cheeks heating up and she took a step back, edging out of the crowd. The whispers around her were growing louder and more intense, and several people were pointing at her. One woman spit at her, and flecks of her saliva sprayed Davis's arm.

Davis turned and ran.

She flew past the monorail checkpoint in the opposite direction of the house, her heart pounding and her breath ragged. She couldn't go home. She couldn't face her dad. He would be devastated and furious. Everywhere she looked, there were evil faces. Grimacing, leering, judging. But how had they gotten those pictures? Had Cole been setting her up? No, he couldn't have—this was suicide for him. What if he'd already been arrested? What if he was facing imprisonment or worse?

Davis felt sweat trickle down her forehead and along her breastbone. She felt her back dampen and her breathing grow shallower with every step. She felt sick now, truly sick, as though she could throw up even while running. What was wrong with her?

Davis didn't even think about where her feet were taking her until she reached the bank of the river. She'd been heading toward Cole all along, without even thinking about it—but, of course, it wasn't surprising. She needed answers. The urgency with which she felt she had to see him was overwhelming. All she wanted in the world was to let him know that she had forgiven him. It was time to stop fighting it—it wasn't even within her power. She'd forgiven him because somewhere inside, she knew none of this was his fault. She knew he was her only ally in all of this. She had to warn him; she couldn't *not*. If she didn't, she was as bad as they were, with their secrets and lies.

She looked behind her, but no one had followed. Maybe not everyone had seen the tabloids yet—it was still early in the day. Eventually, the very same motie she'd seen the other day idled up to her spot on the bank.

"You back for more, pretty girl?" he asked. Another sharp wave of nausea rolled through Davis's stomach, and this time she didn't fight it off—she gagged into the weeds at the bank, but nothing came out. There was nothing in her to expel. She righted herself, wiping tears from her eyes. She made an effort to straighten her shoulders, and she zipped her jacket, pulling the hood up to conceal her face for the second time in less than twenty-four hours. Then she faced the motie, nodding back at his toothless grin. She stepped inside the rickety vessel and steeled herself for another passage to the Slants.

# 14

## COLE

The banging on the front door was frantic. Cole moved the curtains aside and, when he saw who it was, yanked the door open without a second's hesitation.

"Get in here!" he whispered harshly, pulling Davis in by a trembling forearm. She winced and he pulled back—he hadn't meant to be rough with her. But if anyone had seen her, he couldn't guarantee he'd be able to protect her a second time—she'd be torn to shreds. Her very act of coming to him could result in her murder.

Her temples bore beads of sweat, and she looked exhausted. Her normally porcelain complexion was almost translucent, her eyes were watering, and she had bits of leaves stuck in her hair. Still, Cole's heart lifted at the sight of her. She looked pretty even now, even in the apparent height of her despair. "You can't be here," Cole told her after he helped her inside and she'd settled herself on the low wooden bench that bordered the dining table. Cole checked out the curtains that bordered either side of the trailer, just to make sure no one had seen her arrive. "You could get yourself killed!"

"I know," she said, resting her head in her hands. "But I didn't know where else to go! If I go home, I'm dead. Have you seen them yet, Cole?"

"Seen what?"

"You and me. All over the tabloids." Cole's jaw dropped. He felt his cheeks begin to flame, and fear penetrated every part of his body. Everyone knew. He'd be executed, or at the very least thrown in prison. It was only a matter of time; it had to be. He thought fast; he had to pretend to be as shocked as she was. He struggled to maintain an expression of surprise, which wasn't so difficult, given that he *was* surprised it had happened like this, so fast.

Above all, Davis couldn't know that he knew it was a setup. "Oh, God," he said, running a hand through his hair. "This is bad. This is really, really bad." He paused, gauging her reaction. He was struggling to sound surprised, but his voice sounded false and had even shaken a little. Still, she seemed oblivious. Her eyes were trained on his. He looked for hints of suspicion but found none. "We have to get you out of here," he told her, his voice tense. It was all his fault. He'd been responsible for dragging her into this mess—he'd get her out of it or die trying. He racked his brain for places to take her. If someone found her—if anything happened to her—he'd never forgive himself. "I have no idea who could walk through here—Hamilton's friends are always in and out—and if people recognize you like they did at the riot, I'm pretty sure they're not letting you get away this time. At least not without a million questions. Come with me." He put a hand on her shoulder, attempting to urge her from the bench, and her back felt as brittle as a bird's under his touch.

"Can I just . . . can I have some water first?"

"Sure." Cole filled a glass from his tap and handed it to Davis, waiting. She stared into its rippling surface but made no attempt to bring it to her lips. "Davis," he said gently, "I know you're freaked out, but we have to go. I know somewhere where we can talk." She looked up from the glass, guilt creasing her features, and all at once he understood: she was *afraid* of the water. Afraid of the Gens' filtration system, that it might not be clean, that it might give her something contagious. The irony almost made Cole laugh, but her fear was too palpable for him to make light of it.

"I think I have bottled water here somewhere," he told her. "Here," he said, grabbing a bottle from the minifridge in the corner. "You can take it with you." Bottled water was expensive, but Cole's mom had been coughing so much lately that he'd used some FEUDS money to invest in a case. Davis had been right to be a little concerned—the filtration system hadn't been updated in who knew how long.

After she took a couple of sips, she looked slightly better, and some of the color began to return to her face. Cole helped her stand, and then he gave her one of his hoodies, which hung all the way down to her knees—but it was the best he could do for a disguise. They left the trailer together and made a sharp left, heading away from the center of the Slants. Cole didn't want to go too far from the riverbank—it was important that Davis be able to return home quickly—so he headed for the decrepit, abandoned carousel on the outskirts of the trailer clusters.

They were just twenty or thirty feet from the carousel when he heard voices headed in their direction. Davis's eyes, wide with panic, moved to his. He grabbed her arm and pulled her underneath a small, makeshift deck that stretched from the back of a trailer. It was really just a few boards of plywood supported by cement blocks, and they struggled to fit their bodies under it, squirming against the dirt. Cole made sure Davis was concealed first; then he wiggled in after her, pulling himself against the ground using his forearms. They lay there, their breathing louder than he'd have liked, as the footsteps drew nearer. He heard laughter; there were maybe two or three men, their voices unfamiliar.

As they lay there, Cole became aware of Davis's body pressed against his: her shoulders and hips and waist and thighs filling the negative space between them. He couldn't see her in the dark, but Cole had the sense that her face was only inches from his. That if he moved just slightly—

"I think they're gone," she whispered, breaking the silence. Her breath was hot on his cheek, but he forced himself to move. They had to keep going. Her safety was most important right then.

"I think you're right," he said. "Let me check first." He scooted from under the deck and took inventory of the area before coming all the way out and motioning for her to follow. She emerged from under the building, her clothes and face covered in dirt. A smudge of dirt crossed her cheek near her mouth, and he reached out to brush it away. She took his hand as if to stop him, but then to his surprise, she held it in her own, squeezing it tight.

"Let's go," he said. Hand in hand, they ran the rest of the way to the carousel. Priors had dumped the broken structure in the Slants years and years ago, like they did with most of their junkyard items. That's what the Slants really was to them—a place to chuck their trash, to get rid of things they didn't want to see, including the Gens themselves. But the carousel had become a staple in the community. Kids had liked to climb all over the painted animals, even though it wasn't running. Not anymore, though. Over the years, parts had rusted and metal had corroded and it was no longer very safe.

"This place used to seem amazing to me," he told her, a trace of nostalgia in his voice. "It's funny how even the crappiest stuff can seem that way when you're a kid with an imagination. But now it's all just junk. Perfect for getting away from everything, though," he added with a smile. He ducked into a car shaped like an elephant, and motioned for Davis to sit next to him. The stuffing on the seat was moldy and popping out, but the elephant car was dark and deep and offered the greatest shelter, in case anyone happened by. Not that anyone loved wandering by the old fairgrounds. No one liked to linger in the more dismal parts of the Slants. And everyone's parents were keeping them on lockdown these days, since the latest body dumping.

To her credit, Davis didn't look disgusted. Just terrified and exhausted. Davis's shoulder pressed against his—another benefit of the close quarters of the elephant car—and Cole tried not to focus on how the contact made him feel.

"Cole," she started, "did you *know* people were photographing us?"

"Of course not!" He moved away, startled. "Why would I lie about that? I'd basically be throwing myself to the wolves." He held her gaze, struggling to stay calm. If she figured out the truth, he'd lose her for sure.

She sighed, and a new torrent of tears made their way down her face. Cole reached out and carefully wiped her cheek. She responded, leaning into his touch. So she wasn't mad at him. She still wanted him as badly as he wanted her, he thought.

"I'm so scared," she said. Her body looked slight inside the carousel car—child-sized, as if it had been designed for her. "I'm scared, but I hate this feeling. I don't want to sit here, helpless. I want to *do* something! But I can't go home. I'm so scared. Cole, my family is ruined. My father's whole career is over because of those photos. I can't face him. And what about . . ." She stopped, choking back a sob. "I'm worried about Narxis. I'm worried you were right."

"Come here." Cole placed an arm around her shoulder and drew her body toward his. She felt stiff, like her whole torso was encased in some protective shield. She slowly relaxed into him. "I wanted to tell you last night," he continued, "but there wasn't time. Gens weren't allowed past the Slants, so I couldn't even have reached you if I'd tried."

"What do you mean, 'Gens weren't allowed past the Slants'?" Davis drew back, her eyes full of worry. "Why not? Because of the riots?"

"No." Cole shook his head. "Because there was another death last night. One that couldn't . . . go unnoticed."

"Who was it? A Prior?"

"They're all Priors," Cole reminded her. "It was Marcus Eastman," he said. Davis's body tensed.

"The swimmer? Four-time winner of the Olympiads?"

Cole met her eyes and nodded.

"But . . . I met Marcus once. At an athletic conference two summers ago. They brought him in to talk to us. He seemed so solid. He was invincible."

"No one's invincible," Cole said. "They dropped his body just past the city limits, and now we're on quarantine. I'm not even sure how you got in here." He paused. "I'm not sure I want to know, actually. They think Gens are infecting everyone. But none of us are sick—look around. There haven't been any Gen deaths, only Priors. It's not something that's starting with us, Davis."

"Narxis is real," she breathed.

Cole nodded. "I think so." He hugged her again, and this time she melted into him, but only for a second.

"There's one thing I need to know," she said, pushing away again. "Why me, Cole? Why did you choose me? You had to have known who my father is. You knew you were ruining my life by doing this."

"I didn't know, I swear!" Cole fought to steady his breath. At least that much was true—he hadn't known Davis was Robert Morrow's daughter. "I never would have come after you if I'd known." That part probably wasn't true. Cole swallowed back his guilt. The truth was, he would have gone after anyone Parson told him to, no matter who it was. He'd had to, in order to get Parson on his side and secure his place in the FEUDS. It had been the only way out of the Slants and the life he'd been born into—the only way of creating a better future for the family he loved. He might have gone after anyone . . . but he wouldn't have fallen in love with anyone. For that, Davis was entirely responsible. It wasn't just her beauty and the attraction he felt for her. It was her way of looking at the world, her ability to see a different future, to question everything that had been fed to her all her life. It was her curiosity, and her empathy, and the way she still loved her mother so much after so many years. It was even in the way she was hard on herself, and the way she wanted to please everyone. It was the way she smiled up at him, like she trusted him more than anyone else ever had. And the way she held his hand that showed him they were in it together. It was a closeness he'd never felt with anyone else—had never even imagined feeling. And a strength he sensed in her, this indomitable force that was far more powerful than any brute strength he could show in the cages. It was a combination of all of these things that made her different from anyone he'd ever met. He wanted to treasure her, and love her, and protect her forever.

Could he tell her about Parson? Cole opened his mouth, but nothing came out. Davis looked at him expectantly. When he didn't say anything, her lips formed a grim line. He had to say something, fast. But if she knew everything . . . if she knew her father's rival had *paid* him to get close to her—she'd never in a million years believe his feelings for her were real. And they were. They were the strongest, most intense feelings he'd ever felt for anyone in his life. He couldn't lose her.

He swallowed. He'd made his decision.

"This is going to sound really pathetic," he said carefully, wincing as the lies poured from his lips. "But I just . . . I really wanted to see what life would be like as a Prior." He waited, seeing if she was buying it. She didn't respond, but her expression softened. "I'd never really been outside the Slants except to fight in the FEUDS. I wanted to see what it was like. Some friends of mine . . . we joked around that I could maybe pass for a Prior. So I tried, and it worked. And I met you. And Davis . . ." There he paused, swallowing the lies and hurrying ahead to the truth, wanting to feel good about himself again and to tell her how he really felt. "I connected with you the second I saw you. I wanted to know everything about you. When I saw you first, you weren't facing me—you were turned away, and even though I hadn't seen your face, I knew you were the most beautiful girl in the room. Then when you first smiled at me, and we first started to talk, it was like I could talk to you forever. That was real. Everything since then was real. You're everything to me. Every time I touched you, or kissed you, it was because nothing in the world could make me happier." He looked up, meeting her eyes for the first time since he'd begun talking. He had no idea how she'd react.

Davis's green eyes were full, searching. Cole reached out and touched her hand, his pulse pounding in his ears. He leaned forward and she came to him easily; as though this whole time, they'd been fighting against forces so natural, and all it took was breaking down the barrier to let them return to their rightful state: in each other's arms. She melted into him and he found her lips with his, and then his tongue was on her neck, which tasted sweet, and she was running her hands through his hair. He brought her face back up to his and their kiss was fervent, hungry. The emotions that overpowered him were like nothing he'd ever known. He moved his hands to her lower back and lifted her into his lap, wrapping both arms around her. Cradling her was like holding something precious. It was overwhelming, terrifying, and amazing all at once. He almost couldn't handle it; the thought of ever losing her—of her being hurt—ripped through him painfully and he gasped. She whispered to him, telling him it was all okay. Then she had her hands in his hair and then on the sides of his face, touching him gently but with urgency; then she pressed her lips to his, and if he could have consumed her altogether, taken her whole body into his to make them one person, he would have.

"Hey," came a voice from beside the carousel. "Who's that?" Cole and Davis broke apart, breathing hard; she slid off his lap onto the seat next to him and looked at him, her eyes wide with fear. Cole motioned for her to be quiet, and he peered out of the elephant. Maybe he could pretend he was with was Michelle or some other random Gen, if he could block this person's view. He maneuvered himself closer to the opening and looked up to find Worsley standing there with his medical bag, his tall frame half-bent in order to see them better.

"It's you." Cole heaved a sigh of relief, and Worsley straightened back to his full six feet. "Thank God." It wasn't that he was unafraid of Worsley's reaction; it was just that he knew Worsley would always be on his side. He trusted and admired Worsley, maybe even more than his own brother.

"Cole, who's in there with you?" Worsley's voice held a note of warning, and before Cole could stop him, he pushed him aside and peered inside the carousel car.

"Dammit, Cole," Worsley told him. "This is bad. Come here." He motioned for Davis to climb out. "It's fine, there's no one else around. Just let me get a look at you." She climbed out of the elephant and Worsley turned to Cole, his shoulders tense under his plain white button-down. "You're not involved with her, are you? Cole, please tell me you're not."

Cole stepped forward, his fists clenched in rage. For once, he noted Worsley's physical impressiveness. He'd been a FEUDS fighter once, and Cole was always forgetting that and boxing him in as an intellectual. But now, feeling his opposition, he automatically noted every tensed muscle in Worsley's neck and his slightly aggressive stance, legs spread wide and arms crossed. "When did you become so prejudiced?" Cole asked. "What's so bad about being a Prior? Since when do you judge, Worsley? I thought you were all about equality."

Worsley's mouth dropped open and his face flushed. "That's not it at all," he insisted, reaching up to tug at the strap of the signature canvas messenger bag he always wore over one shoulder. "Cole . . ." He trailed off, running one hand through his hair. His eyes wore a worried expression, the blue in them brighter than usual. If Cole hadn't known better, he'd have thought Worsley pitied him.

"What?" Cole said, feeling the sudden, urgent need to know what Worsley was thinking. "Just say it."

"Can't you see it?" Worsley pled. "I don't care if she's a Prior, Cole. Look at her."

"See what?" Cole felt the blood drain from his face, the beginnings of panic. "See *what?*" he demanded again, moving closer to Davis, who looked shaken. Worsley placed a hand on Cole's shoulder. He hesitated before telling Cole what he already knew, what he'd known since Worsley's first shocked expression. Cole's hands shook as he waited for the words.

"The girl has Narxis," Worsley finally said.

# ❧ 15 ❧

## DAVIS

*The girl has Narxis.* Davis blinked and struggled to sit up, squinting into the dim light of the room. She tried to shake off the dream, but something in her refused to let go of the panicky feeling that was taking hold of her. Where was she? She waited impatiently for the hazy shapes to form into her familiar bedside table, her desk, the set of hooks she used for hanging scarves. But unfamiliar lumps and angles remained unfamiliar, until two people-sized forms moved into her line of vision.

Her eyes adjusted more, taking in the cut of Cole's jaw, the worried crease in his brow. And she remembered with a sudden, sick feeling that nearly bowled her over: none of it had been a dream. Cole reached for her hand, but she yanked it away, scooting farther back on the table. "What are you doing?" Her words came out breathy, clipped. "Where are we?"

"We're in my lab." Tom Worsley stepped forward into the narrow beam of sunlight that issued from the window behind her and illuminated a very small portion of the room. "How do you feel?"

"I'm fine." Her tone was guarded—her words sounded clipped—but she didn't care. "There's nothing wrong with me." It was true; she felt fine. A little woozy, but she'd had a shock. It was to be expected. She looked to Cole for reinforcement—surely he'd back her up; Worsley was being nuts—but he only frowned.

"Hit the lights, Cole," Worsley ordered. "Now that she's awake and adjusted, she should be fine." Cole tugged at a long metal chain hanging from the wall, and the room was suddenly flooded with light. Davis gasped as Worsley's lab came into view: it was rife with cold metal contraptions and beakers. She felt like less of a person, perched up there on that table. Her skin crawled. She felt like a *specimen*.

"I'm fine," she said again, louder. She moved to stand up. "Perfect. I'm totally perfect, see?" She stood straight, squaring her shoulders and desperately ignoring a powerful wave of nausea, a result of standing too soon. She tried to meet Worsley's eyes, but he just looked away. *Coward*, she thought. It was almost as if he preferred her as a little lab animal he could poke and prod. Still, her stomach turned, and she could feel moisture forming at her temples.

"Cole," she said. She looked at him. His eyes were large, sad. "I want to go home. I shouldn't have come here."

He reached for her hands, and this time she didn't pull away.

"Davis, please." His voice was soft, so soft she almost cried. "Just let him run a few more tests. If . . ." He trailed off, then swallowed hard, seeming to get his bearings. "If you do have Narxis, Tom Worsley is the best person to help you. Your doctors across the river are denying the disease even exists. You can't turn to them if you need to. Please stay here; let us take care of you."

Davis hesitated. She glanced in Worsley's direction and he moved to the opposite end of the lab, just out of earshot. It took effort to summon her words; what she was about to say felt like a betrayal. Because she couldn't be sick. It couldn't be happening to her. Still . . . this was bigger than her. "Cole, if you're right . . . If Narxis really does exist . . ."

"Then we need to get you help."

Davis shook her head. "No. Maybe. But first I need to talk to my dad."

Cole met her eyes, frowning, but he didn't argue.

She took a breath. "My dad can do something about this." She squeezed his hand, her tone urgent. "You know that. He's the only one who really can. And if this thing is real, it means my friends, my family . . . they could be next. I need to try to help them."

"You need to help yourself first," Cole said, his voice raspy. "You can't do anything for anyone unless you're healthy."

She shook her head. "No," she said firmly. "This is what I need to do. I'll never be able to sit here and think about them over there, not knowing. Besides," she said, rubbing his palm with her thumb. "You know my dad will pull out all the stops for me. He'll get me the very best." She smiled a little. "You know you think I'm a little bit spoiled. Go ahead. Now's your chance to say it because my dad will do everything he can to make sure I'm okay. His entire campaign is based on making Columbus a better place for me and Fia. He'd do anything for us."

"Okay," Cole said reluctantly. "But when can I see you? How will I know you're all right?"

"Cole," Worsley broke in, taking a step toward them. "You can't just let her go."

"I can't keep her here against her will," Cole pointed out. He held out a palm, discouraging Worsley from moving any closer. "There's nothing we can do, Tom. If she wants to go, I'm not going to force her to stay."

Worsley nodded, his face grave.

"I'll come back tonight," Davis said, keeping her voice low. "After I've had a chance to explain everything."

"The carousel?" Cole held her gaze with his, and with his palms grasping her own, it was like he was cradling her with a look. She felt safe, strong.

"Yes." She leaned forward, allowing herself to relax against his shoulders. He stood in front of her, cupping her cheeks in his hands. He drew her toward him, tilting her chin up so that when he bent low over her, their lips touched. The kiss was brief but sweet, and it sent a surge of energy through her. Davis closed her eyes, then let go of his hand. She gave him one last glance as she left the lab. Worsley stood behind him, his arms at his sides, looking resigned. Cole looked anything but. His shoulders were squared and his face determined.

"Good-bye," she said softly.

"Tonight," he said back—not as a reminder, she knew. As a promise.

"Oh, thank God!" Davis's dad rushed toward her, his face a mask of worry and confusion. He wrapped her in his arms so forcefully that Davis felt pressure against her lungs, and her breath came short. "I was so worried! Davis, where have you been? We were frantic. Terri's been calling—well, never mind that. After the articles . . . I thought something awful had happened to you."

"So you're not mad?" Davis hadn't been sure what to expect from her father—shock, at best.

"Mad? Sweetheart, no. It's obvious you've been taken advantage of. Worried, though. My God." He ran a hand through his lightly graying hair. "I've never been so worried in my life."

She felt her eyes well with tears but willed them away. "I have to talk to you," Davis said, eager to let him know about Narxis, to get help right away. The urgency she felt was all-consuming, and seeing her dad's concern made her feel empowered. He'd do something to help, she knew it. He was the only one who could, practically.

"Yes, we do need to talk," he agreed. "Come into my study, where we can be alone." He glanced down the hall with a wry smile, and Davis saw Fia's form darting around the corner, away from her hiding spot. She couldn't help smiling, even though her entire body was trembling from adrenaline and fatigue. "I'm not angry," her father began as he settled into the leather wingback chair opposite his desk. "It's clear that you're a victim in this."

"Dad," Davis said, cutting him off. "This isn't about Cole. I mean, I need to talk to you about something else." His eyes narrowed at the familiarity with which she uttered Cole's name, but she forged ahead anyway. "People are disappearing," she started, allowing the words to tumble out, hoping they made sense. "Dying. There's a disease, Narxis. Parson Abel is covering it up." She glanced at her father's face for a reaction; he was staring at her, eyes wide, his mouth pressed into a grim line. "There are Prior bodies lining the Slants, I can show you—"

"You went into the Slants?" Splotches of red appeared on his neck and cheeks.

"Dad, I can take you there! I can show you I'm telling the truth. It's a disease, it's spreading fast, and Parson is making up rumors, blaming the Imps and dumping the bodies. And . . ." She trailed off, looking at her hands, which were damp and clasped tightly in her lap. She whispered the last part. She could hardly bring herself to say it aloud. "I might have the disease. I think I have Narxis."

"What?" Her father was on his feet again. He kneaded his jaw with his right hand, clearly struggling to keep calm. "Davis, these are serious allegations—"

"I know. But I've seen it."

He sighed, rubbing his forehead. "That's another issue. The idea of you wandering over there by yourself—but it must have been that boy. We'll deal with that later. What you're saying now— you feel ill?"

"I think it might be Narxis," she said again. "I've been dizzy. Weaker. Nauseated. Tom Worsley said it's contagious, and some of the ballerinas have been missing—"

"Tom Worsley? Who . . . ? Never mind. If what you're saying is true—if Parson's really covering up some sort of . . . epidemic . . . I've got to expose him. I have to do something."

"I can take you to the bodies," Davis said, leaning forward. She was growing more animated, her words tumbling out faster. This was how she'd hoped he'd react. This was exactly what she'd hoped for.

But he whirled on her. "You're not taking me anywhere," he said firmly. "You're sure as hell not going back into the Slants. I don't know how you got involved with these people, Davis, but it's only brought this family pain." Davis reeled back as if she'd been slapped, but her dad continued, barely noticing. "No. What you need is to stay safe. You need medical attention if you're not feeling well. We'll go now." He jabbed his left palm with his right index finger for emphasis. "We'll get you to the best doctors. Then I'll worry about the rest, with Parson."

"But Dad, I already have a plan—"

"Davis!" He raised his voice, was practically yelling at her. He almost never yelled; it caught her off guard. "It is up to *me* to make these decisions, not you."

"But—"

"No!" He leaned toward her, his face growing red. "You will listen to me. I know what's best for you. My decision is final. I will escort you to the car. Frank will follow with a bag for you."

"You're not even letting me pack my own stuff?" Davis heard herself matching his tone and pitch, and it was an unfamiliar feeling. They were outright fighting; his voice was loud and her face was streaked with tears.

"No. I'm not letting you out of my sight again until I'm certain you're safe."

Just then, the door to the study inched open. Terri's head poked around the corner, looking ashen.

"What's all this?" she asked. "Robert, why are you arguing? Fia's frightened."

"Please take Fia to her room, Terri," he responded. "I'm sorry. I shouldn't have raised my voice. Davis and I are headed to the hospital." Terri drew in a breath, and her eyes widened in alarm. "She's fine," her father reassured Terri. "We just have to visit a doctor. But everything will be okay."

He didn't sound convincing to Davis, but Terri just nodded, moving farther into the room. "Davis, sweetheart," she started, moving toward Davis as if to hug her. Instinctively, Davis took a step back. What if she was contagious?

"Terri." Her father sounded tired. "We're okay in here. Can you get Fia?" Sure enough, Fia's diminutive form had wriggled its way around Terri and into the room. Fia stared up at Davis with plaintive eyes, and Davis gave her what she hoped was a comforting grin. Every part of her wanted to reach out and wrap her sister in her arms, but she knew she couldn't. She steeled herself, keeping away. If Narxis was real, it wasn't worth the risk. Fia had to stay healthy and safe. Her father got on his DirecTalk and paged one of his security men. Fia gave Davis a little wave, then allowed herself to be led from the room. Davis collapsed back in her own leather chair, overwhelmed by fatigue. She felt as if she couldn't stand up ever again.

She didn't have to; a moment later, her father watched as James, one of his security personnel, hoisted Davis's arms around his shoulders and carried her to the elevator and down to the car park and into the waiting car. Her father would immediately follow, he'd said. Davis didn't care anymore. Every step she took toward the car was a step away from Cole. She just had to regain her strength, and then she'd figure something out.

The hospital suite was large and luxurious, nearly twice the size of her bedroom at home and located on an upper floor, high above the city. Floor-to-ceiling windows offered an astounding view of Columbus, its buildings rising impressively in the distance. Davis could barely make out the river and the Slants. It felt like it was on another continent. The suite was more akin to a hotel than a hospital, with a plush carpet and a real bed with a down comforter instead of the standard hospital beds she was familiar with from the time she had visited Fia long ago.

Still, it was frightening. It was an atmosphere of germs and disease.

She knew her father had pulled out all the stops to make sure she was comfortable, but somehow it made her feel worse, know-

ing this sort of luxury wasn't available to everyone. She paced like
a caged animal. For the past several hours, physicians had let
themselves in and out of her room every few minutes to run tests
and check her vitals. Still, no one could tell her exactly what her
condition was—exactly how bad. She had to do something. She
was supposed to go meet Cole. Her father had just stepped out for
a meeting with Frank. This was the moment; she might not have
another chance.

"Miss Morrow?" A pretty young nurse just a few years older
than Davis and clad in a skirt suit entered the room. She wouldn't
have known the girl was a nurse at all if it weren't for the stetho-
scope dangling from her neck. All the nurses wore plainclothes
now, rather than the scrubs they'd still worn when Fia was in the
hospital as a toddler. The nurse smiled in a friendly way, and Davis
forced herself to return the smile. She had to act normal—she
couldn't put anyone on high alert. "Do you mind lying in the bed?
This is the last of it for the evening; then we'll let you get some
rest."

"For the evening," Davis repeated. "So I'm staying here all
night?"

The nurse looked surprised. "Well, yes. Didn't the doctor tell
you? You're being held for observation." Davis tried hard to conceal her panic. She forced herself to nod calmly and smile back at
the nurse.

"Right," Davis said, climbing back atop the bed and allowing
the nurse to tape a thin, circular monitor to the space just above
her heart. "Of course, I knew that." As the nurse bent over her,
squinting at the digital monitor taped to her chest, her laminated
ID badge—affixed to the lower pocket of her green scrubs shirt—
knocked against Davis's leg. The nurse went on checking the read-
ings, pausing to make notes in her digital tablet. Davis wasn't sure

yet how the ID would come in handy, but when the nurse was squinting at her tablet, she shifted her hand slightly to the left and unclipped the ID badge, sliding it under her thigh, where it burned like a brand until the nurse left the room, oblivious to what Davis had done.

Davis waited five minutes to make absolutely certain no one was coming back. Then she edged the ID from under her leg and clipped it onto her own shirt, hoping desperately no one would notice the name. Her dad and Frank would be back soon—probably in fifteen or twenty minutes. It was a small window, and it was by no means safe, but she had to go for it. Davis tiptoed silently to the door, adjusting the badge so it was visible but not prominent. She eased the door open and scanned the hall. The secretary's desk was fully staffed, but Davis knew there were two glassed-in offices with computers just a few yards farther down the hall, between their station and the guest elevators.

She didn't have time to think. She squared her shoulders and walked down the hall, hoping none of the secretaries had been working when she'd checked in. Clearing their desk area, she eased open the door to one of the offices and slid inside. She sat at the single computer—it looked like it was an office belonging to one of the cardiac residents, judging by the paperwork, envelopes, and other paraphernalia spread in a mess alongside the computer. Davis's back prickled; she didn't like not being able to see who walked by. But then, it meant they couldn't see her either. She tapped the front of the computer screen, and the monitor lit up. The words ID NUMBER and PASSWORD flashed insistently against the screen.

Davis panicked. She fumbled for the stolen badge, hoping desperately. There was an employee ID listed beneath the blond girl's picture: 02157FLEET87. Davis typed it in. PASSWORD would be more difficult. Taking a wild guess, she typed in "Mount Co-lumbus Guest," a phrase that was scrawled in pen on a notepad amid the clutter. The screen flashed once, then went dark. Trem-bling, Davis hoped she hadn't somehow triggered an alarm. Then the welcome screen flashed on, and she could again breathe easily. Kind of.

Davis didn't know what she was looking for, not at all.

Seeing a tab for "patients," she clicked. She typed in Emilie's name, and her friend's information flashed across the screen. Davis scanned it quickly, her anxiety levels ratcheting all the while. Emilie had died. Somehow she had known it all along, but this was the first time she was officially facing the fact. She forced herself to read on. Emilie's cause of death was listed as "unknown." But her time of death was clearly stated as being forty-eight hours after she'd been brought in. Davis clicked off that screen and repeated the process with Caitlyn's information. Caitlyn had been dead within twenty-four hours of showing symptoms.

Davis's mind raced. If she had Narxis, she should be dead right now, too. She must have been exposed to Narxis days ago, via Caitlyn, and had definitely begun feeling faint shortly thereafter. None of it added up. She typed in her own name. A small part of her didn't want to. Part of her didn't want to know. Her records flashed on-screen and there, in bold letters, flashed a large error message. Davis's heart stopped.

It was worse than being diagnosed with Narxis. It was worse than anything.

*ERROR,* the message read, in twenty-four-point font across the wide screen, obscuring the other fields. *NOT FULLY A PRIOR.*

Davis read it slowly three more times, stunned. Its meaning failed to compute. What could it mean? Was she an Imp? But that was impossible. She pushed back from the computer desk, terrified.

There was a small scrawl of a signature in the corner of the intake, there where it was scanned on the screen. "L.E.," a set of initials, likely from the nurse who'd signed her in. That was all. The initials, the error, her fear. The letters seemed to flash brighter and larger until she could swear they were leaping from the screen and taking up the entire room, wrapping themselves around her neck and squeezing.

"What are you doing in here?"

Davis hadn't heard the door open.

"You're not allowed to be in here." The grip on her arm was firm, but she barely felt it. She didn't resist as the nurse led her back to her room, practically shoving her into the bed as she left to confer with the staff outside the door.

**NOT FULLY A PRIOR.**

She couldn't stop thinking about it. It was seared over everything else in her brain until nothing mattered anymore. It was the only thing she could think about, the only thing that really mattered.

No.

Cole mattered. She had to pull herself together.

Davis heard the sound of raised voices in the hall, some of them male, and shortly thereafter, her father burst in.

"Davis! I can't understand what you're thinking," he said, dismayed. "How could you assume it was okay to tamper with the staff computers? You have your own tablet right here if you need to check your e-mail."

"I wanted to know what was wrong with me," she whispered, avoiding his gaze. Her dad's expression softened and he moved next to her, sitting on the edge of her bed.

"We'll know soon," he assured her. "Just be patient. This . . . this Narxis you're certain you have. It's just speculation. It could easily be a product of your overactive imagination. You probably just have a cold; maybe you're run-down from the stress. . . ." He kept on going, but Davis tuned him out. She had no idea whether she had Narxis. But what was in her file was almost worse. She tuned back in to hear him say, ". . . Just in case, I'm putting two of my guys outside your room. I'm just not certain I can trust you right now, Davis. Maybe I shouldn't have given you so many liber-ties growing up. I think you'll agree when I say that this is for your own good."

"Dad, no!" The words escaped her before she could think about their implication.

"It's not up for debate," her dad said. "And it shouldn't matter anyway, since you're just resting. It only matters if you planned to sneak around again. I want you to think about what it is you need so badly, Davis. If it's that boy . . ." He swallowed hard. "It's not acceptable. I won't have it. You'll stay right here, under my watch, until you're better." With that, he left the room, and through the open doorway, Davis could see two hulking men guarding the only entrance to the room. They were two of her father's best, most trusted men. She was trapped. There was no way out.

Davis glanced out of her window as the sun's evening rays fil-tered inside, casting a purple-and-pink hue across the room. She blinked hard, trying not to cry. What would Cole think when she didn't show up? Would he be afraid she was in trouble? Or that she was angry, and had given up on him? She hated to think of him worrying. She hated the thought, too, that she might not know where to find him if she ever did get out of this hospital-turned-prison. She had to get him a sign. But how? Davis racked her brain. She scanned the horizon for clues—for anything that could help her. And then she saw it: the steeple to St. Aloysius Church, one of the most beautiful remnants of Old Columbus. Her favorite refuge. But there was only one way there.

Before she could think about it—before she could doubt her gut for even a second—Davis pushed open the window, allowing a rush of cold air into the hospital room. She reached outside, pushing it as far as it could go in order to widen the gap. It wasn't much—the hospital likely wanted to take precautions against this very thing—but it was far enough for her to wriggle through. And so Davis pushed her lithe form through her only slim exit to the outside world. She stood finally, breathless, to balance on the outside ledge. Then she started climbing, her only footholds the decorative brick detailing, the closest balcony nearly four stories below.

# ❧ 16 ❧

## COLE

He got to the carousel fifteen minutes early. It felt like fifty. Finally, after an interminable wait, his DirecTalk sounded, letting him know it was 7:15, the time they'd designated to meet. But she was nowhere. Cole slipped inside the elephant car, then jumped out again a second later when he realized she might not see him in there, and if she didn't see him, she might leave, and their moment would be lost.

He felt jumpy. Every nerve was firing. It was the kind of anxiety that only her presence could ease, and every second in her absence amplified it times a million. Cole sat on the elevated platform that held the carousel horses and carriages. He let himself put his head in his hands for just a second; he took a long breath, but the second he let it out, the anxiety was back. It felt like something was wrong.

He didn't want to think that way. He told himself he was just being paranoid. She'd get there any second. But what if the motie had harassed her? What if someone had seen her and prevented her from coming over to the Slants? Should they have met somewhere else? Cole groaned. They definitely should have met elsewhere, somewhere safer for her. The Slants were remote, but if someone recognized her as a Prior . . .

Cole heard a branch crack.

"Davis?" He whirled around, looking for the source of the sound. "Is that you?" He kept his voice low. Another crack rang out. It may as well have been gunfire for how it sounded against the silence of the carousel. Another crack, closer.

Hands were everywhere. On his shoulders, his wrists, the back of his shirt. They weren't hers—gentle. They were rough, confident, strong. He fought to wriggle from their grasp.

"Cole Everett. You're coming with us." A policeman came into view in his periphery as the officer pulled Cole's hands behind his back. Confusion gave way to panic, and Cole struggled with every muscle in his body, but the cop held him.

"What is this? What's going on?" Cole shouted. He struggled. He pulled one arm free, and the cop swore. He wouldn't go down without trying. Cole swiveled partway, throwing a desperate punch that connected with a cop's nose. The cop cried out and released him, and Cole turned, intending to run—but a second cop was on him, pinning him to the ground. Cole twisted, kneeing the cop in the stomach. His heart thudded and his entire body pulsed with adrenaline. He struggled on the ground against the second cop.

They were now engaged in a sort of wrestling match, and Cole was surprised by how well the guy fought.

Another set of arms came down and pinned Cole to the ground, but not before Cole got in another good kick. "Forgot this guy's a cage fighter," one of the cops grunted. Then Cole was on the ground, his face pressed firmly against dirt, his arms twisted firmly behind him. Cole winced against the pain as the cop pulled back his arms and cuffed him. The cop hauled him to his feet, twisting his arms hard in the process.

"You're under arrest," he said, "on charges of unlawful fraternization with a Prior."

Cole hung his head, allowing himself to be led to the cop car. His heart sank; there was no way out now, not even a way to get a message to Davis. Her life depended on them finding some way to counteract the illness. He couldn't rot in some prison and hope she'd be okay on her own. He racked his brain for some solution, some way out. There was nothing, only desperation and devastation where there had once been the greatest happiness he'd ever felt.

The detention center was cold and gray, a makeshift facility that looked cobbled out of cinder blocks. Cole thought that it had probably once been a hospital—the cells weren't cells at all but little individual rooms, all in a row, with locked metal doors. The cops hadn't talked on the way over and they didn't talk now—just shoved him into one of the rooms so hard that he stumbled and fell. He struggled to stand with his arms tied behind him, and he heard laughter through the door; he turned and saw the pudgy face of one of the cops frozen in a wide grin. Jeering. Exhausted, Cole sat on a cot in the corner; it represented the only furnishings in the room. It was cold, and he could feel the metal springs through the thin mat that covered it. He couldn't see any of the other in-mates, only a heavy stone door with a small window that faced another stone wall.

An hour—or maybe two—passed. Cole couldn't tell; his thoughts were racing in circles. Everything came back to the fact that the tabloids showed his face with Davis's. There was no way out of the situation. It didn't matter anymore that the only reason any of this had happened was because he wanted something better for his family—a happier life, away from the losing battle they were all fighting to survive. If he hadn't fallen for Davis, it might all have worked out. But it was impossible to think back to a time when he hadn't cared about her. None of it was her fault; he'd brought it on her. The thought of Davis suffering, possibly in pain—it made Cole rise to his feet, pace the room. He couldn't sit still and do nothing while she was in danger. He *had* to make things right. She'd been so scared when he saw her last. Her eyes, wide and bright with panic; her hands, trembling. Her mouth, her lips . . .

Finally the door cracked open, and a gruff voice ordered Cole to follow. He was led into a room only slightly larger than the one with the cot and instructed to sit down. He sat, and the cop sat across from him.

"You're being released on bail," the cop informed him. Cole straightened, his mind racing.

"But who—"

"Don't interrupt," the cop ordered, obviously irritated. He clenched and unclenched his jaw, shuffling through some paper-work on the desk. "It's important that you know that you're re-stricted to the Slants. Under *no* circumstances can you leave the Slants until your case has been closed." Cole struggled to his feet, his legs weak with adrenaline. Had his family collected money from the others in the Slants? But even with the help of friends, how had they come up with enough, and so fast? He felt sick, imagining what they'd probably gone through to get him out, how much they had to have put on the line.

"Sign here," the cop said, thrusting a piece of paper at him along with a pen. "I guess I'll have to uncuff you first." Cole's blood boiled. The cop was enjoying every second of this, and he was making no attempt to hide it. He strode over to Cole and unlocked the cuffs roughly, yanking Cole's shoulders hard in the process. His arms would be in bad shape for the FEUDS—if the FEUDS were even a possibility for him now. The thought hit him with such urgency that he nearly lost his balance. The cop glanced up at him, noticing him falter. Cole fought to appear calm, in control. He'd figure it out—there was always a way. He shook out his wrists and massaged his shoulders, glancing over the release form.

"I don't have all day," the cop informed him. "Sign it and leave, or get yourself back to the cell." Cole skimmed the text, which seemed pretty standard—it stated that he'd be staying in the Slants until the trial was concluded, and that any attempts to leave would result in immediate arrest. He signed.

The cop opened the door and gestured with his head for Cole to get lost.

A man in a suit awaited him in the lobby. One of Parson Abel's nameless, faceless staffers. The guy chomped down on some gum, or maybe candy, and held the door open for Cole.

There was a sleek black car waiting. Cole slid inside and faced Parson Abel. Very few Priors let their hair go gray, Cole had noted, but Parson's was so silver it was practically metallic.

"Got yourself into some trouble, huh, kid?" Parson grinned, and his prominent jaw showcased a crowning cleft at his chin.

"Have you heard anything about Davis?" It was the first thing

Cole could think to say, and his urgency was clear. Parson laughed, and Cole tried hard not to show his embarrassment. He'd laid all his cards on the table for Parson to exploit.

"She really got under your skin, didn't she?" he wanted to know. "Well, your little 'girlfriend,'" he said, using air quotes around the word, "turned you in. Betcha didn't know that, did you?"

"No." Cole reeled. It wasn't possible. "You're lying," he said, but Parson only laughed again.

"Yeah? I don't think so, buddy. Better just shake it off. Women are trouble every time." He clapped Cole on the shoulder, laughing, and Cole jerked away from his touch, which only amused Parson further. Cole felt sick inside. So she'd betrayed him. She could have kicked him, punched him, inflicted any bodily harm. Nothing physical could compare to the pain of her giving up on them. His mind reeled. He couldn't focus.

All he could do was glare at Parson Abel, refusing to speak. His skin crawled at the sight of his shiny forehead, his enhanced skin tone, his lab-rat lips. Parson Abel was broad, but not muscular. Powerful seeming, but it was just a carefully cultivated aura, Cole knew. Parson did not have the frame of an athlete.

"Shake off that anger, son," Parson said. "It's time to get back to training. I'm taking you straight to the Swings."

"And if I don't want to fight for you anymore?" Cole challenged.

"Oh," said Parson, raising his eyebrows. "You must be confused. I wasn't asking for your preferences, Cole. I've got a lot of money riding on this thing. You're fighting for me whether you want to or not."

Cole turned from him, staring out the window. He was trapped. He felt it all throughout his body. His head throbbed and he wanted to scream.

A hint of gold glimmered from inside Parson's suit, and as Parson leaned back, his jacket moved to reveal the gold-handled knife he always wore in his shirt pocket.

For an instant, Cole fantasized about grabbing that knife. He could easily swipe it from Parson's pocket. In less than one minute, Parson could be dead. Cole's body tensed, and he felt his hands begging to inch closer across the seat. Parson Abel didn't stand a chance against him; he knew it. Those broad shoulders and strong jaw hid a weak character and physique. Cole read him as a coward a mile away.

But then he realized: when it came down to it, without Davis, what did it matter? There was nothing left in Columbus for him if Davis was no longer a part of his future.

He'd win the fight. He'd get his family out of there, get out of town. He'd try to find a way to live a life without Davis, somewhere where everything around him didn't remind him of her. For now, he'd do the only thing he really knew how to do. He'd fight.

Cole could barely recognize downtown Columbus from the air as he made his way to the FEUDS in Parson's helicopter. "Protecting my investment," Parson had told him with a clap to his back, and although Cole had felt dirty—had cringed from the contact—the ride itself was taking his breath away. Cole was alone in the helicopter, as Parson himself had stayed back, instructing the pilot to deliver Cole to the FEUDS. It was smart, too; the violence was everywhere. Priors and Gens swarmed the streets. Cole might not have been able to fight his way through the masses of people to the FEUDS otherwise. The city spread out below him, beautiful despite the turmoil. The towers in the downtown segment rose above masses of rioters. He couldn't identify even an inch of extra space in the streets beneath him. The rioters looked like tiny dots from his vantage point, but they were clustered so tightly that the streets themselves were almost completely obscured.

As they drew closer to the landing pad, Cole could see Prior cops struggling to maintain control of the crowd. He squinted: from the variations in uniforms—some green, some an unfamiliar dark blue—it seemed like reinforcements had been called in from outside Columbus. They wore militia-grade guns and Cole suspected they had any number of other advanced weaponry on them: tear gas, paralytics, grenade launchers, digital revolvers. The Gens, Cole knew, had nothing that could compete with that. If the Prior cops decided to fire on the crowd, hundreds could die in a matter of minutes. He didn't understand why anyone would even want to come see him fight Noah when people were killing each other in the streets. But that was ridiculous; he knew it the second he thought it. They wanted to come see him fight, because they wanted to see him die. The thought sent panic spiraling through Cole's limbs, and he was glad they hadn't touched down yet, glad he still had a minute to himself.

Getting to the FEUDS would have been suicide without Parson's helicopter. *I'm lucky not to die* before *the fight,* he thought grimly. Parson Abel had promised not to let anything happen to him, and so far he'd made good on the promise. But what would happen after the fights were finished?

It would be hard for him to muster the energy to fight when every breath in light of Davis's betrayal was painful. He couldn't believe she'd turned him in. He literally couldn't comprehend it, not after everything they'd been through. Hadn't he shown her how much he cared? How could she take that and throw it all away? He wouldn't think about it—he couldn't. It would ruin him.

The helicopter touched down on top of a building directly across the street from the FEUDS, and when he approached, the crowds parted to let him in. They recognized him. It'd be impossible not to—he was shirtless, wearing a mouth guard along with low-slung shorts and taped wrists. With the sweat and filthy sheen of that afternoon still coating his body, he knew he looked menacing. Parson's guards ushered him roughly to a back office, standing guard outside the door while he shadowboxed.

He climbed into the cage to the sound of taunts and cheers. He moved in place, bouncing from one foot to the next, playing to the crowd. Cole couldn't help it; despite the brutality of the fights, he loved it. He loved knowing what his body could do if he let it. He loved that no-holds-barred sensation. And now, after everything that had happened with Davis, he was extra angry. Extra hungry to expel those emotions. Noah was already there, stretching and warming up. The cage door slammed behind him, and Cole heard its automatic lock click into place. There was no time for him to warm up. The clock was already marking down each second until the start, the crowd chanting along with it. Adrenaline coursed through him; all his nerves were on fire. His heart pounded in his ears.

*Three. Two. One.*

A burst of smoke, released for effect, filled the room. It clouded Cole's vision. Noah reacted more easily, going in for a punch. His fist connected just beneath Cole's rib cage, knocking him back a few steps. Cole bounced on the balls of his feet, landing a solid punch of his own to Noah's jaw. It knocked him on his back for a second. And then another smoke screen clouded his vision, complete with the thrumming of some kind of hypno-beat, designed to get the crowd wild.

And they were going wild. He could hear them screaming, feel their body heat from where they pressed up against the cage, wanting to be as close to the fighters as possible. As the smoke began to clear, he saw a glint of light in the cage. Then it disappeared. He squinted through the screen, blindly punching in order to keep Noah at bay until he could see well enough to place his jabs accurately.

"You're dead either way you look at it," Noah grunted between jabs. Cole didn't bother answering. Noah was trying to get in his head. It was obvious. "You'll die here or you'll rot in jail."

Cole hesitated. How did Noah know he'd just come from prison? The hesitation was enough to allow Noah to push him against the sides of the cage. "Guess your girlfriend didn't like it when she saw photos of you kissing that Prior slut," he growled, his face next to Cole's ear. His arm was positioned against Cole's windpipe, nearly cutting off his access to oxygen. "Maybe I'm actually doing you a little favor."

Something inside Cole clicked. Something wasn't right. Noah's words sank in.

Davis hadn't set him up. *Michelle* had! For an instant, his heart stopped. It was as if someone had hit pause for a millisecond. Then his vision cleared, and he was filled with an intense rush of adrenaline fueled by the need to see Davis, to find her and clear everything up as soon as possible. The adrenaline was enough for him to dislodge Noah's arm from his throat. He gained a little bit of leverage and managed to upset Noah's balance just slightly, regaining his own offensive stance, but it was too late.

He felt a sharp slash against his forearm, and the pain that followed was enough to make him gasp. The smoke cleared and he saw it: a gold knife, slim but razor-sharp, clutched in Noah's sweaty palm. Cole lifted his eyes to Noah's face. Noah's own eyes were wild and desperate. He thought back to the stories about Noah's prison time. Noah wasn't just fighting streetwise or dirty. He was fighting to kill.

The gold handle of the knife was etched with a familiar-looking crest. Cole's memories flashed through his head: there was the knife, glinting in the pocket of a sports jacket. There was the knife, every time Parson Abel tapped out his cigar and reached for his wallet in order to withdraw Cole's prize money. The same etched logo: a star above a scorpion. The same exact knife.

*I've got a lot of money riding on this fight.* Cole heard the words echoing in his brain, ricocheting around the sides of his skull. Parson had a lot of money riding on the fight. But not on Cole's victory. Not after the last fight, anyway. On this one, Cole realized in horror, Parson had money riding on the underdog. Cole forgot about everything as the truth of it sank in. All he could see were Parson Abel's beady eyes, his trademark cigar, his dimpled chin, and the way he was probably salivating with greed at that very moment. Everything faded—except the truth, now crystal clear.

He forgot about Noah, until Noah kneed him in the chest, sending him flying backward.

And then he was back in it.

Everyone was on their feet, going crazy with bloodlust. No one seemed to care that there was an illegal weapon in the cage. Cole leaped to his feet, barely avoiding a kick to the skull. He still had speed on his side, but he had to get the knife out of there.

He drew on his own knowledge of martial arts, vestiges of the research he'd done on Noah's fighting techniques, to land a karate chop to Noah's wrist, and then a second blow in the same place. The knife clattered to the floor of the cage. Cole and Noah rolled over each other punching wherever they could connect as they both scrambled for the weapon. Cole landed a right hook to Noah's temple, stunning him. Noah was on his back, and Cole used two or three seconds to roll atop him, pinning him. Noah struggled under his weight. He was still strong, still fighting. The knife was on the floor between Noah's head and his massive shoulders. Cole knew he had to get it, even if he didn't use it. He couldn't fight if Noah had it. He'd die.

Using all of his strength to hold Noah down, Cole leaned over and bit down on the knife handle, hard, just as Noah pushed Cole upward and over, shoving him backward. Cole held on to him, and they were both falling together, Cole on his back and Noah, having lost his balance, falling toward Cole. They both realized the same thing at the same time, but by the time they did, it was too late.

Cole had maintained his grip on the knife between his teeth. Noah was hurtling toward Cole's chest, powerless against the weight and velocity of his own body. Cole registered the panic in Noah's eyes just as the tip of the knife plunged into Noah's neck. It punctured and moved deeper as Noah's weight fell on it, its hilt sliding backward into Cole's throat at the same time. Noah let out a choked gurgle, blood pouring from his wound. Cole shoved Noah off him as hard as he could, releasing the knife from his mouth. His throat and teeth ached. His mind felt numb. Noah rolled to the ground, his eyes wide and lifeless, while Cole spit Noah's blood onto the floor.

The crowd went wild.

Noah.

Noah was *dead*.

Cole lurched to the side and vomited. They were long, hacking heaves that wouldn't stop. His sickness was the deep and searing kind, born of self-loathing. He hadn't meant to kill Noah. He hadn't meant for that to come of it. He had won, but the floor had fallen out from under him. The door to the cage clicked open, and three shirtless men entered the small enclosure to remove Noah's body. Cole dragged his gaze to the crowd. An eerie silence had fallen in the minute he'd taken to recover. Cole felt a sense of horror welling up from the pit of his stomach. What had he done? What would happen to him now?

But as he focused on the individual faces of the audience—the Gen girls in their bikinis, the Prior businessmen in their elevated seats—he realized they weren't looking at him, or the mess on the cage floor. No one was. Instead, their eyes were trained on the glass-enclosed loges where the major FEUDS donors sat. Cole could just make out the forms of several policemen surrounding the center loge. Then he saw Parson's form rising from his seat. Fury and relief and confusion overcame Cole in a rush as he saw Parson extend his hands, saw the Prior policemen clamp handcuffs over his wrists.

Now there were murmurs in the crowd, whispers, and rustling. Why had Parson been arrested? Cole couldn't make sense of it. If it was about FEUDS, stacking the bets—there was a good chance he'd be next. Cole took his chance while the crowd was still focused on Parson being led away by the police. He ran.

Cole ran until his lungs were burning more than they'd ever burned during any fight. He was certain he'd run for several miles by the time he saw Davis's sign. But it took him a long while to recognize it for what it was.

His mind felt thick with every emotion known to man: horror over what he'd done to Noah; dismay at what was almost certainly a loss of the FEUDS money now that Parson had been arrested; devastation at seeing his dream for his family ripped away; fear at his inability to control himself in the arena; confusion over what exactly had happened with Parson. But most of all, a strong undercurrent of hope. Because Davis hadn't sold him out. It meant somewhere in the city, she still loved him.

He'd never stop loving her. He wouldn't have stopped even if he'd always believed she'd sold him out, if he'd moved to another continent. Distance couldn't betray what he felt for her; it was so vast and selfless. It was what was propelling his feet through the streets of Columbus—streets he was technically banned from—when a flashing light began to beam in the sky.

Why hadn't she shown up? Why hadn't she come to him, knowing he'd be there? How would he ever find her now? He needed a sign from her. Anything. It was a moment when, if he'd believed in prayer—if he'd thought God existed—he would have prayed with all his heart. Instead, he hoped. And finally, after the light in the sky flashed for the third, then the fourth time . . . he knew.

This was his sign. It was her. The light was Davis, calling him to her. He couldn't explain the certainty with which he felt it; he just knew.

# 17

## DAVIS

She wondered how long it would take for someone to notice the spotlight and tell her to stop. How long would it take for someone to discover she wasn't asleep in her bed, how long could she sit here, shivering, before she could accept that he hadn't read her sign at all—and he wasn't coming?

It had been at least an hour. The sun had fully set, and all that was left was the clear night sky, dappled with clusters of stars. There was a chill in the air, but although Davis knew she should go inside and warm up—accept that Cole hadn't and wouldn't see her signal—she couldn't bring herself to leave the hospital rooftop. She'd never managed to replace her DirecTalk, and she didn't even know if Cole had a working one of his own. There was no way to reach him. No way except this. So Davis flicked the switch on, flicked it off, over and over, a mechanical manifestation of her hope.

Her arm was stiff and sore, her fingers frozen and practically powerless to manipulate the switch. Still, she forced herself to keep going. Her eyes were growing heavier by the minute, so much so that she didn't even trust herself to climb back to her room. Not that it was possible. Above the mini roof deck where she sat, there was a fire escape that led three more stories up. Her room was two above that—she'd had to dangle and drop onto the next lowest fire escape. Now, with her limbs stiff and cold, she couldn't hope to hoist herself up again. She'd have to enter through another floor. Once her father found out she'd managed to escape again, he'd probably take extra measures to make sure it couldn't happen a third time. Davis felt a strange sense of anxiety mixed with an awful lethargy that threatened to overcome her. She felt her arm drop to her side. She couldn't keep up with the signal; it was too much. She folded into herself, huddling in the corner of the roof deck, willing herself not to fall asleep. Trying by sheer force of determination to keep her eyes open. It was dark on the roof now that she'd stopped operating the spotlight.

When she saw the hand, dirt-encrusted and bloody, wrapping itself over the top of the wall nearest the fire escape, she thought it was a nightmare. She shrieked, scooting backward on the roof until her back hit the wall. Then the rest of the form emerged, climbing up the fire escape and over the low wall that bordered the roof. It was ominous and bloody in the dark, and . . . familiar. Davis opened her mouth to scream again.

"Davis! Don't. It's me." Cole's voice emerged from the hulking figure. "It's me." He moved toward her, and all of a sudden her entire body was trembling, and she let out several choking sobs. It was him. He'd found her.

She moved toward him, all fears evaporating. "What happened?" she asked as he pulled her to his bare chest. She was on her knees and he was reaching for her, then kneeling down also, until they were both hugging like that, the cold pavement pressing up through their legs while they knelt on the roof. Somehow, it felt like heaven. It felt like everything was going to be okay again. She was gasp-sobbing into his chest; he smelled like sweat and dirt and she realized there was nothing better than Cole in any state at all. When he was with her, she felt okay.

But the blood . . .

"What happened to you?" She pushed back, scrutinizing his torso for wounds, which seemed to be everywhere. "Oh my God. The FEUDS. Cole." He turned away, but from the pain she caught in his eyes just before he did, she knew something wasn't right. That was when she noticed he was breathing hard. His movements seemed jerky, and all of that calm composure he'd always had was gone, replaced by something panicked and animalistic. He took two ragged breaths in and she waited, keeping her hand on his forearm.

"He's dead," he told her, clenching his jaw. He blinked rapidly; he was clearly fighting tears. Davis's heart stilled.

"Who?" she said. "Cole, who?"

"Noah. Guy from the FEUDS. Davis," he whispered, moving toward her—and this time it was he who needed comfort—"I killed him."

She tried not to pull away in shock, but she couldn't keep her face impassive.

He laughed bitterly, hopelessly. "How can you look at me after this? Of course you can't. I didn't mean to," he said, his voice thick with desperation. "He pulled a knife on me . . . I didn't know what I was doing until it was over." He stopped, fighting for breath. His next words came out in a rush. "I'm a monster," he spit out, choking on a sob. "I must disgust you." He pulled away from her, kneading his forehead with one hand. And then he cried, freely.

Davis had never seen a man lose control. But she wasn't afraid or repulsed. She'd always needed him more than he needed her, but here he was, asking for her help. She moved toward him, wrapping her arms around his shoulders and burying her face in his neck. She didn't care about his blood or the way he looked or what he'd done because his heart was pure, and it was hers. "Shh," she told him, running her hands through his hair. "It's going to be okay. You didn't have a choice. You'll be okay." She meant it. She didn't know how, but she'd do anything to make it happen.

He wiped his eyes roughly and kissed her cheek. He ran his hands through her hair. "This is all I wanted," he said. "I saw your signal and I—I didn't know for sure it was you, but I felt it, and I went after it, and all I wanted was to see you again. I had to run, I had to see you. And now . . . Oh, God."

"What, Cole? It'll be okay, I promise. Whatever it is, we'll work it out."

He shook his head violently. "How can it? Not after this. I'm as good as dead. Parson, the police—they'll never rest until I'm hanged."

His words pierced her. It couldn't happen. She was filled with a profound urgency. She wouldn't let it happen. She put one hand on his face, one on the back of his neck, forcing him to look at her. "Cole," she said. "You're not a monster. And you're not going to die. We're together. You know how we make things work when we're together. No one can stop us. You can't give up." He laughed a little, palming his eyes.

"I won't," he whispered, meeting her gaze. "I'll never give up if you're beside me."

She looked hard into his eyes, which were wide and earnest. She knew he meant it. He cared about her more than anything else—she could feel it in every word, every touch. She leaned closer to him. She was finally certain of everything she'd been feeling; it had come together upon seeing him, focusing itself in her heart.

"I love you," she whispered. "I love you so much." He drew in a breath, then pulled her to him, kissing her urgently.

"You're cold," he said, pulling back, breathless.

"You, too. You're the one without a shirt on," she pointed out, smiling a little.

"I'm okay. But your skin . . . you're so cold." He scanned the roof deck, and she followed his gaze to a tiny glass enclosure on the opposite end of the roof. "There," he said, helping her stand up. "We'll be warmer inside." They walked over to the enclosure, his arms wrapped around her waist, steadying her.

Once inside, she realized exactly how cold she'd been. Her body was shaking uncontrollably, and although he was shaking, too, her discomfort was more violent. She felt weak and tired, yet charged by his presence. "What is this?" she asked, looking around the tiny cubicle.

"I'm not sure. A lookout point?" The room was bare aside from a set of high-definition, magnifying goggles. "Yeah, it's gotta be a lookout of some sort. Here, come here." He sat cross-legged against the glass, pulling her onto his lap. She leaned her back against him, and he nestled his chin in the crook of her neck. "I don't deserve you," he breathed into her skin. She felt goose bumps rise along her neck and shoulders and spine in response.

"That isn't true," she heard herself insist. "It's the other way around. I could be dying. If you were smart, you'd leave me. You'd run away before you're found." She pulled away from him a little, but he wrestled her back into him. Their body heat was slowly warming her, and she found herself wriggling closer into his embrace. "I won't let you stay here and die for me," she whispered.

"You don't even know." He laughed. "I don't have a choice. I love you." He paused, and she let the words wash over her in a warm rush. "I'd die without you. Don't you get it?" She turned a little so her torso was angled sideways against his, and he cradled her head to his chest. "No matter what, I'll be with you. I'm not going to leave you again. I'd die sooner than let anything happen to you. No matter how bad things get. I'm immune to Narxis, Davis. Without you, there's nothing. I'll find you a cure. I'll protect you. Leaving you isn't an option."

She twisted toward him and looked up, and his lips were there, on hers, and his tongue was searching her mouth, and everything around them was electrified.

"We can't be together always," she told him, finally pulling apart. She struggled to find the words; her breath was uneven, and all she wanted to do was bury herself inside him. But she had to say this one thing. "You *need* to go in the morning, Cole. Stay for now, but then you have to go. It's the only way for us to have a chance. If they catch you with me in the morning..." Her words trailed off, but they both knew the implications.

"But if I go, this might be it. Our last night together." He didn't say "forever," but the word hung between them, unspoken.

"If you don't go, it *will* be our last night together. If you go—and try to save yourself—we have a chance." Davis felt tears flowing down her cheeks and neck, and he bent to kiss them away, starting at her collarbone until she was gasping for breath. He pulled her face to his, ever so gently, but his mouth found hers with an intensity she'd never felt. She moved backward until she was lying on the cold cement rooftop, and she brought his body with her. He pulled back for a brief second, his eyes searching. But she'd never wanted anything more. She didn't have to answer him; he saw it, and then he was on top of her, strong but as gentle as she'd ever been touched. It was more and bigger than anything she'd ever felt. Every brush of his lips on her skin made her feel whole and alive, more so than anything ever had—even dancing, even leaping across the stage in the most exhilarating of highs.

He was hers, and every touch conveyed it. He ran his finger down her neck, onto her collarbone, her breastbone, her stomach. She pulled him to her, pressing her body against his, fully aware of how warm his skin felt. She kissed his stomach and chest, tasting the salt from his fight. He cradled her to him, kissing her lips and cheeks and forehead and finally just holding her there in the night until they were charged, both so charged, but unbearably exhausted.

She didn't want to fall asleep. She wanted to hit pause on this night forever, just live in these moments. But finally she felt herself fading into the comfort of his embrace. "I love you," she whispered . . . or at least she thought she had said it, but it was hard now to distinguish reality from a dream. He kissed her shoulder and pulled her tighter, and she let herself relax into him, allowing the whole world to fade away.

# 18

## COLE

When he woke, Davis was stirring and the darkness of the night was just beginning to fade. At first it seemed like a miracle, waking with her small, beautiful body in his arms. Her face was pressed against his arm, and he never wanted to move it. But the fluttering of her eyelashes as she blinked away sleep tickled, and when he moved just a little, she opened her pretty green eyes.

"I love you," he whispered, just as she whispered, "You have to leave."

He laughed ruefully. "Not exactly the kind of good morning I hoped to hear." She smiled up at him and kissed him once, then twice on the lips, but he could tell she was serious and he knew she was right. "I'll leave," he told her. "But only because it's the best way for me to make sure we have more nights like this one." She nodded, burying her head against his chest. He felt her silky brown waves against his skin and tried to memorize the sensation so he could play it on repeat after he'd gone.

"God," he groaned, pulling her toward him. "Life was much easier without you, Ms. Morrow. Much easier and much less amazing." She shoved him lightly with one hand and pried herself from his arms, which was a good thing, because he didn't trust himself to let her go.

"Get out of here," she ordered, her voice firm. Still, she couldn't meet his gaze. "The sooner you leave, the sooner we'll be together again."

"Promise me," he pleaded, "that you'll take care of yourself. We'll find you a cure. But promise you'll stay in the hospital and let them take care of you until I can come back for you." He grasped her hand, squeezing it tighter as he spoke.

She nodded, pulling her gaze to his. "I promise," she said. The sun's first rays began to filter over the rooftop, and they both saw it at the same time. "Go," she told him. "You need to go right now."

"I'll look for you, forever," he told her. "I love you." He bent over her for one last, lingering kiss. And then he was gone.

Cole went home first. He had to disappear entirely, but if he left any kind of note, he'd be putting his family in danger, too. He had to say his good-byes quickly, and in person. As soon as he stepped inside his mother's bedroom and saw her sleeping figure, he knew he'd made the right choice in taking the risk. He gave her a quick kiss on the forehead, careful not to wake her. He wanted to say good-bye, and that he was sorry for putting her through all the worry and stress she must be feeling. He wanted to explain to her that everything was about to get better, with just a little time . . . if she could only give him some time, he'd fix it all. But waking her—and fielding her questions—would be a mistake. Instead, he gave her hand a gentle squeeze and walked as soundlessly as possible from the room.

Outside the house, the air was blustery. Cole's only thought was how to disappear, and where. He stood for a second in front of the house, trying to sort out his thoughts. It was still early enough that not many people were out and about, so he was startled when he heard a loud "Hey," and swiveled quickly, instantly on his guard.

Michelle stood before him, tearful and disheveled, her thick hair tangled and crazy looking. She'd obviously been hoping to catch him—she lived a five-minute walk away, but she must have been staking out the place, hoping he'd show up. "Hi," he said, his tone guarded. He looked left and right, trying to judge whether this was another trap—whether Michelle was out for the ultimate revenge, locking him away for good.

"Cole, I—" She moved toward him and winced when he took a step back, away from her.

"What do you want, Michelle?"

She lifted a fist to her mouth, her red-rimmed eyes tearing up for what clearly wasn't the first time. She had dark circles under the red. "So you know," she said.

Cole nodded, feeling his jaw tense up.

"I'm so sorry," she choked out. "I thought I was protecting you. I thought . . . I thought if I told them, I'd save you from Noah. I thought if you were in jail, at least you'd be alive."

"That's fucked-up logic, Michelle," Cole said, but he was al-

ready losing some of the anger that had fueled him a moment ago.
She looked a mess. And she looked sincere. Somewhere inside, she
probably really *had* been trying to look out for him.

"I know," she said, struggling to speak through her tears. "And
I'm so sorry. You have no idea. You have to believe me, Cole. I
thought you were going to die. Please believe me—I don't care
what happened between us. I just care about you. I heard a ru-
mor. Noah was talking to some of the guys . . ." She trailed off,
but Cole perked up.

"Yeah? About the knife?"

She bit her lip, nodding. "He said he wanted to kill you. That
he *would* kill you. Please believe I never thought it would wind up
like this. I thought you'd be safe in jail . . . and now Noah's dead.
It's all my fault." Michelle broke down, sobbing. She stood there,
her hands covering her face, and she looked so sad, so hopeless.
Cole felt his guard crack. She'd caused so much trouble, but she'd
been confused—trying to help in her own misguided way. He
couldn't help going to her.

"Hey," he said, wrapping her in a hug. "It's not your fault. You
were trying to do the right thing." Even as he said it, he knew
part of her motives probably had stemmed from something misguided. Anger, or revenge. But she looked so miserable and sorry
that he couldn't find it in himself to be angry. "It's not your fault,"
he told her. "I'm so sorry. I never meant for you to get involved in
any of this. You were never supposed to get hurt.' His words
sounded wooden. The problem was, no one was supposed to get
hurt. But it was starting to feel like he could no longer control the
fallout. He wondered how many more people would be casualties
of what he'd started.

Michelle pulled back, wiping her eyes roughly. "Where are you
going to go?" she asked.

Cole shrugged. "I'll figure it out."

"You don't have a plan? Cole, what . . . ?" She trailed off, biting her lip. Her expression mirrored his desperation. He had no plan, and winging it hadn't gotten him anywhere good so far. He felt backed into a corner, trapped, and time was running out. A cold sense of terror washed over him as he realized exactly how bad this was. He *had* to go somewhere safe while he contemplated what to do about Davis. He had so few choices and no time at all. Nowhere in the Slants was completely safe, he realized. Nowhere in Columbus was safe. He racked his brain for solutions and came up short.

"They won't stop looking until they've tracked you down," Michelle said softly. *Tracked.* The word settled under his skin, triggering some visceral reaction. He was being hunted.

"They won't stop until I'm dead," he realized. Michelle met his eyes; she didn't say anything, but he could see from her somber expression that he was right.

"I'm afraid for you," she told him.

"Wait a second," he said. "They really won't quit until they know I'm dead," he said, thinking aloud. He felt himself getting excited; it was the key to everything. If he couldn't win by fighting against them, he'd have to work *with* them. "Don't you see?" he asked Michelle. She looked blank. "I have to give them what they want. I have to die."

Michelle's jaw dropped and she shook her head, hard. "Cole, what are you saying?"

"No, no. I don't really have to die. I just have to make it look like I did. If I stage it convincingly enough," he said, "they'll call off the hunt. I can be free to disappear."

She nodded, but she still looked doubtful. "How are you going to pull that off?" she asked.

"I'll need your help," he responded.

"No." Michelle took a step back, looking over her shoulder. "I took a huge risk just meeting you here. I just wanted to apologize. I don't want to get involved in any of this. If they think I'm helping you . . . I could be dead, too."

"Michelle," Cole said. "Please, Michelle. If we do this right, it's the safest possible way. It might be the only way out of this mess."

"It's the only way you can see her again," she responded, her voice getting hard. A flash of pain crossed her eyes, but Cole nodded. It was time for him to be as honest as possible with Michelle. "You care about her a lot," she continued.

"I do."

"Then I'll help." Her chin trembled slightly, but she didn't cry. He was reminded of a time when they were both kids, when Michelle had fallen from the top of the slide that used to exist at the Swings, back when it was still a playground. She'd been so brave, while Cole had been the one to panic.

Cole pulled her into another hug. He'd known Michelle nearly all his life. Her willingness to help despite everything that had happened between them—despite the feelings she carried, which had long gone unanswered—touched him in a way he couldn't articulate.

Five minutes later, they were knocking lightly on the door to Worsley's lab. It was still early morning, but in another twenty minutes or so, people would be rising for the day. Cole had to put his plan in motion, fast. Worsley answered, bright-eyed. He was a hard worker; Cole guessed he'd probably been up for hours already. Surprise crossed his face when he registered Cole and Michelle. Surprise turned to shock when Cole said, "We need a body."

"No. Absolutely not." Worsley shook his head but ushered them inside anyway. "What are you thinking, Cole? Haven't you gotten yourself into enough trouble?"

"Just listen." Cole laid out his plan point by point, watching Worsley's face shift to skepticism and, finally, to reluctant agreement.

"There is a body," he said, sucking down his second cup of coffee. Cole had accepted his own gratefully, only to find that nerves and adrenaline had made his stomach too hopped up to drink anything at all. Cole breathed a sigh of relief, then hated himself for doing so. Another body meant another victim. The virus was continuing to spread. "It was dumped yesterday. Still hasn't been identified."

"How bad is it?" Cole felt like such a jerk asking it, but it was essential that the body be damaged enough that it couldn't be identified on sight alone.

"Bad," Worsley said. "Completely mangled." Michelle winced. "But you know how it is, Cole. These families are so eager to disassociate themselves from the disease. No Prior wants to admit what's happening."

"It would be easy enough to switch identities," Cole said, and Tom nodded.

"No one will care to ask questions. We just have to get your information into the system."

"But who's in charge of doing that?" Cole wondered aloud. This was the crucial part of his plan. He knew Worsley had something to do with identifying and tagging the bodies, but he didn't know how easy it would be to circumvent the system. To his surprise, Worsley shrugged.

"I'm handling most of it," he said. "No one else in the Slants understands DNA coding. It would be easy for me to make this happen. I'm not on board ethically, but . . ." He trailed off, his eyes softening as he looked at Cole. "You know I'd do anything for you.

No one's claiming these bodies anyway." Cole's throat tightened, and he swallowed hard. Worsley was like a brother to him, but Cole was asking a lot. The fact that Worsley was on board—even enthusiastic—was the key to his survival.

"So what do I have to do?" he asked, his voice gruff.

"I can do it right now," Worsley said. "I don't have the body in my lab, but I can get your information sorted out here and link it to the photos of the body. They're already registered in our database. I'll find a way to leak the news to the media later today."

"That's perfect," Cole told him. "You have no idea how much—"

"Don't worry," Worsley told him, clapping him on the shoulder. "I would have done much more. You two need to get out of here now, before there are too many people out there."

"Who are you, now that you're 'dead'?" Michelle asked as they exited Worsley's lab en route for Michelle's dad's general store.

Cole took furtive glances around them; people were definitely awake—he could see shadows in profile through trailer windows and smell coffee in the air—but so far, the streets were still empty. Still, he quickened his pace. "We'll figure that part out later," he said. "A new name is all I need, really."

"You can stay here as long as you want," she said, unlocking the door to the store, a small, one-story concrete structure. "No one ever goes down to the basement, even with deliveries. It's too damp down there. Food was rotting and all the paperwork was mildewed. Just don't make too much noise. It opens at ten A.M. every day, and closes at seven. If my dad hears you . . ." She hesitated. "I can't be sure he won't turn you in."

"I'll be careful," Cole assured her. She opened the trapdoor to the basement and the stench of mold and rot assaulted his nostrils. He took a deep breath and began to lower himself down the rickety wooden ladder into the darkness. "If he does catch me, I'll tell him you had nothing to do with it," he said. "I'll make sure he thinks I broke in myself."

"Okay," she said, already backing away. "Okay."

"Wait," Cole called out, pulling himself back up the few steps to say good-bye.

"Thank you." He gave her a kiss on the cheek. When he pulled away, her eyes were sad.

"Aren't you forgetting something?" she asked. Cole looked at her, questioning. "If I were your girlfriend," she started, not meeting his eyes, "and I heard that you were dead, I'd be heartbroken." She stopped, but Cole was still confused. Then it dawned on him.

"I have to get her a message," he said. Michelle was right. But how? "It's so risky."

"I can get it to her." He looked at her in shock, but now she was looking at him directly, her gaze steady. "You have to tell her. Believe me. I know what it would be like." Her tone was firm, but her eyes looked pained. He knew what this offer was costing her.

"I want to," he said. "But you've already done so much. If someone finds the note, finds out it's a lie . . ." He trailed off, shaking his head. "If someone finds out you're involved, I'd never forgive myself." There was so much at stake. But she was right. Davis would be devastated if she thought he was dead. She might leave the hospital . . . she might forget her promise to him to keep herself safe. "Are you sure?" he asked. Michelle was so brave. And this, he knew, was the ultimate sacrifice.

Michelle nodded. "You're forgetting who you're dealing with," she said, cracking a smile. "I don't *get* caught." She dug a pen and paper out of her satchel and he scrawled a quick note to Davis. *I love you*, he wrote. *I'm okay*. He was hoping it was direct enough for Davis to understand but vague enough that, if it were found, it wouldn't mean much of anything to anyone else. He handed the note to Michelle. Giving him a wave, she lowered the trapdoor hatch over him as he descended again, careful not to pull the latch.

Then she was gone, and he was left alone in total darkness.

## ❧ 19 ❧

### DAVIS

Davis climbed back through the window, wriggling her form through the narrow gap and awkwardly descending, hands first, into the room. Thoughts of Cole consumed her: how to clear his name, how to get him out of trouble. She was so distracted that she was nearly to her feet by the time she looked up and caught sight of the silent figure sitting in a chair on the left side of the room. Davis had to clap a hand over her mouth to stifle a gut-reaction scream. But it wasn't one of the security guards sitting there, or her father, waiting to take even more extreme measures to keep her locked up. It was Vera.

Vera raised an eyebrow, smirking at Davis's disheveled appearance. "I've never seen you look so ungraceful," she commented, careful to keep her voice low. Davis half laughed, half gasped, her pulse thrumming wildly. Then she covered the narrow expanse of the room in just a step or two and threw herself into her best friend's arms.

"How are you here?" she wanted to know, pulling back to look at Vera. Vera looked as beautiful as ever; her dark hair swept into a careless knot atop her head, her slight frame dwarfed by a green tunic over tights. Slouchy black boots completed her style, which Davis had long ago dubbed "accidental chic," like Vera had just happened to throw on the exact random things that worked together and worked on her. But Vera's face was creased with worry, and her smile seemed more tempered than usual.

"What's up? Why *are* you here?" Davis asked again, pulling back to examine her friend's face. "It's got to be"—she took a quick glance at the digital monitor on her wall—"oh, my gosh. It's barely eight. You're late for class."

"I was worried," Vera said, bringing a thumb to her mouth and gnawing on its cuticle. Davis could see that her other fingernails were ragged. Vera had grown out of the habit years ago. It touched Davis to know that her friend's distress was so real. "You weren't answering your DirecTalk, so I called Terri. You just left the other night, without any explanation. You could have waited to say good-bye . . ."

"I'm sorry." Davis shook her head. She'd been an awful friend; there was no question of that. "I just . . . there's been so much going on. I've wanted to tell you, but it's like it's happening faster than I can control it. I'm so sorry. I haven't known how to handle it. But I should have talked to you sooner."

"Why are you here? Are you sick?" Vera wanted to know. Davis took several steps back, nodding. She realized belatedly that she'd hugged Vera, maybe risking her friend's exposure. Even being in this room could be a threat to Vera's health.

"I think so," Davis explained, wary of being too specific. She settled on the edge of her bed. It seemed like a safe enough distance from where her friend stood in the living area of the room. "You probably shouldn't be here. It might be contagious." Vera's eyes widened at this. "Where are the security guards?" Davis continued. "I'm surprised they let you in here."

"They weren't too hard to convince." Vera shrugged. "I just smiled a lot. I think they put in a call to your dad and he okay'd it as long as you stay inside."

"Didn't they see the window?" Davis gestured to the windowpane, which was still ajar, causing the flimsy white curtains that bordered it to lift in the breeze.

Vera shook her head. "They didn't watch me; I came in alone. And when I saw it I figured you'd climbed up to the roof." She smiled a little, her eyes warming. "We used to do it all the time," she reminded her. "It's kind of your MO."

Davis smiled. It was true. Climbing things had always sort of been the easiest way to circumvent authority. The roof of her apartment building had practically been their secret headquarters. Going up there undiscovered had always given her a rush, kind of like roofing. And Vera had never shied from adventure.

"So," Davis said, wanting to address the obvious elephant in the room. She looked at her own hands, her own cuticles—ragged not from chewing but from climbing, and just generally being places she wasn't supposed to be. "I guess you've seen the pictures."

Vera was silent for so long that Davis thought she hadn't heard her. Then she spoke, staring Davis straight in the eye. "I wish you'd told me."

Her words conveyed the hurt she must have been feeling for a while. Davis realized how it must look from her friend's perspective. She'd been secretive, distant. Vera probably felt cut out. "I'm sorry," she told her. "I wanted to say something. I just . . . didn't know how. And I didn't want to get you in trouble."

"You know, Davis," Vera said, her eyes troubled, "I'm stronger than I look. I've met Cole. I don't think he's a bad guy. The papers . . . I think they're exaggerating all of it. Because they don't know him. I understand why you've kept it a secret, but I wish you'd trusted me. I've . . . I've really needed you lately. I feel like you just up and disappeared when everything's been such a mess."

"What do you mean?" Davis felt alarmed; was Vera sick, too?

"Olympiad results came in," Vera said. "But you already knew that."

"No," Davis told her, shocked. "I didn't have any idea."

"Really?" Vera wrinkled her brow. "I can't believe no one said anything. Because you qualified." She paused, and Davis waited for some sort of reaction to sink in. But the news felt wooden, meaningless. Vera could have told her it was about to rain and generated the same response. It just didn't matter. None of it mattered when Cole was in danger, and she might be fighting Narxis, and her fate and her love hung in the balance. The Olympiads felt trivial, like a problem from someone else's life. It was amazing that it had once been the most important thing in her life, Davis realized.

"Davis?" Vera looked at her, astonished. "Aren't you happy?"

"Of course," Davis said, mustering a smile. A month ago, she would have been deliriously happy at the prospect of dancing with the best, like her mother did, and making her father proud. But now the news just felt inconsequential. Still, it mattered to Vera. The Olympiads always had. Her dreams of becoming a classical musician rested on it, and her family was counting on her. They'd always had that in common. "But what about you? What's a mess? What's going on?" A growing feeling of dread had begun to form in the pit of her stomach. Vera looked miserable. Her heart went out to her friend; all she wanted to do was wrap her in her arms, but the knowledge that she might be contagious held her back.

"I didn't qualify," Vera whispered, tears forming in the corners of her eyes. "I—I was distracted. Nervous. I screwed up."

"Oh, Vera."

"My parents won't talk to me," she went on, choking out the words. "Oscar can barely look at me. Everything's horrible." She broke down, sobbing.

"It'll be okay," Davis told her, trying her best to soothe her friend, wanting desperately to wrap her in her arms. Davis felt herself tearing up at the thought of the pain Vera had been going through, and how alone her friend must have felt. "I'm so sorry, Vera. I wish I'd been there for you right away. I'm so sorry you've been dealing with this alone. Your parents will get over it, though, I promise." Even as she said it, she wasn't sure; Vera's parents were strict, dogmatic. They had never been as sympathetic to Vera as Davis's dad had been to her.

"It's okay," Vera said, wiping her eyes with the back of her hand. "I know you've had your own things going on. Clearly." She laughed a little. "But it's just . . . I wanted to talk to you. I've been feeling weird lately."

"Weird how?" Davis felt panic forming in a tight knot in her chest. If Vera had Narxis . . .

"Just, I don't know. Off."

"Dizzy? Nauseated?"

Vera shook her head. "No. It's . . . it's something else. Not sick, exactly. I'm just . . ." She hesitated, seeming uncertain of how to continue. "I don't want to worry you. I'm sure it's nothing. I don't want to talk about it quite yet."

"Okay," Davis said doubtfully. "But I'm here when you're ready. And I'm not going to let anything bad happen to you. Cole was a secret because . . . I didn't want to hurt you, or get you in trouble. I was worried I couldn't trust him. But I should have trusted you. I know better now. No secrets."

Vera smiled through her tears and nodded at Davis. "No secrets. D.M. plus V.S. equals BFF, right?" She extended her wrist to show Davis that she was wearing the little charm bracelet they'd both worn every single day as kids. Vera's was a red rope with a heart charm and their secret motto etched in the heart. Davis's own was blue, and it was home in her jewelry box, where it had lain for most of high school, after they'd grown out of that sort of sentimental thing. It touched her now that Vera had remembered, had cared enough to put it on.

"Remember how we used to scribble it everywhere?" she asked.

"Desks, walls . . . we got in trouble all the time," Vera responded, laughing. It had seemed important at the time to write it on every surface, like the message was one everyone should see. They'd been so innocent then, Davis realized. They'd had no idea what was waiting in their futures. A nurse walked by the room and Davis was jolted from her reverie. She glanced at the clock, realizing nearly twenty minutes had passed. Her dad would be back soon to check on her now that it was morning. Vera followed her gaze.

"Security guards were easy to flirt past. Doctors . . . probably not so much," she said. "I should go." Davis nodded, and before she could stop her, Vera had crossed the room and wrapped her in a final hug. "Stay strong," she told her. "And get yourself a new DirecTalk. We haven't gone this long without talking in . . ."

"Ever," Davis finished. "You stay strong, too, Ver. Chin up." Vera flashed her a wan smile and was gone before Davis could say anything else.

Davis was alone.

Something about Vera's memory, her bracelet—the initials, etched in that cheap metal charm—had bothered her. It was sitting in the back of her brain, refusing to be ignored. She fought to think why it was bothering her.

Then she realized, leaping to her feet. The initials.

The Imp orderly had signed initials at the bottom of her birth record: "L.E." What if that person was still working at the hospital and knew what the error code meant? And if he or she did, maybe she'd also be able to tell Davis why Narxis wasn't affecting her. Even better, Davis thought, heart pounding as she moved toward the door, maybe the orderly knew enough about it to help her find a cure. But she had to move fast. Her father would be back soon. She stopped herself just before reaching the door; there was no way she'd get past the guards, who had just seen Vera out. Instead she backed away, heading for the window. She had to do it. She didn't care if her father showed up while she was gone. She didn't have a choice.

Davis exited through the window again and scaled the wall down to the balcony below. On the balcony was a door she hadn't noticed before, and she pushed through it, praying it wouldn't trigger an alarm. Instead, it opened soundlessly to reveal another small staircase leading downward to a second door and a hallway.

Davis slipped through the door and down the hallway, keeping her head low; her palms were sweating and every nerve in her body was on high alert. She did a lap around this floor—the fifteenth— before finding an unattended computer in a tiny office labeled 1531. She entered the username and passcode she'd memorized from before, and sure enough, the screen lit up. It didn't take long to access the employee directory.

Davis scrolled through hundreds of names, growing more desperate by the minute. She sorted them by "last initial E." That narrowed it down a little—but there was no one listed with a last name beginning with *E* whose first name started with an *L*. Then she realized these listings were of current employees only. Maybe the person who'd checked her in no longer worked there. She clicked on another tab, sorting staff records by year. From there she could access records from previous employees.

She quickly scrolled to the year of her birth. With every second that passed, she felt the window of opportunity closing. Finally, her hands shaking so much she could barely manipulate the system, she found it: the staff profile of a woman named Leslie Eide, who had quit working the very week Davis was born. It could not have been a coincidence. It was her. The directory listed an address in the Slants.

This was it, she realized. This was her only lead, the most promising lead. But what if the address was no longer current? Davis realized it was a long shot, but it was enough to give her hope. It was her one chance to figure out why she hadn't succumbed to the disease like everyone else. With trembling fingers, she exited the system and moved from the room without looking back.

"Hey," she heard someone call out behind her. "Hey. Stop!" But she didn't pause to look back. Instead she ducked her head and ran for the guest elevators. She wasn't going back to her room. Not when they'd probably lock her up there for good. She was going to the Slants.

The journey to the Slants wasn't as difficult, now that she'd been there a few times before. She knew the best dark corners to duck into, and, with her long auburn hair loose and tangled around her face, she felt relatively anonymous. Her clothes were ripped and her skin scratched from where she'd slid in and out of the hospital window, and she was almost certain her face was flushed from exertion. But these things, she reasoned, would work in her favor once she got to the Slants. She crossed the river by motie easily, no longer afraid of the leering old men who had once terrified her so. It was only once she stepped off the vessel to the other side of the water and eyed the ramshackle communities stretching out ahead of her for a mile that she realized how hard it would be to track down Leslie Eide's house on her own.

She'd have to ask for help. She thought about trying Worsley's lab, but she didn't want to waste any time, and there were rows of houses right there in front of her, presumably containing dozens of people who could help. If she made her way to Worsley's—and it turned out to be out of the way—she'd be wasting time and risking getting caught. Plus, she ran the risk of Worsley trying to convince her to stay for testing. She didn't want him to sniff after her plan. She needed to do this on her own.

Davis ran her hand through her hair, tousling it so it would be even gnarlier looking than it already was. Then she approached the first fully lit house she saw: a tiny cinder-block structure that looked like it couldn't contain more than two small rooms. She knocked lightly on the door, and an old man in a dirty wifebeater answered. Davis just barely stopped herself from uttering a sigh of relief—an old man like this might not keep up with the news. Maybe he wouldn't recognize her.

"Eide," he said thoughtfully, tugging at his few remaining strands of white hair, which hung lank above his left ear. "Sounds f'miliar. Rae," he shouted over his shoulder. "Rae-Rae? You know an Eide family? Someone by the name of Leslie?"

"Sure do." The mature, feminine voice preceded a heavyset woman wearing jeans and a long-sleeved T-shirt. She approached the door and clapped her hands twice as if to rid them of flour or dust. "Who's asking?" She leaned in, squinting at Davis. "You look familiar," she said finally. "Do I know you?"

"No," Davis said. "Well . . ." She scrambled to think. "I'm Tom Worsley's cousin. We've seen each other around, I'm sure."

"Yes! Of course." The woman's eyes lit up, though they betrayed a lingering hint of confusion. "Tommy's cousin. Okay then. Why didn't you just ask Tommy? Well, never mind. The Eides have been over by the band shell for years. I want to say house number ten or twelve. It's, you know, one of those trailer ones, but it's green colored, from what I recall. She's been there for years, and her mother before her."

"By the band shell?" Davis was relieved to know where that was.

"Yep. Second row in. There are only four rows, five or six houses per row. It's a small cluster."

"Thank you," Davis said. "Thanks a lot."

"Anything for a cousin of Tommy's," the woman said. Her tone was leading, though, like she wanted to ask more. So Davis waved and ran off, hoping desperately she'd be long gone from the Slants before the lady put together where she'd really seen Davis before—on the news channel.

Leslie Eide's house, assuming it was still the only green one in the cluster, was boarded up. A look at the mailbox near the front door—clearly labeled EIDE—confirmed that she'd found the right place. But it wasn't good news—it looked like no one had lived there in years. Weeds were growing up over the porch steps, and a tarp hung over one window. Davis peered behind the tarp to see a cracked windowpane and darkness behind it. Her heart sank. The place was abandoned. Decrepit. Davis fought hard not to burst into tears right there. The loss of her only lead was crushing, and she couldn't think where to go from there.

She didn't know how much longer she'd be alive. Or whether she'd ever see Cole again. Davis turned to leave, tears blurring her vision, when something fluttering from around the side of the house, near a small paved alley, caught her eye. She moved closer, and as she rounded the side of the house, she saw a clothesline draped between a window at the Eides' and a window at the neighboring house. There was a row of freshly laundered shirts hung carefully with clothespins on the cord.

Her heart lifted. There was a fifty-fifty shot that someone lived there after all, had just done their laundry. It might have been the neighbors, but one glance at their house showed darkened, dead rooms. The laundry could very well be Leslie Eide's. Someone might live there after all, and there was only one way to find out.

Davis ran back around to the front of the house, and with two swift kicks to the flimsy metal door, she forced her way in . . . only to face down the barrel of a gun pointed directly at her head.

# ❦ 20 ❧

## DAVIS

"What do you want?" The woman holding the gun looked about thirty. But the creases on her forehead and near her eyes indicated a difficult life. Those eyes were narrowed now, and the hand holding the gun was steady. Davis's thoughts raced. If she said the wrong thing—any tiny misstep—this woman would shoot her. She knew it as certainly as she knew her own name. Davis lifted her hands slowly, palms out, to show the woman she meant no harm—couldn't inflict any even if she wanted to.

"I'm not here to cause trouble," she started.

The woman took a step closer, jabbing the air a few inches from Davis's chest with the gun. Davis took a breath but didn't step backward in response. She had to let this woman know she was strong. Still, her whole body felt on the verge of collapse. She was weak, tired. But she had to stay strong—she had no choice. "My name is Davis Morrow," she said. "My father is Robert Morrow. My mother was Elisabeth Morrow. I'm looking for someone named Leslie Eide, who may have worked at the hospital about sixteen years ago. I just need to ask a couple of questions."

The woman snorted, lowering the gun only slightly. "Well, sixteen years ago might've been a good time to come around," she said, her tone cold. "My mother's been dead since they decided Elisabeth Morrow's—*your mother's*—life was more important than my mother's. I'm Racquelle Eide. Leslie's daughter."

"There must be some mistake." Davis felt confused, foggy. Her thoughts were all mixed together—and with the gun still in her face, she didn't know how to react. This wasn't how this was supposed to go at all. "My mother died in childbirth," she told the gun. "Please? Can you put that down? I'm not going to do anything to hurt you."

Racquelle stared at her for a long minute before lowering the weapon. Then she gestured to Davis with her chin, and moved toward a tiny wooden table in the corner of the room. A small television—a luxury in the Slants—played on mute behind them.

"Well, come on," she said. "What are you waiting for?" She pulled out a rickety chair, its woven seating broken and frayed, and gestured for Davis to do the same. "Your father gave my mother a thousand dollars and the promise of her own safety to get Elisabeth safely out of the hospital. All my mother got was a death sentence. She was charged with aiding and abetting."

Davis felt her face flush. "But surely . . . I'm sure my dad tried his best . . ." She trailed off, knowing how inadequate it sounded.

Racquelle stared at her, her face hard.

It hit Davis all at once: Racquelle had spent her whole life blaming Davis for her mother's death. Her resentment was sixteen years old. "That can't be right," Davis insisted. "My father wouldn't lie to me. What could he have been trying to hide? My father is a good person."

Racquelle scoffed at that. "Good to the people *he* cares about," she told her. Davis recoiled as if stung. "Who knows what he was trying to hide." Racquelle went on. "I never got the details. But none of it matters. It won't bring my mother back. And I'm not like my mother. I'm not going to meddle in Prior affairs and wind up dead for it."

Davis opened her mouth to respond, but nothing came out. Her shock was too overwhelming. Her mother hadn't died at the hospital? She'd escaped, alive? And her father had let an innocent woman die?

She slumped weakly against her seat, staring up at Racquelle, whose face softened.

"We're just the fallout of this mess," Racquelle said then. "I can tell you didn't know about any of it. It's not your fault even if you did. It's not mine, either. That's why we need to stay out of it, stop asking questions. It only leads to trouble. You seem like an okay kid," she started just as an alert appeared on the television behind them. Davis saw Cole's name flash across the screen in red.

"Turn it up," she told Racquelle. When the woman didn't respond right away, Davis reached across the table herself and switched on the volume.

". . . was found dead near the Slants. His was positively identified as of eight A.M. this morning, and his remains have been deposited in the morgue, scheduled for cremation tonight. A citywide search is out for Davis Morrow, who disappeared from her hospital room this morning. REPEAT: BREAKING ALERT. Cole Everett, the Imp accused of fraternizing with—and kidnapping—the daughter of CPM candidate Robert Morrow, has been found . . ."

"No," Davis whispered. "It can't be true."

Recognition registered on Racquelle's face, and a flicker of fear, too. "You need to go," Racquelle ordered, rising to her feet. "Right now. Before they come looking for you. I put all this behind me years ago, and now you show up . . . I'm not going to let you ruin my life for the second time."

Davis stood, staring, until Racquelle moved toward her, giving her a hard shove. "Get out," Racquelle said, louder now. "Go!"

Somehow, she found a way to move her feet. She ran blindly out the door and around the side of the house, far away from the center of the town. She took off toward a field, barely able to see the ground in front of her, not caring what she looked like, half wanting to die.

It had to be a lie, all of it: Cole, her father, her mother. Cole. Cole, dead, his body in a morgue. She'd truly believed that with him, nothing else mattered. They'd felt invincible, even when everything was falling apart. She hadn't realized exactly the extent of her hopes and feelings for him, the way her entire world rested on his existence, on them being together. Now she had nothing. This was what happened. It was her fault for breaking all the rules. She'd loved someone she shouldn't have. Their love had caused so much pain. If he'd never met her, he'd still be alive.

Her tears obscured her vision, but she kept her feet moving. She had to get away, far away; she didn't know where. Trees and grass blurred together into one sweep of brown in her periphery, but blinking through it, she could just make out several hulking figures leaping out of their vehicles and running toward her. They were close, so close. She tried to move faster, but her lungs were about to explode, and she didn't know where she was running to.

When they caught her—jerking her arms painfully behind her

back—it was a kind of relief. Now she could die, too. Without him, she had no reason to run.

They dragged her toward their waiting vehicles. One truck rose out from the rest, bigger and more intimidating. They moved her toward it, but all she could see was Cole in her mind. Cole, kissing her tenderly. Promising he'd see her again. Cradling her to him in the cold of the rooftop. They'd known it might be their last night. But she hadn't *known*. Not really. There'd always been hope, until now.

"Wait!"

She turned at the sound of a girl's voice, but the officers didn't even pause. She blinked tears from her eyes, struggling to make out the girl's familiar features. She was running toward them, still maybe a city block's length away. She had waist-length, coal-black hair and dark skin. Her long hair streamed behind her as she ran. Davis fought to place her. She was the Gen girl, the one from the FEUDS who'd been there to see Cole. She'd seemed upset, Davis recalled now. It was definitely her, shouting Davis's name and waving something in the air—some small scrap, paper, maybe?—as she ran. Davis looked back at her, struggling to dig in her heels to slow the burly men pulling her along, but they shoved her all the more forcefully toward the waiting vehicle. They pushed her up against the side of it. The girl was running hard, she was so close. Davis looked up just in time to see the metallic lettering across the side of the van: QUARANTINE. Then they shoved her headfirst into the vehicle, slamming the door after her.

Davis just managed to struggle to her feet to look out the window and see the girl stop, still a good distance away and half bent over, her palms resting on her thighs as she admitted defeat. Then the van started to move, and the girl and the landscape receded until Davis could no longer see anyone at all.

What had the girl wanted to tell her?

Life without Cole, without love, seemed like its own version of death. Davis felt void, dark, hopeless. But there was this girl, and there was the fact that maybe her mother was still alive. Without Cole, none of it mattered.

Still. Something in the girl's movements had seemed frantic.

In the darkness of the van, Davis had the choice to succumb to it if she wanted, to let it envelop her. But Cole's last words to her echoed in her ears. They were enough to keep her on this side of giving up. Cole had said, *I'll look for you, forever. I love you.* She believed him. She didn't know how, but it wasn't over. Not until she had more answers. The truck labeled QUARANTINE moved forward over bumpy roads and ditches, and all Davis could make out from where she lay was the bright blue sky.

# ACKNOWLEDGMENTS

The process of writing this novel was such a joy, and I look back on it as an example of what a collaboration can be at its most exciting. I'd love to thank Angela Velez, Lexa Hillyer, and Laura Schechter of Paper Lantern Lit, all of whom I've known in so many capacities for nearly seven years: as colleagues, friends, and now editors. You are three brilliant women for whom I have much admiration and respect. Without your notes and creative insights—and without the way you relentlessly pushed me to be a better writer—this book would not have come together the way it has.

My sincere thanks to Jen Weis, whose brilliant editorial instincts have helped mold this novel into something I can take pride in.

My writer friends in both New York and Paris, where I wrote the bulk of this novel, have provided me with endless support. Your constant encouragement and the sense of community you provide mean more than I can say.

Thank you to all those who welcomed me in France, in particular Amy Plum, who generously invited me into her Loire Valley home (providing evening cocktails and afternoon baguettes/pâtes/terrines and an endless coffee supply in the morning) for two writing retreats, shepherded me toward several deadlines with my sanity and sense of humor intact, and made me chicken soup when my romantic endeavors crashed and burned. Morgan Matson, who visited for six weeks in Paris, scouted out the best shopping spots and writing-friendly cafés (Les Emporte Pièces!), coined Falafel Sundays, introduced me to the best crepe man in Paris, loaned out her kitchen for mashed-potato-making and her Internet for Web-perusing, guided me toward what will be an everlasting love for Mindy Kaling, and became my number one Paris sidekick and a friend whom I treasure. Finally, Celeste Rhoads: I can't enumerate the many ways you helped me settle in and grow to love Paris! As a writer, you supported me in so many ways (by organizing events and introducing me to fellow creatives). As a friend, you made all the difference: from your initial advice over our first lunch regarding music venues and dance party–friendly bars and thrift stores, to nights hanging out at the library for hours after closing (a strange yet welcome iteration of my nerdy childhood dream), to picnics in the park, to piña colada–fueled dinners—you are a part of so many of my favorite memories. You're a huge part of why I came to love Paris, and why I'll miss it wholeheartedly. To the American Library in Paris, and in particular my teen writing group at the ALP: your support and friendship will always be remembered and appreciated. I look forward to returning for many visits (and to Skype-crashing future writing group sessions').

Much love and many thanks to my friends and family in New York and elsewhere who invited me into their homes when I was in transition, and of course to those who offered me constant love and friendship in one way or another throughout the period of time in which I was writing this novel: Jessica Palette, Lauren Palette, Marielle Spangler, Jackie Resnick, Kourtney Bitterly, Caroline Donofrio, Katherine Lofts, Jocelyn Davies, Rachel Abrams, Kristen Sylvester, Maggie Hazboun, and Katie Brunetti.

Lastly, thank you always to my parents—excellent and devoted readers (in every way), as well as two of the best editors I've ever had.

sometimes the heart
is the greatest enemy . . .

Don't miss

# rival

a Feuds Series e-original novella

AVAILABLE DECEMBER 2014

## can love survive?

Davis and Cole battle for truth and each other in

# torn

the finale of the Feuds Series

AVAILABLE JUNE 2015